THE JUDGE
OF ORPHANS

**Books by
Rosemary Aubert**

Novels:

Song of Eden
A Red Bird in Winter
Garden of Lions
Firebrand
A Thousand to One
Free Reign
The Feast of Stephen
The Ferryman Will Be There
Leave Me By Dying
The Red Mass

Poetry:

Two Kinds of Honey
Picking Wild Raspberries

Non-Fiction:

Copper Jack (with Jack Webster)

THE JUDGE OF ORPHANS

A Novel

Rosemary Aubert

Rosemary Aubert (signature)

iUniverse, Inc.

New York Lincoln Shanghai

THE JUDGE OF ORPHANS

iUniverse books may be ordered through booksellers or by contacting:

iUniverse
2021 Pine Lake Road, Suite 100
Lincoln, NE 68512
www.iuniverse.com
1-800-Authors (1-800-288-4677)

Because of the dynamic nature of the Internet, any Web addresses or links contained in this book may have changed since publication and may no longer be valid.

ISBN: 978-0-595-45412-9 (pbk)
ISBN: 978-0-595-89725-4 (ebk)

Printed in the United States of America

This novel is the result of extensive research on the street as well as years of delving into my family history and the history of Italian immigrants collected by such historians as John E. Zucchi, Robert F. Harney, Justin Ferate, Anthony Robins and Teresa D'Amico—to all of whom I am grateful. However, the characters, offices, institutions, incidents and objects depicted here are the products of my imagination. None is intended to represent any real thing or any actual person alive or dead.

Front cover photo used by permission of Joseph A. Proe, Jr.

Author photo used by permission of Wilf Iles.

 **Canada Council   Conseil des Arts
for the Arts   du Canada**

I acknowledge the support of the Canada Council for the Arts which last year invested $20.1 million in writing and publishing throughout Canada.

Je remerce de son soutien le Conseil des Arts du Canada, qui a investi 20,1 millions de dollars l'an dernier dans les lettres et l'édition à travers le Canada.

This book is dedicated to J. Douglas Purdon

CHAPTER 1

▼

The present.

Mary Rose Cabrini stared out over the crowd gathered in Nathan Phillips Square. She glanced at her Rolex, at the clock between the gargoyles on the pinnacle of Old City Hall, at the red digital numerals on the office tower across Queen Street. They all said the same thing. Nine fifty-six. Four more minutes to go.

She adjusted the white linen tabs at her throat, smoothed her back wool robe. A cold October wind snapped the Maple Leaf on its flagpole in the center of the square. Mary Rose ran her fingers through her straight, streaked hair. She didn't care about the breeze or the cold. She was too nervous for that.

At nine fifty-seven, she noticed the run in her pantyhose. At nine fifty-eight, she asked herself one last time *Why me?* At ten, the bell of Old City Hall jolted her. She dropped her gold-engraved program and bent to pick it up. Too late. A gust of wind caught the paper and propelled it out into the crowd.

Beside her, His Worship the Mayor, John Franklin, stood hiding the fact that he had forgotten the words to the national anthem! Out of the corner of her eye, she caught him mouthing, faking. His deputy, a short, stout man, held Franklin's printed speech in his chubby hand. With an impatient jerk, the mayor pulled it from his assistant's fingers. The fourth person on the platform was a tall, striking, middle-aged dignitary. He looked vaguely familiar. Feeling her watching, he smiled. *Lizard,* Mary Rose thought, but she didn't know why.

The painful singing of the anthem over, the dignitaries sat down. Mary Rose pulled her robe over her knee to hide the run and folded her hands in her lap to hide her nervousness. It had been decades since the nuns had taught her how to sit properly and she'd been doing it ever since.

"Today," the mayor began, "we are gathered here for the ground-breaking of a new courthouse ..."

Blah, blah, blah.

Mary Rose felt as if she had heard it all before.

"Thanks to a small number of dedicated citizens of this city," he said, "this project will revitalize the legal landscape of Toronto, uniting the old and the new. When contractors excavated the site of the former Land Titles Office, they found artifacts that we will eventually incorporate into the building we initiate today. But …" He turned his dark, handsome head away from the crowd and nodded toward Mary Rose, "more importantly, today we announce that Mary Rose Cabrini will be our first Judge of Orphans."

"Why?"

Mary Rose saw the mayor's head whip around to find the questioner. A small figure hunkered down on the cold cement of the square. A boy, ten or twelve years old, his eyes locked on Franklin, glared at the mayor, who grinned, a smile as fake as his anthem singing. The boy frowned. The mayor fumbled with his papers, and the sound was amplified into a thundering rustle that filled the square, sending hands to cover ears.

Mary Rose stifled a laugh. *Good question!* She didn't know the heckler, but in her role as a children's lawyer, she'd seen a lot of elephants frightened by mice. Served the pompous mayor right.

Franklin regained his composure, resumed his talk. Now he was going on about how this part of the city, twenty acres in the center of town, had always been the heart of Toronto's legal life.

Amazingly, the boy in the front row shook his head. Could he possibly know what Mary Rose knew? That the mayor was mistaken—or lying.

Suddenly it seemed to her that a hundred years sped away. New City Hall before which she sat, Nathan Phillips Square, Old City Hall across the way, the skyscrapers, even the courthouse in which she worked and the law library in which she researched disappeared. In their place stood a steaming neighbourhood of single-story, run-down wooden houses, many made by their occupants out of scraps. Narrow streets teemed with vendors of ribbons and fruit, pots and stockings, rosary beads and yarmulkes. Italian, Yiddish and Chinese voices yelled and sang across the crowded alleys. A tambourine and a concertina accompanied the dancing of dark-skinned women. In the midst of a tattered knot of urchins, a newsboy stood clutching his last remaining copy of the Toronto *Star*. A man tried to snatch the paper away, but the boy turned sharply and scurried off, leaving the man cursing at the curb.

Mary Rose blinked and the past evaporated. She heard her own name spoken again. What had Franklin just said? Was it her turn to talk?

Rising, she glanced down. The little boy in the front row had edged even closer. She saw that he was expensively dressed, good-looking and intense. What was he doing alone at the ceremony?

His eyes followed her as she took her place at the podium. There was pleading in his face, in his posture, his entire young body straining forward as if to try to touch her. She had spent years responding to the pleas for rescue of innocent children and some not-so-innocent children, too.

"Despite all my years working in this very neighborhood," she began, "I can say few things for certain, but one thing I can say is that somewhere, at this moment, in this city, there is a child in need of protection."

The boy in the front row shook his head. It unnerved her, but she went on.

"Somewhere a defenceless person waits to be saved. A small boy tormented by bullies. A little girl afraid of the intimacy of her father. A teenager brought to this city against his or her will and forced into a lifestyle he or she cannot abide …"

A gust blew Mary Rose's hair across her face, and she raised her hand to push the strands away. As she did so, she made a sweeping gesture that took in the square and the city that surrounded it.

"Before these buildings stood here," she said, "there was a huge factory in which poor little girls sewed clothes for rich women. Before the factory, there were forests where little boys wielded axes to help their fathers hew wood. Long, long before the woodsmen, the land on which you stand was submerged beneath a vast inland sea on which children set out in boats to catch fish for their families to cook over open fires on the beach. I don't know what was here before the inland sea. But I do know that in factory and forest, on the sea then and in the city now, somewhere there is a child in need of protection."

She paused and looked out over the mass of people. They were listening with rapt attention. A movement caught her eye. Now, at the edge of the crowd, near the back, she saw the intense little boy, or thought she did. How had he moved so quickly? He was still watching her.

"You have chosen to honor me today," she went on, "by asking me to lay the cornerstone of a magnificent new courthouse that will be dedicated to serving the needs of children in conflict with the law. I have no children of my own, so I am free to serve the children of this city. They do not vote. They do not pay tax. They do not demonstrate or litigate. They don't strike or publish or make speeches. So in this place and at this moment, let us speak for them. And let us dedicate this building to their rights as full citizens of this country, worthy of its protection. Let this new courthouse stand as a symbol of our dedication, our determination that no child in need of rescue will ever be ignored by us."

The crowd erupted in applause. The grinning mayor handed her a trowel with a red ribbon around the handle, and she scooped a little cement from a silver tray and rubbed it onto a piece of stone. When she handed the trowel back, it was not the mayor who took it, but the mysterious man who'd eyed her earlier. With a trowel in his hand, she recognized him and blushed with embarrassment at the cliché of the whole ceremony. He was Antonio Di Marino Bianco, a major developer, an Italian-Canadian whose family had built half the skyscrapers in the city.

While he made a speech about how honored he was that his firm had been chosen to build the new courthouse, Mary Rose searched the crowd.

The haunting little boy was nowhere to be seen.

CHAPTER 2

▼

New York. 1873.

Giuseppe Di Buonna had a choice. Hang onto his hat or his harp. He didn't know which he hated more: the stupid hat that sat like a black cone on top of his ten-year-old head, or the harp, which he was obliged to play every day from six in the morning to nine at night on the dusty corner of Crosby Street and Grand.

Billbone Benson the newsboy, his arch enemy and best friend, was the culprit who made Giuseppe's life a misery. Sixty or seventy times a day, he knocked the hat off. When Giuseppe bent to pick it up, Billbone grabbed his harp and held it high over his head until Giuseppe was forced to give Billbone a good swift kick in the shin. This Billbone considered hilarious, especially when, by late afternoon, Giuseppe was in tears.

Today, however, there was no time for tears or even for the fear that usually gripped Giuseppe whenever he left his corner, which was seldom. Leaving the corner meant he'd have to fight bigger street musicians for it when he got back. Plus his grandfather didn't like him to lose money by, as the old man put it, walking the street for free. Giuseppe had to get home and fast regardless of the consequences.

Billbone, a Negro, told Giuseppe, an I-talian, that someday he'd be a rich I-talian. Giuseppe wasn't sure how this could be true, but Billbone told him that when Old Man Di Buonna kicked the bucket he, Giuseppe, would get everything. Monkeys, musical instruments and all the money Old Man Di Buonna's street kids—all forty of them—brought in every day. Maybe it was true, but Giuseppe wasn't stupid. Old Man Di Buonna was old all right—at least fifty, but he wasn't going to die anytime soon, even if he was, as Billbone said, in a whole lot of trouble.

By the time he'd reached his house on Crosby, Giuseppe was out of breath and out of nerve. Gingerly, he climbed the stairs to the top of the front tenement. Behind, there was another house on the lot. The boy knew better than to go back there, even though he couldn't quite figure out what went on. The groans and screams coming from the back building didn't scare him, but the idea of disobeying the old man did.

There were only four windows on each floor of the tenement, no air-shafts, no ventilators. The air in the narrow unlighted stairwell smelled of dust, urine, tomato paste, animal dung, coal smoke and burning human flesh. It was no worse than the smell of horses in the street, of saliva baked onto the sidewalk, the smell of clothes and hair never washed, the smell of bad meat roasted outside all year long. The boy was used to the smells, but he didn't think he could ever get used to the cries that filled the whole dank building, the cries of screaming monkeys, and screaming children, too.

Giuseppe loved the monkeys, so when he got to the second-floor landing, he couldn't resist peeking into the room that covered the entire floor. All the walls had been knocked out so that the monkeys had plenty of space to run around. They were everywhere, swinging from the gas fixtures that hung from the ceiling, balancing on the windowsills, bouncing into and out of the holes in the floorboards. They spun on one of their little feet, then fell dizzy to the floor. One or two were old and mangy, and the old man said he only kept them because he had a soft heart for animals and children. Most of the monkeys were small, healthy and handsome. The old man always made sure the monkeys ate first. "In America," he said, "there's only one letter between monkey and money."

The old man also said that when Giuseppe got to be twelve, he could learn the accordion and have a monkey of his own, but the boy didn't believe this promise because he knew there had never been a Giuseppe Di Buonna who played anything but a stringed instrument, including his dead father, who'd been a violinist.

Today the monkeys were more frantic than usual. In the middle of the room stood a tiny boy named Petuccini, bawling his eyes out. Giuseppe was crazy about this four-year-old. He liked to pet him, the way he petted the monkeys. Petuccini's sister, Aldelina, was always washing him, and he had soft, black curls that felt warm under Giuseppe's fingers. It killed him to see the kid's cute face all screwed up with fear and crying, but in truth, Giuseppe felt sorrier for the monkey.

"*Non posso mai.* No. No. No!" Petuccini screamed. He was no younger than Giuseppe had been when he'd first begun to dance with a monkey, but Giuseppe had gotten along with the animals from the first.

As Giuseppe watched, one of the older street boys grabbed an empty wooden grape crate, stood it on end, and sat down. He began to play a cheery ditty on his concertina, his fingers flying over the pearlescent keys.

Immediately, the monkey beside Petuccini lifted its face, alert to the music. It began to sway, taking a few prancing steps toward and away from the little boy. Then the monkey spun in a neat circle, and Petuccini spun, tripping and giving up before his circle was complete. The monkey stopped, confused, disgusted.

The unrelenting tune played on. The boy tried again. Again he tripped. But this time the monkey kept dancing. Until he noticed that Petuccini had stopped. He let out a loud squeal, jumped up and down, hopped onto the shoulder of the concertina player, who laughed and started the song all over again.

When Petuccini tripped a third time, the enraged monkey sprang over to the boy and bit him hard on the thigh.

Petuccini howled.

A large dark woman, who had been working in the shadowed corners of the room, noticed the commotion. Her name was Madonna, like the name of the Blessed Virgin, and at that name all resemblance ended. Giuseppe pulled back further into the recess of the doorway, torn between saving Petucinni's hide and his own.

Madonna stomped toward Petuccini. There were no fat people in Giuseppe's world. Nobody had enough money to be fat. But there were large people, and Madonna was one of them. She towered over the tiny failed dancer, who quaked in silence.

Then she reached down and belted Petuccini a good one across the back of his head.

He stopped screaming. Big tears made tracks in the dust on his round, red cheeks.

Madonna got down on one big knee. She embraced the tiny child. Her apron was brown with the dirt of feeding the monkeys and cleaning up after any of them that were sick, but Petuccini sobbed against it as if it were white as the sheets that his mother washed for the nuns.

Giuseppe smiled and moved on.

He could hear other children making a racket further up, and he wished he could go back to the corner of Crosby and Grand, much as he hated it. But he wasn't going back until he could tell his grandfather the awful thing that Billbone Benson had told him. The Negro was a tease, but he was no liar.

He hurried up the dirty, rickety, foul-smelling stairs with burn marks all over them from the cigarettes and pipes of men too tired, lazy or drunk to care where their ashes and butts landed, even in a building made entirely of wood. Above him, the hysterical, sobbing screams intensified.

He covered his ears with his hands. But he quickly gave that up in order to fend off a rat that jumped on him from above, landing on his chest and having the nerve to stare him in the face as if Giuseppe, and not the rat himself were the intruder.

With a violent shake, Giuseppe dislodged the rodent and sent him scurrying into the reeking darkness. His ten-year-old heart was pounding, and he had to stop to catch his breath, ducking into a doorway on the third floor.

He didn't realize the magnitude of his mistake until one second too late. Half a hundred hands reached out to snare him. Though it was the middle of the day, twenty-five men lay sprawled on straw mattresses that twenty-five other men had slept in all night. Both sets of men stewed in the bodily fluids of themselves and their co-sleepers, since neither group had any intention of getting up in the dark of night or the light of day to relieve themselves three floors down in the rank back yard.

Young as he was, Giuseppe already knew that men without women console themselves with boys.

Veni qui, bello ragazzo!

The filthy men laughed as they jostled him, throwing him from one vile pallet to the next. He struggled to stay upright, his feet slipping on the slimy straw mattresses. Strong, rough-skinned fingers grasped his ankles. He kicked as hard as he could, but the effort cost him his balance and he fell atop a squirming mass of muscle, hair and dirt-encrusted cloth. He felt a rain of garlicky kisses on his hair, his cheeks, his neck. He spit and bit and kicked again.

This time, he won release. A deep-throated voice mocked, *vergine Americana,* little American virgin, little Yankee *putanna!*

Eager as he was to get out of there, Giuseppe turned back. He leaned down and swung at the dim outlines of the men on the beds. One of the men reached up and clasped his flailing wrist. With a strength he didn't know he had, Giuseppe yanked his own arm toward his mouth and bit down hard on the hand that held him. Rats weren't the only creatures with sharp teeth.

He ran up another flight of stairs, breathless from fear and exertion. His heaving lungs pulled hard on the fetid air of the stairwell. But the strench he had first noticed at the very bottom, the unmistakable smell of burning human flesh, assailed him more strongly than before and he had to stop. He gagged. Like everybody he knew, he tried hard never to vomit. Because it left you so hungry. But he couldn't help it. A stream of thin fluid flew from his young mouth and joined the splatters that covered the tenement walls more effectively than the decades-old paint that had turned to lead dust and flecked away with the years.

Weak with revulsion, he had to stop at the large room on the fourth floor. He didn't mean to, but he looked in anyway, as if drawn by something he hated but recognized as part of his history, of himself.

In the center of the room stood a huge black iron stove with a crooked, rusted, oily black pipe snaking out of it and disappearing into the browned tiles of the tin ceiling. Despite the blistering heat of the late summer day, a blazing fire roared in the belly of the stove.

Two women, each bigger and—Giuseppe knew—a lot meaner than Madonna of the monkey room, stood on either side of the stove. They had towering masses of greasy black hair and powerful arms visible beneath the rolled-back sleeves of blue work shirts. One held a tiny girl hard against her dirty gray apron. The other held a red-hot iron over the head of the child.

The little girl knew what was coming. She didn't even try to fight, just stood calmly, awaiting her fate. No doubt she had been given a little wine to drink. Giuseppe detested wine, not because of the taste, but because whenever one of his grandfather's helpers came at a child with a bit of wine, it meant that something horrible was about to happen, some tooth yanked out of your head, some bath with burning soap to try and kill the lice, some bad news, like that Giuseppe's beloved father had been killed by runaway horses in the street.

Both children, Giuseppe and the girl, watched as the radiant rod of iron came down with deadly precision and landed on the white cheek of the victim, branding her with an indelible mark: the letter "D" superimposed on the image of a harp.

Like Petuccini, the little girl howled. Her screams seemed to shake the whole wooden tenement tower.

Furious, the two huge women grabbed her and tossed her away like a rag doll.

Giuseppe's fingers strayed to his own cheek and sought the raised outline of the harp and the "D" on his skin. Rage filled him. He dove into the room, tenderly lifted the little girl and cradled her in his arms, cooing words of comfort.

One of the women caught sight of this touching tableau, the one with the iron still in her hand. She made for Giuseppe.

Defiantly, he stared up at her, not releasing his hold on the girl. He could feel the child heave with silent crying.

The woman raised her huge hand, lifted the iron rod over her head.

But before she could strike, the other woman was on her.

Basta! Questo ragazzo e il nipote del padrone!

Giuseppe understood what the woman said, "He's the old man's grandson. Leave him alone."

But his special place in the family didn't make him any less afraid of facing the old man upstairs.

CHAPTER 3

▼

Giuseppe had been to the fifth floor of the house on Crosby Street only a few times in his ten years of life. When his father had died, his grandfather called him up there and informed him that now he was a man and responsible for his mother's well-being. Given that Giuseppe had been six years old at the time, he'd had only a vague notion of what that responsibility might mean. He, mistakenly as it turned out, had concluded that being fatherless meant he'd get his own corner and his own monkey right away.

Instead, what it had really meant was that his uncle, Ambrogio, his father's brother, had begun to keep tabs on Giuseppe. He always showed up when Giuseppe least expected. Take now, for instance. No doubt Zio Ambrogio had already sauntered by the corner of Crosby and Grand and realized that Giuseppe wasn't standing there with his harp.

Tough. Giuseppe had something more important to do.

Unlike every other in the tenement, the sole door on the fifth floor was always closed. It was not pale, peeling and flaking onto a filthy and scarred floor. No. Here the door was dark polished wood—and so was the floor. Giuseppe had seen his own mother just the day before, and the day before that, too, on her knees polishing that floor. The thought made his fingers tremble as he formed them into the fist he lifted toward the door.

He hesitated a fraction of a second before knocking. Sometimes when he stood in the yard outside, he could hear music coming from this room. But not today. He hoped the silence didn't mean his grandfather was exceptionally busy and would therefore be exceptionally angry at being interrupted. At least there were no voices behind the door. The old man was alone.

Giuseppe knocked.

"Chi viene?" The old man's voice was deep and rough.

Pulling back his shoulders, as though to increase the capacity of his lungs and the volume of his own voice, Giuseppe answered, *"C'e Giuseppe nonno."*

Giuseppe waited. It seemed like hours before the gruff voice commanded, *"Avvenga"*

The shining brass doorknob was even with Giuseppe's nose, and the door itself so heavy that he could hardly push it, but nonetheless, he managed to open it a crack without disgracing himself by having to wait for the old man to come and help him, which is what had always happened before.

Squeezing through, Giuseppe was startled to see that his grandfather wasn't sitting behind his massive wooden desk. It took the boy a minute to locate the man in the huge room. He was standing beside the ornate fireplace with its mantle of carved white marble. Surprised by his own courage, Giuseppe walked right up to his grandfather and looked him straight in the eye.

Had he known before this moment that his grandfather's eyes were blue? Surely he'd not forget something as unusual as that.

The boy's eyes skittered away from the gaze of the old man and took in the magnificent paintings that adorned the walls: Madonnas and Christ Childs, fruit baskets and castles, landscapes in which mists hid the sweet hills of Italy, seas that receded into impossible distances.

High over his head, pedestals rose and on them teetered statues—real statues—not fakes like the little white imitation plaster things his cousins sold on the street. The carpet beneath his feet was thick with amazing patterns and colors. Balanced against the wall in one corner stood a white and gold harp a hundred times the size of the tiny dingy harp Giuseppe and the other harpers played on the corner. Beside it, a spindly music stand magically remained upright under its burden of white pages covered in black dots.

"Parla pronto. Che cosa?" his grandfather demanded.

Giuseppe swallowed hard.

"I ... We ... You ..."

Old Man Di Buonna frowned. Giuseppe suddenly felt the sting of the man's palm against his ear. His eyes blurred, making the sheets of music on the stand seem to dance. There were a lot of things in the world, like those sheets, that were magic. If only you could read what they were trying to tell you. The songs he played on the street were old songs from the old country. The music on the stand was new music—from America. Like himself.

"You're in big trouble," Giuseppe found the courage to say, "and you better wise up."

He'd never spoken like that to his grandfather before. He liked the feel of the brash words in his mouth. He liked the fact that his grandfather perked up, like the monkey downstairs had done at the first sound of music.

"What are you saying?"

"I never read a newspaper—or anything else," Giuseppe began. "But newspapers can cause trouble …"

His grandfather was staring at him, and Giuseppe began to lose his nerve. He watched as the nonno moved toward his beautiful desk, its wood decorated with scrolls of gold like the gold in the fairy tales his mother showed him in a big book she found in the garbage. Nonno wasn't so old that his hair was white. In fact, he had dark curls, like Petuccini, and a neat black moustache, like Ambrogio. Unlike Giuseppe's silly little jacket from the old country, Nonno's was from an American store and fit him perfectly.

Giuseppe had time to think about all this because time slowed to a halt as Nonno studied the golden objects on top of his desk. From among the pens and little boxes, and timepieces and gleaming statuettes, he selected one object and picked it up. It glinted in the light from the window—a dagger. *"Parli, ragazzo,"* the man said. "Talk, boy."

Giuseppe watched the dagger slide between his grandfather's fingers, as if the old man were immune from the blade's sharp edge. He drew in a ragged breath and began to tell his tale.

"I got a friend on the street," he said, "Billbone Benson. He's a Negro, but he's been to school and he can read."

His grandfather sighed and Giuseppe glanced up, waiting for the man to say something, but he said nothing, just made a gesture for the boy to go on.

"Billbone knows what everybody's name looks like written down, our name included. He sells the *Times* and sometimes he reads it. A little while ago I was playing my harp and Billbone come running up to me. He says he seen my name in the paper."

The words were spilling out of him now, and Giuseppe just let them flow. "He started to read to me. I liked hearing it because it told all about our house here on Crosby—even the monkeys. It was so good I thought Billbone was pulling my leg, making it all up. But he showed me the exact words. He showed me the name Crosby in the paper and then on the street sign, and I saw it was the same. I started to get scared. In the *Times*, it told about all the children who live here, about how sometimes they run away. It even said that you put words in the paper to get people to find the boys that run away and bring them back. It said you tell people that the children who live here are your own and that they ran away because they are bad …"

Giuseppe stopped. His grandfather was a good-looking man. People told him that and he could see it with his own eyes. Maybe that was the reason why, even when he was terrified of him, he never hated him. Even now, when the blade of the knife slid back and forth between the nonno's finger and his thumb, Giuseppe almost felt sorry for him. After all, Giuseppe didn't owe any loyalty to Billbone Benson or to *The New York Times*, either. But he owed everything to the old man.

"What else?"

"The paper said they gotta do something about it—about us."

"Who?" the old man said. "Who's gotta do something about us?"

Giuseppe glanced at the knife. "The cops," he said, "the paper said the cops gotta do something."

Old Man Di Buonna came around from behind the big desk. Giuseppe looked toward the door. What if he ran? For all he knew, Zio Ambrogio was around. If he didn't grab him, one of the old witches downstairs surely would. Escape was not an option.

He was prepared for a tirade or a smack, but not for what really happened, which was that his grandfather suddenly fell to one knee and took him by the shoulders. He drew Giuseppe near and held him close, his face even with the boy's face. He smelled good, like flowers or herbs, and he was smiling with his mouth, though not with those scary blue eyes.

"You're a good boy, Giuseppe," he said. "You were right to come here and tell me these things. I want you to tell me more …"

"There isn't any more," Giuseppe said, wishing that he, like his friend Billbone, could make up stories when required. Suddenly, he felt a jab of fear. What if Billbone had made up this story? What if that Crosby word thing had been another of Billbone's stupid tricks?

"Nonno," Giuseppe said, fighting hard to keep his voice steady, "I think the best thing would be for you to go down on the street and read the *Times* for yourself."

The old man held him tighter. Giuseppe's shoulders started to hurt. When the nonno gave him a shake, Giuseppe decided to keep talking, even if he had to make some of it up.

"What they said in the papers is that the cops are on to you. They know about everything that happens here. They got society ladies that are gonna come down here and see for themselves … Then the cops will arrest us all. The little kids will go to the orphanage and the big kids, like me, will go to reform school. And you …"

He didn't have the nerve to look his grandfather in the eye now. "And you," he finally said, "are going to jail."

Silence. From down in the street, Giuseppe could hear the clomp of horses. In the yard, the women were washing clothes, beating and splashing and singing in the dialect of Naples. Infants cried. In the distance, he could hear the newsboys shouting. In that moment, he wanted to kill Billbone Benson.

CHAPTER 4

▼

Giuseppe's grandfather let go of the boy's shoulders. He stood and ran his long fingers through the tangles of his own black curls. For the first time, Giuseppe noticed gray at the man's temples. Seeing that, the boy felt less afraid, but he was still surprised when he heard the sudden softness in his grandfather's tone.

"*Viene qui, ragazzo,*" he said, motioning toward the window.

Reluctantly, Giuseppe moved forward. What was the old man going to do—throw him out?

"*Ora!*" Now.

The boy leapt toward the old man, stopping just in front of his feet, which, Giuseppe noticed, were shod in soft-looking leather that caught the gleam of the light from the window. Here, unlike any other room in the place, there were drapes, heavy green silk things with a pattern that appeared to young Giuseppe like monsters eating other monsters.

"Look out this window, boy."

Giuseppe rose on the tips of his toes. Clutching the sill with his fingers, he managed to balance just long enough to follow his grandfather's instructions.

"Tell me what you see."

He could see the women in the yard and the forbidden back building, which was a little higher and a little shabbier than the one in which he stood. He could make out buildings that he knew were on Spring Street, but he couldn't see Hester where the Jews lived or the Bowery either. He knew the river was somewhere not too far away. Was he supposed to be looking at that? What was he supposed to say?

"A bunch of buildings. I see a whole lot of buildings."

The old man nodded. "See how high? Five floors," he said. "Six, even." He shook his head as if overcome by the monumentality of it all. "Where we came from, there were no buildings like these. Sometimes there were no real buildings at all. In the winter, we slept in the goat huts built by the rich farmer who owned every bit of land around our village. I had thirteen brothers and I don't know how many sisters. In summer, we worked in the fields during the day, and we sang for coins in the village streets at night. Then we slept in the woods or the fields. Sometimes the only thing we had to eat was whatever was left after the farmer dug up the vegetables and let his pigs root in the fields. First the pigs, then us. We were always starving."

Giuseppe felt a frightening ripple in the pit of his stomach. He stood taller and put his chin on the windowsill and pressed down hard to keep his face as still as he could.

The old man went on, "we roamed the streets of Laurenzana from first light until after the last drunken slob went home to his fat wife. Once in a while, someone would throw us a scrap of bread ..."

The ripple became a rumble, a bubbling up. Giuseppe pressed his chin down harder. He could feel the rough grain of the wood against the skin of his neck.

"We were too poor to go to school, too dirty to go to church."

The bubble of laughter in his lungs burst and only by burying his face in his hands could Giuseppe hide his inappropriate reaction to his grandfather's sad tale. For the boy had heard the same story a thousand times before. From the women whose arms were raw from the rough soap they used to wash other people's dirty clothes. From the men on the street whose legs buckled beneath the weight of their peddler's wagon. Even from Zio Ambrogio. If things were so much better in America, why were they all working night and day? And why, the little boy wondered, was he still hungry all the time?

Luckily, his grandfather was too absorbed in his own memories to notice how Giuseppe had reacted. The boy gathered himself and listened. He realized he was being talked to as though he were an adult. A feeling of great privilege began to replace his doubt and disrespect. "In Italy," the old man went on, "we had no future. In America ..." He gestured toward the window, "Everything will be ours. The day I came here, I saw the great ships in the harbor, their sails like the white wings of angels. We had come across the wild sea, packed in the boat *come i pesci*, like fish. But I knew from that day, that we had something in Amercia we could never have in the old country. We had hope."

The little boy only vaguely comprehended the words of this grand speech, but he got the gist of the emotion. It made him feel almost tender toward his grandfather. But it did not make him forget the reason he had come.

"Nonno," he said, "we won't have any more hope if we have to go to jail, like it says we will in *The New York Times*."

"We won't have to go to jail," his grandfather responded. He glanced out the window a final time. Then he walked toward the carved white marble fireplace. In the grate, despite the heat of the afternoon, a small fire burned, like the brander's fire in the room downstairs. He grabbed a poker, reached down and stirred the red embers.

Giuseppe was sweating. He wiped his brow. He wanted to get out of there. He'd said what he'd come to say.

From the top of the mantle, far above the boy's head, Giuseppe's grandfather reached for some unseen object. Did he have something up there that he was going to use to punish the boy for his insolence? Giuseppe fought the urge to cower. He was a street boy and no sissy. Whatever his grandfather was about to dish out, he was prepared to stand and take it. He planted his feet more firmly on the richly colored rug.

The old man lifted down a golden box. It was the size of a loaf of bread. A whole loaf of fresh bread was something Giuseppe had only seen in the possession of others, so the image sprang readily to his mind as a measure of great value. He gazed in wonderment as his grandfather carried the golden box to his desk. The object was covered with figures of angels and flowers and leaves that looked real except for their glittering splendor.

Giuseppe longed to ask what this was. He could see a tiny door in the side of the box. Was his grandfather about to open it?

Not without another speech about America, it seemed.

The old man set down the box. He fiddled with it a bit. There was no key, Giuseppe noticed. Boys who worked on the street were always thinking about keys—dropped, carelessly left dangling from a lock, mindlessly shoved into a pocket that was easy to pick. To a boy like Giuseppe, a key was not a symbol of safekeeping, but of weakness.

So he wasn't surprised that there was no key to open this magnificent object. His grandfather somehow managed to open the little door without one.

But before he took anything out, he turned to Giuseppe. "Boy," he said, "Maybe you don't know how lucky you are. Maybe you don't know how other boys have to work in factories. You ever think about those big machines? A boy your size would have to crawl underneath to pick up lint from the threads—or even inside to fix any bolts that come lose. You ever think about that?"

In fact, Giuseppe *did* think about working indoors, especially on cold days when the mist off the river made its way even over to Crosby Street and soaked his stupid black jacket until it hung on his shoulders like a wet blanket. But he answered, "No, Nonno."

"You got everything," the old man went on. "You got a nice place to stand and a lot of fresh air and you don't ever have to work for nobody but your own family. No *padrone*."

"Yes, Nonno."

"You got my mark on you, son, and you're going to thank me for it until the day you die."

At these words, Giuseppe remembered the screams of the little girl, somehow remembered the searing pain of his own branding, though it had happened so long ago. He was filled with revulsion, anger and fear. Let the old man go to jail. It would serve him right.

"Those men from the newspapers, they listen to fancy women from uptown who come down here spying on us," the grandfather said, shaking his head, his fingers still on the door to the box. "But they don't know what they're talking about. I come to this country to give hope to my children and the children of my children, and I can prove it."

Giuseppe moved closer.

His grandfather reached into the box and pulled out a piece of paper. At first, Giuseppe thought it must be money, but then he saw that it couldn't be. It was too white, too square and too small.

The boy figured something had to be written on that paper, and though he couldn't read, he nonetheless strained closer still to see whether he was right, but his grandfather held the paper over his head. He gave the paper a little shake and said, "Boy, if those police come, I will give them this and they will have to leave us alone."

Giuseppe wanted to believe him, in fact, he might have told him he *did* believe, except that at that moment, he suddenly became aware of a sound vaguely audible—at first—over all the other sounds in the building, over the monkeys screaming and the children crying and the women cursing indoors and singing outdoors. Somewhere in the house, there was a commotion even greater than the usual commotion of that place. Both the boy and the old man stood still, listening.

In the distance, then growing ever closer, came the heavy breathing of men straining against gravity and time, the push of stout boots against creaking floors, the crack of the thick wooden door as it was blasted open and bashed against the wall.

Before Giuseppe or his grandfather fully realized what was happening, the room was full of New York City police, their faces red with heat and exertion, their expressions grim, their arms aloft and their truncheons raised.

Thinking fast, Giuseppe grabbed the nearest uniformed leg and held on tight. At first the cop ignored him because the nonno was struggling, too. The old man swung and squirmed and swore, and though he was older and smaller than the New York City police, he was just as determined.

Even when young Giuseppe felt the smack of the billy club on his slim shoulders, he didn't give up. He'd been hit by somebody every day of his life. No big deal.

But when he heard another sharp crack of the club, followed by his grandfather's heart-rending scream, Giuseppe involuntarily let go of the blue uniform trousers and reached out toward his nonno.

It did no good. The constables had him now, one holding each of the old man's arms, a third going in front, a fourth behind. They frog-marched him out of the room. Two other officers dawdled behind. They surveyed the chamber and all its treasures. For a moment, Giuseppe was sure they were going to steal his grandfather's fine things, but then one cop shook his head and laughed. "Typical Tally," he said mockingly. The other constable laughed, too. "A whole lot of trash!" he commented. Without so much as glancing at the boy, the two left the room.

Relieved, Giuseppe rushed out behind them. He tried to close the door, but its broken hinges hung loose from the wall.

Leaving it, Giuseppe headed for the stairwell. He quickly caught up with the retreating officers and followed them down to the street, where they lost no time in shoving his grandfather into a paddy wagon with a great deal of brutal pushing and poking. Regardless of the rough treatment, the old man seemed resigned. He was no longer fighting back.

But he was the only one who *wasn't* fighting.

On both sides of narrow Crosby Street, pandemonium had broken out. Screaming women hurled insults at the officers and flung whatever they had in their hands. A wet sock, black with the street dirt that never washes out, hit one of the cops. Shocked, he spat and spat as if to get all the dirt of Little Italy out of his mouth.

Every child from every corner in the neighborhood had run to see the action. Now they picked up whatever refuse the street offered: stones and bottles and old rusted horseshoes, throwing them at the police. Remarkably, the little girls were more accurate in their aim than the boys.

Even a few of the monkeys got into the act, jumping on the shoulders of the cops, pulling the police hats down over the cops' eyes, plucking at their copper buttons—all the time yelling at the top of their simian lungs.

None of this did any good. The six cops and their captive trundled off along Spring Street toward wherever it was that cops took prisoners. Defeated, all the denizens of Crosby Street stood in silence watching for a brief moment. Then, as if on cue, they all turned away and went back to their various labors. There was no use worrying over something nobody could do anything about.

Terrified and defeated, Giuseppe turned back toward the house. He drew in a sharp breath to make himself stop shaking and to prevent himself from crying. He didn't mind crying when it made people give him more money for playing a sad song from old Italy, but he had never cried except for pay and he had no intention of doing so now. He squared his skinny shoulders, ignoring the stabbing pain from where the truncheon had struck, and headed back into the house.

Once again, he climbed the filthy stairs to the fifth floor.

The door to the nonno's room was as he had left it. Gingerly, not wanting to dislodge the door and have it fall on his head, he pushed it open. He glanced around the beautiful room. By the fireplace, the tool his grandfather used to prod the embers lay on the carpet and black soot stained the lovely pattern. Giuseppe bent down, picked up the poker and put it back in the wrought iron stand where it belonged. He wet his fingers with his own saliva and tried to rub the black soot from the rug, but his efforts only made it worse.

Looking toward his grandfather's desk, he saw that a few things had been displaced there, too, but he decided not to touch anything else. Nonetheless, he walked behind the desk. On the top, hard for him to see, but not impossible, sat the golden box with its little door open. He stood on his toes to get a better look. The effort hurt his neck, and he dropped his chin, then his eyes.

At his feet lay the piece of paper his grandfather said the police had to see if they were all to be saved.

He picked up the small square of paper. It felt heavy, but then he was used to touching newspapers, not documents written on fine stationery. Also, unlike newspaper, the words on this paper were not printed. He knew handwriting when he saw it, even if there was no way in the world he could decipher what it said.

There was, however, someone who could read it for him.

Not wasting another second, Giuseppe ran back down the five flights of stairs and out into the street.

CHAPTER 5

▼

Giuseppe looked for Billbone Benson all over Little Italy. He went as far as Chinatown and over to Hester Street, but he had no luck.

The boy wasn't selling his newspapers on the corner of Crosby and Broome. Giuseppe didn't know what time it was. Maybe the afternoon edition was sold out and the evening edition not yet ready. If so, Billbone would be with the other newsboys hanging around the big iron gate of the press room. Much as he hated that place—the roar of the presses, the steam escaping into the air with an evil hiss, the taunting of the bigger, older newsboys, the jeers of the rugged, ink-stained pressmen, Giuseppe nonetheless headed in the direction of Park Row and Printing House Square.

When he finally got there, the area was deserted. The only person he saw was an agent from the Society for the Prevention of Cruelty to Children lurking in the shadows of a doorway across the street. If he did find Billbone, Giuseppe could warn him to watch out. Saving his friend from being snatched by the society was a good way to thank Billbone for a favor.

Frustrated but determined, he left Newspaper Row and, scouring the darkening streets as he went, he put Mulberry Bend behind him, trekking northwest. The Bend was the worst slum of Manhattan, but at least it was a place where the streets never failed to offer a boy a place to sleep. Giuseppe glanced through rusted iron railings into dingy stairwells. Lots of boys were gathering now. The first to scramble down the stone steps would have the best spot. He'd be able to prop his back against the wall of the building and stretch his legs straight out in front of him—a luxurious use of space that would not be available to late-comers in the stairwell who would have to sleep curled on top of each other.

But it was just little boys who usually bedded down so early. Once a boy got to be eleven or twelve, he could only make real money working after midnight. And if he had the courage to work in the black-and-tan dives at Thompson and Broome, then he could earn enough for slick hats and sharp coats and fine new leather boots like the ones Giuseppe's pal Billbone Benson wore. Working black-and-tan might well mean that an Italian boy armed only with a small stiletto would have to go up against a Negro boy with a razor. Giuseppe was terrified of razors, considering them no match for his little knife. As far as he was concerned, being Negro made it easier for Billbone to hang around Thompson Street. The fact that Billbone was afraid of nobody and nothing helped too.

On the odd chance that he might find his friend before he got to Thompson, Giuseppe checked a few back alleys off Centre Street. There were a couple of abandoned wagons parked there—a perfect place for twenty or so boys to camp out for the night.

But they were empty as yet. So was the big pipe behind the tenement near the corner of Centre and Grand. He peeked in and saw blackened remnants of rags and gray piles of newspapers spread on the "floor" to soak up whatever foul liquids had pooled there. The stinking refuse formed a thick, soft mat for the boys to lie on. Thinking about that, Giuseppe felt a pang of sorrow and a renewed determination to save his grandfather from the police and jail. No matter how dangerous *The New York Times* might say that the house on Crosby Street was, at least the building had a roof that the nonno put over the head of every single man, woman, child, monkey and rat that lived there.

When he reached Broome Street, Giuseppe turned west. It was dark now and he no longer risked checking alleys and hidey-holes. He had to keep his wits about him.

A boy with no possessions to his name doesn't need pockets, and Giuseppe didn't have any. Instead, he carried the precious piece of paper tucked under a torn place in the leather band inside his old black hat. He looked to the left and the right, and seeing no one, he slipped the hat from his head and peeked inside. The paper that could save his grandfather was still safe.

But he wasn't.

Suddenly, boys seemed to appear everywhere, dashing out from behind trash cans, darting out of shadowed doorways, leaping down from the dozens of balconies that hung low over the narrow street.

Giuseppe was used to being pursued, though not by so many. Fear gave him added agility. He wove and darted and got away.

For a moment.

The Negro boys were older, bigger and faster. Every time he took a step, there was another one in front of him. He thought about the knife tucked up his sleeve, but pulling it out, even if he could get to it, would only encourage his tormentors to reach for their own terrifying weapons.

Flailing his arms and kicking out when he could, Giuseppe made slow progress, but he did manage to move a few yards along Broome. If he could just make it to West Broadway, he might have a chance to take a sharp right and run up that street. He wasn't crazy about cops or social workers, but there was at least a chance that one of those would be strolling Broadway. The Negros would run if they saw a cop. It was Giuseppe's only hope.

His attackers were circling in on him now, grabbing at his clothes and kicking his shins and the backs of his legs. He was shorter than any of them, which meant he could duck down and take quick glances between their legs, trying to catch sight of the glow of the gaslights on the corner he so desperately wanted to reach.

But when he got to West Broadway, it was neither police officer nor social worker who met him. Instead, reinforcements waited to add power to the gang of toughs already attacking him. These boys, even stronger than the others, wasted no time. They rushed Giuseppe, grabbed him the same way the cops had grabbed his grandfather. They jabbed rough fingers into his side, making him gasp. They seemed to find it hilarious that their rough treatment robbed the little boy of breath.

Laughing and joking in their deep rolling voices, they swept him along Broome, not letting his bare feet touch the sidewalk.

He fought his fear and then he fought them, squirming and kicking and yelling in Italian.

"Easy, little dago," one advised, "take it easy now."

Giuseppe tried to spit at him, but terror had dried his mouth. Instead, he kicked out as savagely as he could, catching the crotch of one of the boys who held him.

The Negro screamed and let go, seeming disabled, but in the next instant, he managed to snatch Giuseppe's hat.

Giuseppe watched in agony as the tattered object sailed up toward the gaslights, made an arc, then began to fall. Instinctively, he reached for it, but his arms were now pinned to his side and he was trapped.

CHAPTER 6

▼

It all flashed before his eyes. The toughs running away with the hat. The paper being lost or destroyed. His grandfather going to jail. His mother and his uncle disappearing from Crosby as the mothers and uncles of his pals on the street had disappeared so often before.

He could so clearly see what *might* happen that he failed to see what *did* happen.

A ringing voice called his name. A black hand waved in front of his face.

Startled, Giuseppe looked up to see something he had dared not hope for.

In front of him stood Billbone Benson and in his hand was Giuseppe's hat.

Dizzy with relief, Giuseppe stretched out his own hand to retrieve it.

But of course Billbone pulled it away and held it high over Giuseppe's head—the way he always did.

"Give it back!" Giuseppe jumped up, like one of the little monkeys. All the toughs started to laugh, but with a scowl, Billbone snapped his fingers and they dissolved back into the darkness.

"Come on," Giuseppe whined.

"Not until I'm finished," Billbone teased. He grabbed Giuseppe by the ear, as if he were disciplining him and pulled him along the sidewalk toward the corner of Thompson Street.

Giuseppe dug in the heels of his bare feet. "No! I'm not going over there."

"Don't be such as sissy," Billbone mocked. "Come on."

On Crosby Street the rumor was that black men had guns and black women had diseases. Giuseppe didn't believe the disease part because the women of Thompson Street, unlike the women of Crosby Street, were clean—and curvy and wore beautiful clothes with beads and feathers and embroidery. They had plumed hats and their ears sparkled with jewels. Billbone made a fortune running errands for them, acting as a go-between for one dame in particular. That was because Billbone could do two things faster than anyone else that Giuseppe knew: read and run.

As for the men, Giuseppe believed tales about the guns. Billbone had told him that if a person made one false move in the black-and-tan, he'd be shot dead. Which was not the reason Giuseppe believed. He believed because he'd seen at least one gun for himself.

"What are you doin' down here anyways?" Billbone asked, as he dragged his little friend toward the house on Thompson that he "serviced."

"Give me back my hat, and I'll tell you," Giuseppe answered.

Billbone laughed. "I got something to finish first," he said. "You can run or you can stick around and watch me. Then I'll give you back your hat." He pointed to a spot on the curb, and Giuseppe sat down. As if from nowhere, five or six other boys joined Billbone, but none of them were from the gang that had attacked before. Giuseppe breathed a sigh of relief. He realized what was going on. Billbone, as usual, had been shooting craps. His game had been interrupted and until it was done, there'd be no further talking to him.

While he waited, Giuseppe watched the action on the street in front of the building on Thompson. He saw more than one fine carriage pull up, the sleek flanks of the horses shining in the gaslight of the street lamps. All the men who stepped out of the carriages were white and well-dressed. They looked very up-town. Giuseppe had a hunch that what went on in this building was the same thing that went on in the back building on Crosby. That hunch told him that it wouldn't be long before all of this would be part of his life, too, though he couldn't yet guess how.

Once or twice, a man who had gone into the house came out shortly after with a striking woman on his arm, headed, Giuseppe guessed, for some club nearby, since no white man would be seen with a Negro woman other than in a black-and-tan area.

He was gazing at a particularly beautiful woman dressed all in pale lavender, when she noticed him, stopped her escort, asked him to wait, and came right toward Giuseppe.

The little boy stood, waited for the woman to speak.

"Ain't you the precious little dago!" she breathed in her dusky voice. "You wanna do a lady a favor?"

Dumbfounded, Giuseppe nodded.

Smiling, the woman reached into her reticule, a handbag that seemed to be made of nothing but two lavender feathers. She pulled out a little note. "You bring this to the address I wrote here, okay?"

Giuseppe stared at the words written there. Of course they meant nothing to him. He shook his head in dismay.

Seeing his discomfort, the beautiful doxy stroked his cheek. "Can't read?"

Giuseppe shook his head.

"Well, cutie, you all come back here some day and I'll teach you!" She laughed, a sweet, liquid sound that was like the warm coffee his mother gave him when he was cold, but before he could say anything, the doxy and her beau where off sauntering up Thompson Steet.

"Nice bit, that one," Billbone said, coming up behind Giuseppe and startling him. The boy turned in time to see Billbone stuff a handful of heavy coins into his pocket. Billbone was a wiz at craps. "You gotta be good lookin' to run errands for that one. Pretty particular for a doxy if you ask me."

"Billbone, I come down here because I need your help right away," Giuseppe said, not wanting to waste any more time.

"What's up?"

Giuseppe related to Billbone how he had told his grandfather about what the *Times* had said about children being held against their will and that the police had come and taken his grandfather away.

"Did the newspaper send the cops?" Giuseppe asked the older boy. "Is that what happened?"

Billbone shrugged. "Who knows?" He studied Giuseppe. "Did the cops get your harp?" He shoved Giuseppe's cap under his arm, crooked the arm and made a strumming gesture with his other hand. It was his usual way of mocking Giuseppe's playing.

Despite his difficulties, Giuseppe couldn't help smiling. "No, they didn't get my harp."

"Then what's your beef? You got a way to earn your bread. And you can sleep on the street. What do you need the old man for anyway? Don't he take all the money you make?"

"Yes, but ..."

"Ain't he on your back day and night?"

"Yes, but ..."

"So what's the problem?"

"Give me back my hat and I'll let you know," Giuseppe managed to get out, mimicking the wise-ass attitude of the older boy.

Billbone handed over the hat.

"Listen," Giuseppe said, "I don't want my nonno to go to jail. If he goes down, we all go down. My mother, my uncle. I don't want to sleep on the street. I don't want to be by myself. Not yet."

"Geez, but you're a baby," Billbone said. "Anyhow, what's all this got to do with me?"

"I need you to read me something."

"Aw," Billbone mocked, "the little baby needs a bed-time story. Want me to read you a bed-time story, baby?"

"Shut up," Giuseppe yelled. "Just shut up for once and read me this piece of paper." He reached inside his hat and extracted the tiny document. He unfolded it and handed it to Billbone as if he were handing him a sawbuck.

Billbone took the paper with due respect. He held it at an angle so that the gaslight fell on it. He made a great gob of spit and ejected it with terrific violence onto the pavement. He studied the paper some more.

"No way I'm reading this," he finally said.

"What? What do you mean you ain't reading it?"

"Simple," Billbone said, flicking the page with contempt. "It ain't English. It's dago. In case you forgot, little Tally boy, I'm American. I don't read dago."

"Billbone, please ..."

"No sir. Looks like you are right outta luck. Sorry, boy."

He tossed the paper at Giuseppe, jumped up, and headed toward the door of the whorehouse.

"Unless ..." he said over his shoulder in the whining teasing voice that drove Giuseppe crazy.

"Unless what?"

"Unless we can find the troll," Billbone said. "The troll can read. And everybody says he knows every language in the world, even Chinese."

"*Ho bisogno solo italiano,*" Giuseppe answered wearily. "I only need Italian— Can he do that?"

"Of course, but—" Billbone nodded toward the door to the house.

"But what?"

"Listen, kid," he said, "I got a night's work ahead of me. I can't take you to the troll right now. But we can go in the morning. You can help me now. I'll show you what to do." He gave a lascivious wink and shook his hips in a suggestive way.

"Nah, I ..."

"Don't be such a fool. I can show you how to make as much dough in one night as you make playing that stupid harp of yours all week long."

At the mention of his instrument, Giuseppe was struck with a sinking realization. He hadn't seen the harp since that moment early in the afternoon when Billbone had shown him his own last name in the *Times*.

"Hey," Billbone said, "what's up? You look like you seen your own ghost."

"Maybe I did," Giuseppe answered. "Listen," he went on, "I gotta know what this note says—and if you think the troll can help, I'll come back here tomorrow and we can find him. But I'm not sticking around here. I gotta go."

Had he put his harp away safely—or had he left it on the street? Maybe it was far too late to rescue it, but he had to get to Grand to see whether his instrument was where he usually hid it. Without the harp and without his grandfather, Giuseppe would have no choice but to take Billbone up on the offer to learn how to act as a go-between for the hookers and thugs in the black-and-tan.

"Don't be late, scaredy-cat," Billbone shouted, "because I got to be at Newspaper Row by sunrise!"

Giuseppe lifted a hand in answer to his friend. He didn't have time to turn back.

By the time he got to Crosby and Grand, he was totally out of breath. He'd gone only eight blocks, but he'd been terrified the whole time, holding his hat tightly under his arm, against his body. He'd kept his distance from doorways and from the black entrances of the alleys that opened onto the street between so many of the buildings. Even with the night air whizzing past his ears as he bolted, he could still hear the moans and sighs, the startled gasps and muffled screams of the denizens of midnight. He was a little boy and a lot more innocent than he would ever be again, but he knew the meaning of what he heard: screams of pain and stolen pleasure, sighs of satisfaction and of agony.

Hands reached to grab his clothing, feet extended to trip his steps, but he ran on, one more gaslit figure in streets full of fellow fugitives.

At last, he reached his own intersection. The building before which he usually played had a cornerstone set into the wall. The date on that stone had long since worn away, and so had the mortar that had held it fast. With fingers made eager by fear, Giuseppe clawed at the stone.

It quickly came free, and he jumped back as it crashed to the sidewalk inches from his bare toes.

He reached into the hole the stone had left.

Frantically, he stretched his small, agile fingers. At first he felt nothing but a few sprinkles of crumbly dust.

Then his hand touched the smooth, worn, painted wood of his harp. Relief filled him, and for the second time that day, he had to remind himself that tears nobody sees are tears wasted.

He sat down and did something else that was a total waste. He played a song to himself. It was a tune his father had taught him before he died, a song about a farm in Italy, in Laurenzana. Giuseppe had never seen Italy and knew he never would, but the song calmed him and he played it over and over until he started to fall asleep.

It was too dangerous to sleep on that corner, too dangerous to go back to his grandfather's house. For all he knew, the cops were waiting to take him, the way they'd taken the old man.

But he couldn't keep his eyes open much longer.

So, crawling with exhaustion, and now protective of both his hat and his harp and still wary of the dangers of the night, he walked another few blocks to Mott Street, where he found a stairwell full of slumbering waifs.

They slept too soundly to notice a stranger. When Giuseppe curled up on top of the heap of them and dozed off, they offered not the least objection, neither knowing nor caring that he didn't belong among them.

Not yet, anyway.

CHAPTER 7

▼

He woke up when the body beneath his began to squirm.

Rubbing his eyes, he saw the sky lightening over the East River. At first, he felt a boy's delight at a summer dawn. But soon the events of the previous day came crashing down on his consciousness and he remembered that he had a mission: to get Billbone to take him to the troll. He stashed his harp in another of his secret places and set out.

In the light of day, however, he felt differently about getting the troll to translate the note he carried in his hat.

Everyone said the troll was a wise old man, but Giuseppe wasn't so sure. For one thing, despite the troll's hunched posture and long beard, he didn't seem all that old. Giuseppe's Uncle Ambrogio, "Zi Gio," was probably older and the nonno was certainly older.

What difference did age make, though? If the old nonno was so smart, how come the cops had him?

Another thing, though: The troll was crazy. Giuseppe and Billbone snuck up on him on a fairly regular basis, watching him talking to stones and rain and dancing in the filthy waves that boats made at the edge of the water. Whatever music he danced to, nobody could hear it but him.

Violent, too. Making him spit and curse and even cry, making him hit his head against the piles of the pier until blood flowed was something Giuseppe and Billbone had done—once and once only.

But still, Billbone was right about the troll speaking other languages than English. So, Giuseppe retraced his steps back toward Thompson.

But when he got there, he learned that Billbone was long gone.

"The *Times* waits for no man," some old hooker just coming in from work told him, cackling like the witch she was.

By the time he got to Broadway, Giuseppe had decided to find the troll on his own.

Beside the banks of the river at the bottom of the city, a great tower was rising, greater than any the river or the city had ever seen. Giuseppe had never been across any of the three great rivers of Manhattan, but he knew there was another big city and another tower on the other side of the East River. Someday those towers would become Brooklyn Bridge. Not everyone believed that day would ever come, but the troll believed. Giuseppe knew because he'd said so, and also because he was already staking his claim beside the tower. He had a house built there of crates that had washed ashore.

And the troll wasn't alone in his faith in the coming of the Brooklyn Bridge and the treasures that lay at its feet. Most days he had neighbors—mudlarks, children as skilled as he was at scavenging in the yards of the docks and warehouses on the river bank.

The boy heard the troll before he saw him. Giuseppe was a musician from a long line of musicians and a tuneless song was torture to him. He felt like holding his hands up over his ears. Or maybe, he thought, over his eyes. Because the way the troll looked was as frightening as the way he sounded. His long straggly hair had seaweed in it and sand and pieces of broken glass. His beard was stiff with spit. His rank, tattered clothes moved in greasy undulations as he swayed his hunched body in jerky rhythm to his singing.

But Giuseppe forced himself to approach the weird man, taking careful steps along the beach with its broken boards, its twisted wire, its glass and shells and pools of oily muck.

The troll stopped singing. He stood stark still and stared at the one who approached. Giuseppe fought the urge to gag, to flee. Awkwardly, he smiled and held out his small hand.

The troll came nearer and stared at the hand as though he might make a tasty snack of it.

Giuseppe smiled harder. "Hello," he said, trying to sound cheerful and unafraid.

The troll grunted. His gruff voice struggled to form words. Giuseppe didn't understand the words, which made him think again that Billbone had to be right. The troll knew foreign tongues.

"I need you to help me," Giuseppe ventured.

The troll, as if he understood, shook his head in a rough gesture of refusal.

"Please," Giuseppe persisted. "I just need you to read something for me. You know, read?" He took the paper from his hat and in exaggerated imitation of Billbone reading the *Times*, pretended to scan and understand the little document.

The troll lunged at him, and Giuseppe jumped back. But then he realized the man was curious. Cautiously, he held the paper out.

The troll took it between his dirt-encrusted fingers and held it to his nose, which Giuseppe now noticed was covered with oozing sores. The troll held the paper so close to his face that Giuseppe cringed. He fought against grabbing the paper and running with it. Instead, he stood still and waited.

He seemed to have to wait a very long time. The sun was full up now, and by its bright light, the hunched figure on the beach seemed to read and read and read. Giuseppe knew that it shouldn't take so long. He began to feel panic, as if he'd made a horrible mistake in coming to this forsaken stretch of the shore. Workers would come here, but not for at least an hour. The troll could do a great deal of damage in an hour.

But Giuseppe dared not interrupt. Finally, with relief, he saw the troll nod in the manner of one who has figured something out to his own great satisfaction.

"It's dago," the troll announced.

"I know but ..."

"Dago, dago, dago," the troll began to chant.

"But what does it *say?*" Giuseppe begged. "Just tell me what it says."

"Dago, dago, dago," was all the troll would answer. His movements became more frantic. He stomped on the sand, his ragged clothes flying now as though stirred by a wind that touched him alone. He began to twirl, all the time yelling the expletive, waving Giuseppe's paper in the air. Within seconds, he was whirling so fast and screaming so loud that Giuseppe was terrified.

But he had to get his paper back. He sprang on the hairy monster and tackled him to the ground.

It was useless of course. The troll was older, bigger and much stronger than the boy. He easily sprang up, tossing Giuseppe onto the beach, and ran.

Before Giuseppe could reach him, the troll crunched Giuseppe's paper into a ball and threw it as hard as he could out into the waters of the river.

Shocked, Giuseppe rushed to retrieve the document. But the troll was behind him. He held the boy, preventing him from entering the water. Giuseppe knew how to fight hard from his life on the street and he knew tricks, too. Kicking and pinching, lifting his heels behind him to wound the troll wherever he could, he did all he could to get away, to get to the paper before the river claimed it.

But all he could do was not nearly enough. The troll grabbed him by the neck of his stupid little black jacket and held him suspended as horrified, he watched his grandfather's only hope of salvation float away.

CHAPTER 8

▼

The troll thought the whole thing was hilarious. He laughed so hard that he loosened his grip. Chuckling and shaking his shaggy head, he made off down the shingle, leaving the devastated Giuseppe on the shore. Behind the boy, the river was coming to life. Schooners lifted their white wings toward the city. Hundreds of smaller boats followed in the wake of the ships, the way rats follow a dog with a piece of meat in its mouth. The boy staggered back up into the streets of the town, back toward the house on Crosby. The running was over. It was time to face whatever awaited.

He was almost at the Bend when he sensed that someone was following him.

He stumbled toward a row of shop windows, hoping to catch the reflection of his pursuer.

No such luck. The sun wasn't at the right angle. All he could see was blazing yellow light. And when he turned again, nobody was there.

The third time he heard the faint steps, he swung around.

A tiny girl covered in mud was walking shyly behind him, keeping a distance of a few feet. She stopped still and stared at him with blue-white eyes surrounded by the grey-brown silt of the river.

"Get away," Giuseppe yelled. "Quit following me, you filthy piece of trash!"

The last thing he would ever have expected was that such a dirty useless little thing would care what anybody thought of her. But at his harsh words, the strange eyes filled with tears.

Despite all he'd been through, Giuseppe melted. No doubt to this poor little mudlark, *he* was a person of fortune and distinction.

He smiled.

And she held up her muddy hand, closed in a fist.

Giuseppe knew that mudlarks often offered some pathetic piece of garbage they'd scraped off the river bottom, hoping someone would give them a coin for their find. He, like every other street musician in Little Italy, had a secret horde he'd managed to keep from the *padrone*, his grandfather.

He took off his funny little conical cap. The sight of the band inside made him cringe when he thought what had been there and what had been lost. He fingered the sweat-stained band that circled the inside of the hat. In the band was a slit. In the slit was a coin.

He offered his only penny to the little girl.

She opened her hand. In it was the crumpled ball of paper that he had so recently given up for lost.

Before he could thank the mudlark, she'd run off, back in the direction of the river.

Giuseppe sat on the stoop of one of the tenements. Soon someone would ask him what he thought he was doing there, but for now, he didn't care about anything except what he held in his hand.

Had the fetid waters washed away what had been written?

Carefully, he unfolded the small document. Carefully, he smoothed it over his bare knee.

The document was wet on the edge, but the thick paper was still dry in the middle. And the writing was as clear as ever—to someone who could read it, that is.

"Move along, son."

The voice startled him out of his contemplation of the inscrutable words. Towering over him was a cop. On any other day, he'd have run. But now he remembered what his grandfather had told him about the power of the paper he held in his hand.

"*Buon giorno poliziotto.*"

"Speak English, son."

The story spilled out of him.

He told the officer about the house and the *Times* and the monkeys and the arrest. He said nothing about the paper, which was still in his hand because he didn't get a chance.

The officer got down on one knee and studied Giuseppe's face. He looked like he was trying not to smile. "Boy," he said, "are you hungry? Do you want something to eat?"

Giuseppe shook his head vigorously. He was starving. He couldn't remember the last time he had eaten. But it was one of the cardinal rules of the street never to accept an invitation to eat from a cop. That was the surest way to end up a captive of the Society for the Prevention of Cruelty to Children.

"Well, then," the cop said, "what exactly is it that you want from me?"

This was not a question Giuseppe was used to hearing.

"Well, lad?"

"What I want," Giuseppe finally answered, "is to know where a person would be—in the city, I mean—if they had to go to jail."

Now the cop did smile. "Somebody you know get rounded-up?" he asked with a knowing wink.

Giuseppe recognized the term. The police were always "rounding up" tramps, bad women and drunks. And boys too stupid or too slow to get away from them.

"Not really," he said evasively. Now that the cop was asking questions, he was getting nervous.

"Look, kid," the cop said, "if somebody of yours was rounded up, you gotta go over to the Elizabeth Street station."

Giuseppe reacted violently to this suggestion. "No," he shouted. "No, I can't …"

Maybe he *was* nothing but the son of a dirty monkey boy, but that didn't mean anybody in his family was the kind of trash that slept in the bug-ridden, urine-washed, tramp-jammed hallways of the vagrant lodgings at the Elizabeth Street police station. Nothing could get Giuseppe to enter that hell-hole, even the idea that his nonno was there.

"Calm down," the cop said. "If your old man—or whoever you're looking for—got picked up for something besides vagrancy, maybe you could try running over to Headquarters."

"Headquarters?"

"I don't know what your problem is, kid," the cop said, standing and shaking his head. He hadn't touched Giuseppe, but he started to rub his big hands as though to wipe something vile off them. He reached into his pocket and pulled out a little black book and a pen.

Giuseppe looked around desperately. How could he escape? Now the cop was going to write his name in the book! That meant arrest. And *that* meant he'd never find his grandfather. Every street kid believed men and boys were separated once the police got hold of them.

He shifted from foot to foot, but the big cop blocked his way. When the man reached down, Giuseppe cringed.

The cop wasn't grabbing for him, though. He was handing Giuseppe a piece of paper torn from his notebook—with writing on it.

Great. Another thing I can't read ...

"You don't need to know anything," the officer said, as though he were reading Giuseppe's mind. "You see that?" He pointed to the writing on the paper.

"Yeah."

"That there's the number of the Headquarters building over on Mulberry. You know Mulberry?"

"Yeah, I do."

"So," the cop said, "you get over to Mulberry and you start walking down the street. You watch the numbers on the doors. When you get to a big building with a number that matches what's on that paper, you're at Headquarters. You got that?"

"And you think my nonno might be there?" Giuseppe asked.

He regretted the words the minute they were out of his mouth. Because the question made him sound like a baby.

His baby days were over. His days as a man were about to begin.

CHAPTER 9

▼

It worked!

For the first time in his life, Giuseppe was able to make sense of something written down. By matching the numbers on buildings, just as the cop had suggested, he was able to find Police Headquarters.

The rounders lounging here were even more pathetic than the Elizabeth Street variety: more raggedly dressed, more vile-smelling, more covered with sores, more drunken, sunken and sad.

Nonetheless, Giuseppe steeled himself, and climbing over several reclining bodies that may have been dead bodies, for all he knew, he reached the front door of the building, pulled at it, and managed to get inside.

The first thing he noticed was the sound.

Giuseppe lived in a world of singing and shouting, of sighing and swearing. But all *that* noise was in the soft, rolling, lolling tongue of Italian.

This noise was American, and it was so loud, so brash, so punctuated with harsh expletives and harsher laughter, that Giuseppe, whose English was perfect, thought he had lost all power to understand that language. What were all these people—for the large central hall was jammed with uniformed cops and men in suits and women in long white dresses—yelling about?

It took him a few minutes to figure out what was going on. He had heard, and now was witnessing for himself, that rich people sometimes came down to Mulberry to watch poor people. Giuseppe was completely mystified by this notion, though he found it amusing to see that the police officers seemed as confused by it all as he was. A line of officers stood arguing with the well-dressed ladies and gentlemen, trying to convince them to leave.

Which was hilarious to the boy, because at the same time, he could see a long string of prisoners, linked by handcuffs and shackles, giving the guards at the front and the back of the line a hard time. They, prisoners and cops alike, would have been very happy to leave.

Giuseppe was a musician, not a pickpocket, but he had friends who were proponents of the light-fingered art, and from them he had learned that the best thing to do in any crowd was to work the fringe.

So he kept to the edge of the large room. His mission was to find his grandfather—if the old man was indeed here. His intention was to figure out which door might lead to regions of the building that were more private and secret than this bustling lobby.

He felt intimidated by the crowd, and though he, having been born on Mulberry Street, was just as American as any of them, he felt like a foreigner. If they caught him, they would call him a "dago" or "wop". But they weren't going to catch him.

Keeping as close to the wall as he could, he began to check out the doors and hallways that opened off the large room.

Skulking along the wood panelling, careful to avoid drawing attention to himself, Giuseppe soon noticed two types of exits from the crowded hall. Some were thick doors. Some were barred gates.

Most of the doors were closed, but he snuck along until he found an open one and peeked in.

Behind a desk higher, wider and more intimidating than his grandfather's desk, sat a man in a suit.

Was this the person the cop had meant when he'd said Giuseppe might be able to get help at Headquarters?

He had almost made up his mind to try to give this man the paper, when he heard a noise a few feet away. It seemed to come from behind one of the barred gates.

In front of that gate stood a mammoth guard whose fingers stroked a ring of heavy keys.

Giuseppe heard the noise again. It sounded like chains dragging on stone. Could this be where they kept the prisoners who were going to jail? Could his grandfather be among them?

Giuseppe remembered Billbone once telling him that the thing to do when you saw a key was to steal it.

But which key to steal?

Anyway, stealing meant running and how was he supposed to run past the guard or through the crowd? If he wasn't careful, he'd end up in chains himself.

Nonetheless, Giuseppe crept closer to the man with the keys.

Just as the boy got within a few feet of the gate, the snaking line of prisoners he'd seen being led earlier reached the gate from the opposite direction. As they drew near, the big guard turned to unlock the gate.

Giuseppe saw his chance.

At the precise moment in which the last shackled convict passed through the open gate, Giuseppe grasped his hat and threw it as hard as he could.

He hit the guard right between the eyes.

The stunned man snorted and stomped like a bull, dragged his meaty hand across his low brow. He didn't even see the small boy at his feet grab a dirty black hat off the floor and scoot into the darkness behind the line of inmates. He slammed the gate shut.

Giuseppe felt a moment's panic. Had he just put himself in jail? Behind him, he saw the shifting crowds in the hall and wished he'd not been so rash.

But it was too late now. He turned and peered ahead into what seemed like a long tunnel made of carved rock. It was very dark and it smelled so bad that he gagged. He knew boys who slept in the sewer. They didn't smell as bad as this rank combination of urine, sweat, feces, mold and fear.

Since he was so small, it didn't bother him that the tunnel was low. It was several feet above his head. But it was dimly lit by only a few gas lamps that gave off an oily, choking smoke.

Already he could no longer see the line of prisoners, which had to mean that the tunnel took a turn a short distance ahead. He shook off his panic and moved on.

About ten feet ahead, he came to the place where the tunnel turned. To his surprise, he saw a bright light and heard laughter. He took the branch of the tunnel that led toward the light.

Twenty or so feet along, he came upon a wooden archway built into the stone. Creeping forward, he found himself staring into yet another crowded room.

He saw a man sitting high above everyone else. Against the wall, in a box made of iron bars, a ragged line of prisoners squinted on the scene, as though every last one of them was unused to light.

Surprisingly, there was plenty of light. It streamed down from tall windows and sputtered behind the frosted globes of the gas lamps. In its dazzle, old cops and rookies buzzed about. Giuseppe had to think before he realized what he was seeing. This was the Magistrate's Court. Billbone used to read him tales from the newspaper of desperate criminals dragged before the bench here. Both he and Billbone loved those stories, especially when the criminals were people that they knew personally.

But now that his own grandfather was under the power of the police, Giuseppe felt differently about this room. If his grandfather was here, he had to go to him. And if he wasn't here, he had to find him.

He studied the squirming prisoners, the cops, the courtroom lackeys, the crowd jamming the benches in the back, craning their necks to see what was happening ...

He jumped back startled when, without warning, a solid iron gate came crashing down between him and the scene in the court.

Cast into complete darkness, he stifled a scream. He reeled with dizziness, reaching out for something to hold onto but touching only the slimy walls of the tunnel. He wretched and fought against vomiting, squeezed his eyes shut and held his breath.

When he opened his eyes, he saw that the blackness revealed something he hadn't noticed before. A faint greenish light shone from somewhere in the distance and voices sounded above other sounds: rats scurrying, water dripping.

At least some of the voices were Italian, and they were all talking at once. When an American voice yelled, "Shut up!" all other voices ceased.

Giuseppe remembered the place where the tunnel turned. He forced himself to keep his hand on the wall to follow its contour until he could get back to that place. The dim greenish light glimmered more strongly ahead of him. He began to hear a rushing, throb and recognized it for what it was—his own blood pounding in his ears.

But he ignored it and moved steadily toward the glow.

CHAPTER 10

▼

The prisoners sat thigh to thigh on a rough bench with their ankles chained into metal loops in the stone floor. Over their heads, lamps with parchment shades green with mold failed to dispel the black shadows on their desperate faces.

Giuseppe's grandfather was the only clean one among them, the only one whose clothes were not tattered rags. The old man flinched each time a guard's black baton swung by his face and missed his eyes by the breadth of a hair.

"What are you so afraid of, wop?" the guard demanded.

Though he had often toppled such a man by diving at his calves and throwing his full weight against them, this time Giuseppe restrained himself despite his instant hatred. He had to keep still until he could figure out what was going on.

He hunkered down behind an overflowing ashcan and spit its dust from his mouth without making a sound.

After only a few minutes, he understood that his grandfather's group was next to be dragged into court.

"Bring the dago bastards along," the American voice he'd heard earlier shouted.

"Whatever you say …" responded the Irish voice of the guard.

With a clanking shuffle, the row of prisoners slowly lurched upward and straggled toward the opening into the tunnel.

Giuseppe, like the sewer rats that scuttled away from his steps, followed the line of prisoners back through the dim tunnel.

When they entered the courtroom and the officers shoved his nonno into the box with the other prisoners, Giuseppe darted across the room. As quickly as he could, he sank to the floor behind a wooden railing that separated the cops and the judge from the spectators at the back.

He gasped when an old woman in a filthy yellow silk dress gave him a hard kick with the toe of her boot. "Get out of here, you stinking street scum," she hissed at him.

The boy scooted farther along the row of observers and cowered at the feet of another stranger, a fat man who perhaps couldn't see past his own paunch. At any rate, he let Giuseppe be.

The boy's small, muscular hands gripped two posts of the railings and he pulled his face close to the space between them. His heart leapt when he heard his grandfather's name called out.

The nonno rose with great difficulty. His hands were dragged down by the weight of the shackles around his wrists and those of his neighbors on either side. He could do no better than to stoop.

"Stand up straight, man," the guard commanded. And he wielded the grandfather a terrible blow with the baton that sent him staggering and pulling the whole line of prisoners askew.

"Leave the man alone," Giuseppe heard the judge warn the guard.

But Giuseppe's grandfather was proud. He wrenched himself up. Pain twisted his mouth. The humiliation of his position was clearly written across his handsome face.

But a worse humiliation was about to come. A bailiff held up a long list and began to chant a litany of nefarious charges.

"Giuseppe Amadeo Ambrogio Di Buonna," the bailiff called out, "you stand charged that you, within the City of New York, for the period from January 23, 1872 up to and including July 7, 1873, at premises situate on Crosby Street in said municipality, did abduct at least fifty children under the age of twelve years and did cause them to labor daily for periods exceeding eighteen hours without recompense, contrary to the laws of the State of New York."

The bailiff looked around the room as though to gauge the reaction of the crowd to the charges. They stared at him expectant but uncomprehending. He squared his narrow shoulders and went on, "You stand further charged that you did wilfully engage in the purchase of said children for certain sums of money tendered in Italy and in the United States of America."

"Slavery!" someone shouted. "Damn dago slave-driver!"

The judge banged his gavel hard, and the noise of the crowd subsided—but only momentarily. They erupted again when the bailiff read, "You stand further charged that you did forcibly confine said children and hold them against their will. You stand further charged that you neglected to provide the necessaries of life, that you exposed such children by way of wilful negligence to moral corruption and …"

His voice was drowned by the jeers and boos of the crowd. Even the banging gavel was no match for the wild yelling that rang from every part of the room.

Giuseppe understood exactly what was going on. His grandfather was being accused of buying and keeping slaves—not negro slaves, but Italian-American slaves. He tried to sink even closer to the floor. Nobody knew who he was, but he still felt the intense shame that centered on his nonno.

Slave-driver. Billbone knew people who had been slaves. Lots of them. And Giuseppe's own mother had shown him pictures of slaves from the war in a magazine she found in the street.

Jumping from his hiding place, Giuseppe waved the magic little document over his head. "*Basta!*" He shouted. "Enough."

He felt a strong shove from behind. He didn't know whether it was an assault or a gesture of support. Whichever, he pushed aside everyone between him and the judge's bench. People shut up and watched in silence as he marched toward the front of the room.

"My grandfather isn't a slave-driver. He's not like these rotten bums." He pointed at the other prisoners in the box. He sought his grandfather's gaze and held the blue eyes with his own. "I can prove that my grandfather didn't do anything wrong!"

Hope lit the old man's face.

Giuseppe saw and was emboldened. He moved closer to the prisoners' box. He stood on his toes and tried to reach through the bars to hand his grandfather the paper.

The old man reached, but the shackles restrained him.

A hand grabbed the paper from the boy. The hand of a cop.

Giuseppe turned. Suddenly, there were four cops where before there had been one. He glanced at their unreadable faces far above him. He took a step, but they moved as he moved. He had lived on the street long enough to read the body language of cops.

It was time to flee, and he did.

But before he escaped, he snatched the paper back from the officer who had grabbed it.

Then he ran, pushing and shoving, swearing and kicking, until he was out of there and as far away from Mulberry Street as he could get before he collapsed.

CHAPTER 11

▼

He wandered the street for hours.

"Heard your old man got rounded up," people told him over and over. Despite the fact that Police Headquarters seemed so far away, everyone on the street seemed to have gotten the news.

"They eat dagoes and spit them out on the sidewalk like a seed," Billbone offered helpfully. "You'll never see your old nonno again."

Giuseppe took a swing at his friend, but it was half-hearted and ineffectual and resulted, as usual in a bout of merciless teasing.

So Giuseppe moved on. He heard so many gruesome stories about what would probably happen to his grandfather, that he finally gave into his fear and decided to go home.

When he got to his usual corner at Crosby and Grand, he saw that another boy had already staked a claim to his spot. He realized he'd have to retrieve his harp and find somewhere else to play it if he ever hoped to earn any money again. Maybe now that his grandfather was in jail, he could keep all the money he made.

The idea was so unusual that it captured his full attention so that he was startled when he looked up the street and saw that police were surrounding his grandfather's house.

Again he fled. Again he wandered the streets for hours.

Again he gave up.

After two days, he returned, carrying his hat and his harp in his hands.

He was relieved to see that no police surrounded the house now. He approached the building. He listened for the sound of the women singing and splashing as they worked in the yard, but he heard nothing.

The door to the house was open. Giuseppe walked slowly toward it and pushed his way into the front hall. It was empty and silent.

He wandered from floor to floor, from room to room.

The cruel women who tended the fire and branded the children were gone.

The dirty men crowded into their beds leered and grabbed no more. They had disappeared.

The room that had housed the monkeys was wrecked. Perches, pens, cages lay broken and strewn across the expanse of floor.

But here, for the first time since he had arrived, Giuseppe heard a sound. From somewhere within the monkey room came the soft sound of weeping.

With trepidation, the boy crept into the room. The sound seemed to be coming from a heap of broken wooden slats in the corner. Gingerly, Giuseppe began to poke among the splintered animal cages.

He jumped back when he felt the touch of a finger on his hand.

Then he had to laugh.

The little monkey that he had seen days before, the one that had bit the kid who had been "training" him, was staring up at him.

The boy reached out. The monkey, with a little cry that sounded like relief, climbed up the boy's body, threw his monkey arms around the boy's neck and clung.

Carrying the tiny fellow, Giuseppe took the stairs to the top of the building. Like the door downstairs, the door to his grandfather's great room was open.

Everything was gone. Every picture, every rug, the big wooden desk. The golden box with the little door.

Giuseppe looked around. He walked to the window and stared out for a moment at the empty yard below.

Then he came back toward the center of the room.

He sat on the bare floor.

He picked up his harp and began to play.

The little monkey knew exactly what to do.

He lifted his tiny foot, spun around one time, caught the beat of the music and danced his heart out.

CHAPTER 12

▼

New York to Toronto. 1910.

"Mangia ..."

Out of the corner of his eye, twelve-year-old Joe Di Buonna snuck a look at the hunk of mozzarella surrounded by nice soft Italian bread with a golden crust that he could feel against his tongue even though his mouth was shut tight in protest.

He was hungry, as usual, and other people on the train were eating, too. Most of them were American. He could tell by the smells that filled the car—mustard and pickles, pastrami, hard-boiled eggs, green apples. Joe was as familiar with that food as he was with Italian food, and he still preferred the latter.

But he'd starve and turn to a wind-blacked corpse before he'd take nothing from the kidnapper thug in the seat beside him.

"Okay, starve you little bastard," the man told him, shoving the bread and cheese into his own mouth.

Boldly, Joe watched the mark on the side of the man's face move up and down with the motion of his chewing. On his cheek, barely visible beneath the black and gray stubble, was a pale red symbol that Joe had seen before.

"What are you starin' at, you mongrel?"

Joe didn't answer. He turned his eyes toward the window beside which he sat. Despite his fear, anger and disgust, he felt his heart leap when he realized what he was seeing out there.

The train was rounding a great curve and in the distance, he could plainly see the engine! Its silver sides gleamed in the sun and a huge cloud of steam rose from it, puffing like the breath of a powerful, but benign dragon.

It was so beautiful out there that Joe nearly forgot to be afraid.

And the trip had been beautiful every moment since the man with the red scar on his cheek had grabbed him, made him jam everything he owned, including his harp, into a small black cloth bag and dragged him off Mulberry and all the way uptown to Thirty-fourth.

Stunned, the boy had allowed himself to be taken inside a palace guarded by great stone eagles and covering more than a whole city block. Not a real palace, though it could have been. In fact, the man had hauled him into Pennsylvania Station. Joe, more used to looking down than up, noticed the marble floors first. And when he did look up, he saw the ceiling soaring toward the sky, the pillars, the carving ... He dawdled then, unable or unwilling to follow the fleet steps of his captor.

The man had raised his hand as if to hit the boy for moving so slowly, but had not hit him after all, letting Joe gaze and gape until his neck hurt.

His reverie was broken by a hard jab on his shoulder. He turned, ready to spit, but stopped himself. In front of his nose, its smell pungent, exotic and too tempting to resist, was an orange the size of a baby's head.

He took it and the captor smiled. Joe forced himself not to smile back.

As he peeled it and let the sweet juice flow into his mouth, Joe thought about how the train had pulled out of the city. He'd never left Manhattan before. Had no idea that the Hudson River went any farther north than Forty-Second Street, which was the farthest from Little Italy that he'd ever been, the day he'd tried to follow his father, Giuseppe, and his father's friend, Billbone Benson, to Harlem.

That had been when he was eight. He'd never seen Harlem at all. And he'd never seen his father or Bill again.

But for sure, the Hudson *did* go farther and, like a miracle, it seemed able to change the city into something else altogether. For the farther the train went, the more the buildings disappeared, the wider the river became, the thicker the trees, the higher the hills, the more numerous the flowers, the birds ... He'd even seen amazing animals that weren't horses or donkeys or dogs. He'd broken down then and asked the captor, who'd laughed and said they were unicorns, and when the boy believed, had laughed again and said softly, "No, *ragazzo*. Cows."

At a place called Albany, the river disappeared, but not the hills.

At a place called Buffalo, they got off the train and slept in a hotel and ate in a restaurant. After supper, they went to a saloon. Everybody in the place seemed to know the captor, whose name, Joe learned, was Ambrogio, nick-named "Gio". The conversation was in Italian and English and Joe understood both perfectly. Ambrogio had come to New York to get him and to bring him to Old Man Di Buonna.

Joe understood that, too, and he knew he had to get away.

That night, he had to sleep in the same bed as Ambrogio.

Such a thing was ordinarily no big deal. But in this hotel, unlike any Joe had seen before, there was only one bed in each room. Which meant it was amazingly quiet.

Which meant that if he moved, Ambrogio would wake up and grab him.

So for a long time, he lay in the dark, listening to a clock somewhere far away strike the hours. He could faintly hear drunken voices in the street. A light from outside shone in the window, casting a bright yellow stripe against the wall. Once, he even heard an automobile. He wished he could go to the window and take a look at the car.

He heard the sound of boat horns, too. And wondered whether somehow the Hudson had mysteriously reappeared.

Of course not!

While he was trying to figure out all the other sounds, he heard one he hadn't figured on.

Ambrogio had started to snore!

Deep, air-sucking, lung-shaking gasps and snorts shook the rickety bed.

Joe almost cried out in gratitude.

Fortunately, the only article of attire that Joe had removed when he'd gotten into bed was his shoes. They were stowed under the rough pillow beneath his head.

Careful not to move any other part of his body, Joe slid his hand beneath the pillow.

A pair of warm, strong fingers snatched his own.

In the light from outside, Ambrogio's eyes looked yellow. They were wide open, locked on Joe's face.

The boy screamed and jumped, but his captor held him fast. The more he struggled to break free, the stronger the grip of man.

"Stop it, boy! Stop this minute," Ambrogio commanded. Somehow the English words sounded so much more forceful than Italian that Joe gave up his thrashing. He lay immobile as the adult's fingers circled his wrists, holding both in one huge hand.

"*Basta. Che fai?*" Ambrogio demanded. "What the hell's the matter with you now?"

As if he didn't know!

"You're a kidnapper!" Joe found the courage to tell him. "You took me away from home and now you're taking me to that awful old man who kills children.

Well, I'm not a child. And I'm not coming with you. I'm going back to New York."

Joe pulled hard, freeing his arms and swinging around to sit on the edge of the bed, his legs dangling. He remembered his black bag and peered into the darkness as though he could find his possessions in the gloom.

A low laugh came from the other side of the bed.

"Tell me if I'm saying something wrong," Ambrogio said, his voice amused rather than gruff, "but I don't remember taking you from home. You don't have a home. You were sleeping in the cellar of a saloon."

Joe didn't answer. Because it was true.

"And as for the old man, why would he harm you? Do you realize what you are to him?"

"A slave," Joe answered. It was the dirtiest word his father had ever taught him.

Joe felt air brush the back of his neck and realized his captor had made a gesture of contempt. "You believe that garbage? There hasn't been a slave in America in fifty years."

"Then he's a murderer!" Joe shouted, jumping off the bed, kneeling on the floor and searching frantically for his bag.

"He never killed in his life," Ambrogio said. "A boy who believes in lies is worse than a liar himself. The man I take you to see is your own blood. The father of your grandfather. The grandfather of your father."

"I don't give a fig who the old man is," Joe answered. "My father told me how his grandfather made him work night and day ..."

"You work night and day yourself," Ambrogio said. "Your great-grandfather wants to change that. He wants you to go to school. To have a decent life. To live like a proper boy and not *come il vagabondo*."

Now it was Joe who made a gesture of contempt, his small fingers forming the vilest sign he could think of. "I don't want to go to school," he said. "I want to go back to New York. I want to go home."

"Tomorrow," Ambrogio said, suddenly sounding sleepy. "I'll take you home tomorrow."

It was the sort of thing you'd say to a baby. Not that it mattered. Joe had already made up his mind. "Fine," he said, "take me home tomorrow." He sat back down, swung his legs up onto the bed, curled his young body. Despite his anger and fear, he fell into sweet, deep sleep.

But the next day, he was as determined as ever to get free and to get back to New York.

He watched for his chance when they went back to the train station and bought bread and milk to carry onto yet another train. It should have been easy to disappear into the crowd there, but just as Joe was about to slip away, a conductor in a blue suit and a funny round cap like a cake grabbed his black bag and insisted on helping him carry it right to the seat he was forced to take beside Ambrogio.

Within minutes the train was chugging along and before the hour was up, Joe was astounded to be crossing over a deep gorge at the bottom of which he could make out a rushing, steaming white river. "Look," his captor told him, pushing the boy's nose up against the window. "Look up the river there. See those clouds of smoke? That's Niagara Falls. People come from all over the world to see that. Look at it, boy! Look at it!"

Joe was no cry-boy. He prided himself on never having cried in his life. But if he were so inclined, that would have been the moment. He had heard of Niagara Falls. Who hadn't? As the train clacked over the bridge all he could think of was that now he was going to have to find some way to climb back over the falls, back across the white river in order to get home to New York.

Despair made him sleepy. He napped and lost track of time. When he woke up, the journey was done.

When he first glanced out the window, he was confused, because the place where the train stopped looked exactly like the place he'd left. A moment's wild joy lifted his heart.

But this was not New York. Beyond the familiar-looking wooden buildings that hugged the railroad tracks, no mammoth buildings rose to hug the sky. There were no great bridges. Above all, there were no ships worth talking about in what Joe could see of the harbor, which was not much. This was a city, all right, but it wasn't home.

And there was no Pennsylvania Station either. Instead, out of the smoke and the mist that the engine had brought with it, rose two eerie white towers with black spikes that seemed to poke the sky as if wanting to make it bleed.

As had been the case now for so many hours, Ambrogio kept the boy close. Every time Joe took a step away, Ambrogio managed to grab his arm or the edge of his jacket or the suspenders of his pants.

It wasn't until they'd dismounted from the train and crossed the tracks to walk toward the station, that Joe finally saw a way to cut loose from his tormentor. Another train had pulled onto the platform. Joe knew nothing of locals or commuter trains, but he could see that the second the doors were thrown open, hundreds of men in what looked like business suits ran as fast as they could off that train and toward the city. They carried no suitcases, like travellers from afar, but instead had newspapers and satchels tucked under their arms. They ran like rats that had smelled a dead chicken, and Joe, his own bag tucked under his arm, ran with them.

He never expected to see Ambrogio again and he was glad.

Until he remembered he had no money, no place to sleep when night came, no friends. He had no idea where he was or even whether he would be able to understand the language the people spoke in this new strange land.

Within moments, he found himself inside the station. It was small and dull compared to what he'd just seen in New York, and he basically went in the back door and came out the front.

The second he stepped out into the street, he was nearly run over by an automobile. He fell to the ground. Dazed he lay there for a moment. When he rose, he found himself surrounded by ragged men and women, all of whom seemed to think he had money, for they shoved things in his face: a newspaper, a bolt of cardboard with shoelaces wound around it, apples, oranges, candles. He shook them all away, but when he'd managed to dust himself off, rise, and take a step or two, he saw a vendor whose wares scared the living daylights out of him.

"Comet pills," shouted a man who wore the black coat and white collar of a priest. "Buy them now before the earth passes through the tail of the great monster of the sky."

Seeing Joe gaping in wonder at the vial in his hands, the priest came closer and shook the little glass bottle in the boy's face. "Comet pills," the priest repeated, his mouth a read gash in his grinning face. "There is time to save yourself, but only just …"

CHAPTER 13

That night Joe saw the comet for the first time. It was nothing but a fuzzy dot in the sky, bright in the middle but with a long pale tail that swept away from it like a veil. He wondered why he hadn't been able to see it in New York. Had it just come into the sky?

That was just one more thing to try to figure out.

He was having a hard time understanding the way people in this town talked. He was used to New York accents—Manhattan and Brooklyn and Queens. But he had heard few if any English accents and for sure had never heard a Scotsman in his life. As he wandered the streets, trying to decide what to do, men spoke to him. Maybe they were being friendly. He really couldn't tell because he couldn't understand a word.

Being hungry was another problem but Joe soon realized that every trick he knew for stealing food in New York would serve him very well in this new town. In fact, he was surprised at how easy it was to filch fruit from the wagons here. In New York, a boy could get his hand stabbed if he got caught lifting an apple or a pear. Here, the vendors seemed almost not to care. They talked to their customers and to fellow vendors, often taking their eye off the merchandise. This place seemed like a street thief's dream.

Still, he had to get his hands on some cash. He picked the first pocket that presented an opportunity, but when he opened the little purse that was his prize, he was shocked.

Nothing in it looked like any money he'd ever seen before. The bills, unlike American money, were all different sizes and funny colors. They had pictures of some guy on them that Joe had never seen the likes of. A fat man with a lot of whiskers. What president was this? Not Teddy Roosevelt. Or Mr. Taft, either. For a minute Joe wished that he'd gone to school. But only for a minute.

At least this place was a city. There were some tall buildings and the streets were jammed with people. They dressed up in this town—the few women on the street wore big hats and most of the men wore suits.

There were a lot of shops and a lot of eateries, too, though, as far as Joe could see, no saloons. Which meant he couldn't make a bit of money washing bottles, which he always did at home when the pickin's were slim on the street, that is, when nobody fell for his little Italian angel with a harp routine.

Speaking of which, he opened his black bag and peeked inside just to make sure his instrument was safe.

He walked up what seemed like the main drag for a while, deciding where he should go next. He kept his eye out for his captor, but the man had disappeared.

After several hours of wandering, hunger struck again. The vendors had long since left the street. In the distance, he could make out a clock tower, guarded by stone statues of weird, threatening figures—gargoyles. The face of the clock was lit. It said ten p.m. He didn't know anything about north or south, so he didn't know what direction he'd been travelling since he'd been snatched and hauled onto the train, but he did know that this place was colder than home. He shivered and pulled his light jacket more tightly around him.

He was beginning to think he'd been wandering in a big circle when he looked up to see something he'd surely not seen before. Directly ahead of him stood a brightly-lit restaurant, busy with the comings and goings of a number of men and even a couple of women. Over the door, a gleaming sign, lit with tiny electric bulbs spelled out several words he could not read and two he could.

"New York!" What could this mean?

As he stood on the sidewalk mystified, a well-dressed woman stepped out on the arm of a gentleman. The man left the lady for a moment to hail a cab. As the horse-drawn hansom drew near, Joe grew bold.

Opening the little change purse he'd stolen, he took out a few of the bills and folded them in his hand so that the colors showed.

He approached the woman. "Madam," he said softly, "could you please tell me which …"

The woman turned at the sound of his voice. She would have been pretty except that she looked so proud and full of her own importance. She wore a small cape that sat on her narrow shoulders. She grasped it in her gloved hand and pulled it tight around her neck as if it were some kind of armor.

Joe's voice froze in his throat. All he had intended to ask was what the money was called and how much it was worth.

But he had no chance.

The woman let go of her cape. She took off one of her gloves. And she slapped Joe as hard as she could—right across his face.

Hurting and stunned, he raised his hand to rub his cheek. The woman cringed and screamed and began to yell, "Police! Police!"

The folded bills flew out of Joe's hand and scattered on the sidewalk. He was no green street arab. He knew it would take time for a cop to show up. So he bent down and began to scoop up the money as fast as he could.

He was so distraught that he didn't even find it strange when a man stooped down beside him and started to help, handing Joe a couple of the wayward bills.

But when the man grabbed Joe's black bag, the boy suddenly came to and realized he'd been careless.

He lunged for the bag.

His hand and the hand of man took hold at the same time. Joe tugged, the man tugged.

Joe looked up, ready to hiss or spit to get the man to let go.

It was then that he saw the red scar on the man's cheek.

With his black bag under his arm, he took off and he ran until the sound of his heart beating in his ears drowned out the sound of the footsteps pursuing him.

Every time he got to a corner he turned. It made no difference to him where he went. Sometimes he sped from the glare of a wide street lit by electricity into a narrow alley lit by gas or by nothing. Blinded, he tripped over ashcans, spilling their acrid contents in his path.

By the time he stopped, slipped into the shadows behind a church, caught his breath and peeked out to see that he was no longer being followed, his eyes had adjusted to the uneven light. The things he had seen: the buildings, the beggars, the newsboys, the toughs and the bully swells, were no different from things he'd been looking at all his life.

"You lookin' for the mission, young man?"

He jumped to find an old woman not three feet away from him in the shadows.

"Because if you are, yer too late for supper. You want something to eat, you gotta come back after the sun come up and before the front door of this church opens. Them's the rules ..."

Joe stared hard into the darkness. All he could make out was a heap of rags. He wanted nothing to do with filthy old women or with missions, either. He drew in his breath and made to run again.

But he hadn't gone two blocks when he heard a sound that stopped him in his tracks.

It was the sound that had stolen his father from him, that had seduced Giuseppe Di Buonna away from the Lower East Side and up into the unknown reaches of Harlem: Ragtime.

He wanted to hate that sound, but he just couldn't. The hot piano cut through the coldness of the northern night and Joe followed his heart toward the song.

The joint was a saloon for sure. He stepped through the door.

Immediately the warmth of the place hit him in the face, the heat of bodies and booze and light. He hoped the funny money would work here. He hoped whoever ran this joint would ignore the fact that he was a kid, not a man.

But he figured he was out of luck when the first person who noticed him was a copper.

Joe sidled back toward the door as the huge constable came toward him.

"Get next door," the cop said, not scowling but not exactly smiling either.

"I—"

"Next door or out …" The cop tipped his head toward an archway that loomed ahead.

Joe weighed his options. He could go back out into the street and sleep hungry, or he could do as the cop demanded. He couldn't see past the arch the cop pointed to, but behind his own back, the raucous voices of drunken men rose in a chorus of shouting and lewd laughter.

He pushed past the cop and into the room beyond.

It was full of ladies. A strong female hand grabbed him and pushed him down hard on a polished wooden chair. "Here ya little cutey, have a bite …"

He stared down at a steaming plate of cabbage and boiled ham. He decided to eat first and ask questions later.

The female sat down beside him and pulled him close to her side. "You need a place to sleep, honey, or are you going back to the Ward?"

Joe pulled away.

"Hey, little dago-boy, don't make strange …"

Another woman sat down on his other side, hemming him in. She reached down and wove her fingers through his thick curls.

"I got money to pay …" He managed to say.

"Money? Let's see."

Joe reached into his pocket and pulled out the bills he'd managed to salvage.

From the expressions on the painted faces of the two women, he could tell that he'd scored big.

One of them snatched at the bills.

Stuck as he was between them, Joe had to move fast to keep them from grabbing all the cash.

"Ladies," he said, unknowingly imitating the charming Billy Benson, friend of his father. "Ladies, let's not be grabby."

He choose two of the bills and gave one to each.

The ladies seemed satisfied. They laughed, called for ale, moved aside and let Joe go.

Back out in the street, he found the nearest doorway and sunk down into the shadows cast by a flickering gas lamp.

At first, he could still hear the ragtime, the shouts of drunkards, the giddy laughter of cheap women, but after a while, all fell still.

But exhausted as he was, he couldn't sleep.

He reached into his little black bag. It was dusty now and sticky from all it had been through over the past few days, but inside, his only possession was exactly as it had been when he'd put it there in New York. He pulled out the small white harp.

The instrument had been in his family as long as he knew.

And so had been the tune he played.

It was an old song from long-lost Laurenzana, which he, being born and raised in America as his father had before him, had never seen. The song was about mountains and clouds and the sun of spring that fell on the houses of an Italian village. He'd heard it all his life, played it sometimes for money and sometimes, though rarely, just to hear it.

It made him feel calm and safe, though he didn't know why.

When he finished playing, he allowed himself to do something else that he did but rarely.

He turned the white harp over.

On the bottom, hidden in the wooden carvings of flowers, fruit and leaves, was a small knob.

He turned the knob. It resisted at first, but then, it gave, and as it turned, a tiny door slid open, revealing a hollow in the base of the instrument.

Joe stuck his finger into the hollow, pressed.

Until he was able to push out a small scroll of old paper. Carefully, he unwound the scroll.

CHAPTER 14

▼

Click. Clack. Click. Clack.

In the dream, Joe was still on the train. Outside the window, the Hudson slid by. Beside him the scarred man slept with one eye open.

Click ...

No!

This was no dream.

Joe jumped awake. The first thing his eye fell on was the empty compartment at the bottom of the harp that sat in his lap.

Where was the scroll?

Click. Clack.

Every part of his body ached when he moved, scrambling to stand in order to search for the tiny piece of paper. His eyes, still bleary with sleep, scanned the deep doorway in which he had spent the night.

Even in the bright light of morning, the shadows were dusky. He had to scoop up the pieces of trash at his feet in order to see them better.

Click.

His fingers fumbled and shards of trash fell from them as he frantically combed the debris.

The steps, light but certain, came closer.

The walker was almost on him when he found the scroll and quickly rolled it back up, jamming it into its hiding place just as the footsteps came to a stop.

Lifting the harp, Joe fingered the strings. A jaunty dancehall tune, out of keeping with the hour, but, Joe hoped, charming and fashionable, spilled out into the bright chill air of morning.

It was his trademark never to lift his eyes toward a customer until the song was finished. That way, he made use of the natural curiosity of people, especially women. As soon as the last note sounded, he would lift his large, dark, heavily lashed eyes, dripping with a soft, heartbreaking but silent plea.

Nine times out of ten, startled by his apparent ability to stare right into their hearts, the marks would cough up.

As he played, he studied his listener's shoes and the hem of her dress. Unusual for him, he could tell nothing from these observations. Was she one of the cheap women from the saloon he'd been in the night before? From the firmness with which her feet were planted on the rough pavement of the street, he doubted she had a hangover.

He finished the tune. Slowly he raised his gaze.

But it was he, not she, who was startled by the directness of their locking eyes. She was no prostitute.

Almost by instinct, he began to play again. *Rock of Ages ...*

She smiled faintly and moved closer. Graceful. Her slim white dress with its narrow lace collar, its delicate cream embroidery, struck him as simple and fine. Joe fought the urge to stop playing. To shrink further into the shadows.

She was young, he thought. Not ten years older than he was. Her hair was thick, red-gold, swept up into a knot on top of her head. Her eyes were wide and green. Pretty.

She reached out and laid her gloved hand on the strings of his instrument.

"*Basta,*" she said sweetly. "*Non ha bisogno di giocare per me. C'e abbastanza.*"

Her words stopped his song more effectively than her fingers. Not because her voice was so soft and gentle. Not even because he was so totally unused to being spoken to kindly by someone of her station. But because she was very clearly not one of his own people, yet she spoke perfect Italian. It was the first time since he'd left New York that Joe felt he was with someone whose speech he could truly understand.

"Come with me, young man," she invited. "You'd be welcome at the mission for breakfast."

The mission! He should have known.

"No!" He said in English. "Forget it. I'm not—"

Startling him, she stooped down so that her face was even with his where he sat on the step. He'd never seen anyone look so beautiful with so little paint on her face.

"You don't need to be afraid," she said. "I know lots of boys like you. I've been to concerts and tea dances. I've been given to understand that once in a while one or more of you arrives from out of town on your own and has difficulty finding the hotel. Is that your problem?"

"What's a dame like you doing out in the street so early in the morning?" he blurted, not wanting to give into the temptation of believing that the kindness in her voice could be genuine and—harder to swallow—directed at him.

She nodded. "That's a fair question, I guess. I do volunteer work at the mission." She gave him a long, hard look. "You're from New York, aren't you?" she asked.

"Yeah."

"Well, then …" She smiled and stood up, extending her hand. Joe studied the white fingers with their short, clean nails. "Why don't you come along? I'll take you to the other boys."

What was she talking about?

"Perhaps you'll meet someone you know right off," she continued, her English as perfect as her Italian, light and rippling. "Won't that be nice?"

"What other boys? Who do you mean?"

She smiled. "Why the Laurenzani, of course. There are harpists, like yourself. And a whole bevy of fine little singers. And then, there's Romano!" She put her hand on her heart and rolled her eyes.

Despite his confusion, Joe had to laugh. It was a gesture that old Italian women performed whenever they talked about some actor in a play, some singer, like the Great Caruso, for example.

"Who's Romano?"

"Only the finest violinist in the city," the young woman answered.

"Hm—And the hotel? What's that?"

The woman looked puzzled. "Isn't that what you came up here from New York to find?" she asked.

"Yeah," Joe answered, beginning to see a number of advantages in playing along with this scenario—the opportunity to mix with a set of people who'd be ripe for the picking when it came to petty theft, for instance … "Yeah, sure," he lied.

"Well, then, step lively!"

He stuffed his harp into its bag, surreptitiously giving the little door at the bottom a light tap to make sure it was securely closed. He stood, brushed himself off a bit and began to follow the woman.

She slowed her step so that he was walking beside her rather than behind. The thought of them walking down the street side by side threw him, but since it was what she seemed to want, he complied.

"The Old Master is a wonder," she said, chatting with merry brightness. "How he manages to take one hundred children and meld them into a single voice, is more than I can figure."

"One hundred?"

"Oh, yes. It's always that many! But it couldn't be unless you people kept coming up from New York, could it?" She slowed and studied him. "Though you're a little older than most of the children, aren't you?"

It was beginning to dawn on Joe that he might be walking into a trap. One hundred boys who could sing and play? Children from New York?

"Who exactly *is* this master guy?"

His lovely escort laughed. "Oh," she said, "you are a bully one, then aren't you?" She leaned over and tweaked his cheek. On any other such occasion, he would have slapped away the hand that tried that trick.

All he did this time was breathe in the scent that emanated from her wrist—the scent of lily-of-the-valley, not that he knew the name of the flower.

"What do you mean?" he asked.

"Pretending not to know the master's name, when it's on everyone's lips these days!" Again, she laughed her merry laugh. "And I suppose you think it's funny to pretend never to have heard of the hotel, eh?"

Joe said nothing. Instinctively, his eyes began to dart, his glance flicking into corners, checking doorways.

They turned from a wide thoroughfare lined with shops into a neighborhood of narrow streets, crowded with shabby wooden houses. He listened for the sound of footsteps following them, glanced suspiciously at rickety porches and lean-to shacks. The place seemed deserted, but he sensed the presence of people behind the scarred doors and the windows greasy with years of accumulated muck.

When they turned back onto a street of commercial brick buildings and storefronts, he saw that, unlike at home, past the main street almost all the buildings here were low—only a couple of stories compared to six or eight, and there were no iron facades or balconies. The absence of the familiar architecture of the Lower East Side stabbed him with a feeling he'd never known before. It took his breath away. Homesickness.

"What's wrong?" the woman beside him asked, as if she could read his mind.

He almost told her that he missed New York, that he wanted to go home, that he didn't want to meet this master and his hundred boys.

But before he opened his mouth, he saw something that gave him hope. On a building a short distance ahead, he saw a sign in a language familiar to him from the streets of New York. He couldn't read that sign, but he knew that it meant that there were Jews nearby. For the first time in four or five days, he felt a sense of relief.

"Where are we?" he asked his companion, but she just smiled.

The next sign he saw he couldn't read either, but this time, he knew it was in Italian.

Albergo Di Buonna.

His own name!

He stared at the magnificent building that commanded the corner of Chestnut and Edward. It would be a while before he learned the names of those streets. For now, he just tried to take in the sight of the wide white marble staircase that led to a double brass door beside which two palm trees in red alabaster vases swayed slightly in the morning breeze.

He let his eyes wander to the doors themselves, and he saw that each held an etched glass window. As if he could touch that glass with his eyes, he went over every detail of the etching—the flowers, the leaves …

And then he realized that the central symbol on each of the two windows was something that he had seen before. The first letter of his own last name, a picture of a harp, like his own harp. The sign he'd seen on his own father's cheek, the sign that had made him trust, at first, the man who had kidnapped him and forced him to come to this city that was not his city.

He didn't waste a second, he turned to run.

But the woman who had brought him put her hand on his shoulder.

And before he could explain to her why he had to get out of there, she pointed to the brass doors.

"Wait," she said.

He didn't have to wait long. In a second, the huge doors creaked open and the master himself appeared.

The old, old man was surrounded by boys. Two boys dressed in fine puffed caps with narrow peaks, wearing knickerbockers and shiny high-button boots, held the doors open for the master to pass through. Another boy in a white silk sailor's middy walked down the stairs one step behind the master, holding his closed umbrella while, on the other side, another boy, similarly dressed, carried his gold-topped cane. There was a boy for his hat and a boy for his bag, a boy to straighten the high collar of his linen shirt and a boy to adjust the white flower in the lapel of his tailored jacket. There was a boy to whistle for the boy who called for a cab and another boy to help the old man down to the curb.

On the master's left was a younger man, young enough to be the old man's son. With a start, Joe recognized him as his kidnapper, the man with the scar on his cheek!

So it must be true: that he had been kidnapped from New York in order to be brought to Old Man Di Buonna—the villain of a life-time of warnings and fearful dreams.

Joe turned on his heel and ran as fast as he could through the narrow, crowded and unfamiliar streets.

He ran head-first into a rag-man, upsetting his cart and scattering bits of cloth all over the sidewalk. The man yelled at him in Yiddish. The sound of that language brought tears to Joe's eyes. This place sounded like home, but it wasn't!

On he rushed, through ashcan-strewn alleys, past the rear doors of saloons, the pungent smell of beer making him thirsty even though it was still morning.

Greater and greater numbers poured into the streets. Everybody was selling something. A skinny girl in a rough, faded dress and no shoes shoved a bunch of wilted flowers in his face. Another girl held up a loaf of golden bread. Joe knew enough about the streets to figure how many days ago the loaf had been baked— and discarded. A little water sprayed on the crust of hard bread made it look quite fresh if you knew how to do it.

More than once, he heard a jolly jig tooted on a tin whistle or a sweet, cloying melody dragged from the strings of an out-of-tune violin. The clack of castanets, the jingle and shake of the tambourine … He could stop right there and play a song that would put every other street musician to shame. But not now.

He stumbled through the crowd, knocking into people with his little black bag, dropping it, scrambling to pick it up, running again.

Until he found himself running full-tilt into a pair of waiting arms.

CHAPTER 15

▼

He caught the scent of her before he felt her breath brush his ear and heard her soft voice whisper, "Stop running. You're not in danger ..."

Instinct told him to tear away, but there was something stronger than instinct that told him to stay.

He let his face fall against her shoulder. If he had ever been this close to a lady, he couldn't remember when.

"I didn't mean to take you to a place you may know nothing about," she said, not pushing him from her. "I thought you were kidding when you said you had never heard of the hotel."

He straightened, moved out of her embrace, ashamed now and feeling childish. "Lying," he said, "not kidding, lying. I've known about that place my whole miserable life." He hesitated. "Maybe you think lying is a sin or something. For me, it's a job."

And at those words an embarrassing thing happened. He started to cry. Not the fake tears he used to get extra money, the way his father had taught him. But real, uncontrollable sobs.

Humiliated to feel such defeat, such weakness—let alone to exhibit it in front of this woman, who, as far as he knew, was now the only friend he had in the world, he struggled to speak. "You shouldn't have found me this morning, or followed me from the old man's hotel, either. I'm not one of his musicians and I don't belong with him. Or with you. Or with the man who brought me here from New York."

He glanced at her. He expected the softness he'd seen in her eyes earlier to still be there, especially since she'd gone to such lengths to stick with him when he'd run.

But her face had become hard.

"Look," she said, "I've got a job to do—"

Now it was *his* face that changed from soft to hard.

"You bitch," he shouted, "you rotten bitch. *He* sent you after me, didn't he? You're just one more of *them*." He shook a fist in her face.

She seemed shocked, maybe even frightened, but she drew in her breath until the white lace at her bosom stopped quivering.

"If by *them* you mean people who care about the children of streets," she said shakily, "you're correct. I *am* from the mission. I don't hide that fact. I'm here to help you, regardless of how you ended up an arab and a waif.

"But," she went on, "I don't take guff from anybody—street arab or no. If you want help, I'll help. If you don't want my help, fine. You're on your own."

"Maybe I can help *you*," he said, not realizing how adult he suddenly sounded.

"How?"

"I can play you a song ..."

"Maybe another time," she answered. "For now, I'd rather get you something to eat."

"Okay." He was still wary, but hunger was getting the best of him.

"Good," she answered, brushing her hands against each other, as if she'd just accomplished a great deal of work.

He expected that they'd have to walk quite a distance before they would find an eatery good enough for a woman like her, but within only a few blocks, the narrow streets changed into a wide boulevard on which both men and women walked at ease in the spring sun.

"In here," the woman said, ushering Joe into a place the likes of which he'd only heard about from boys who'd moved uptown and come back down to Little Italy to brag about their adventures.

"What do you call this place?" Joe asked, not trying to hide his awe. A man he took to be a butler welcomed him and the woman through tall glass doors etched with pictures of fat cherubs and entwined garlands of flowers.

Ahead of him opened a vast room panelled from floor to ceiling in gleaming mahogany. The walls were lined with shelves on which sat bottles full of liquids that shone like jewels—emerald liquids, fluids the color of rubies. Overhead, crystal chandeliers glowed.

A marble counter stretched along one wall, its top a rich golden-veined white, its front amber-colored, decorated with bars of pure black and deep green. Behind the counter three arches stretched to the ceiling and within each arch sat a mirror framed by black marble pillars. Between the pillars, more angels—slender bronze statues—lifted their arms toward a frieze of terra cotta painted with scenes of some mythological landscape.

Of course, Joe knew the words for none of these things. He stood with his mouth open, dazzled.

"You can call me Mattie," the woman was saying. "And in answer to your question, this is a drug store."

"A *what?*"

"Don't tell me they don't have drug stores in New York?"

Joe felt an instant's intense anger, followed by that sickening feeling he'd had before, that homesickness. "They have *everything* in New York," he declared defensively. "You can bet they have bigger, bullier drug stores than this uptown on Fifth Avenue ..."

"I imagine they do," Mattie said with a smile, "but since we are at a soda fountain *here*, I suggest we settle for what we can get."

"I want a banana split!"

"That's not much of a lunch!"

Nonetheless, she ordered it for him.

"Helping runaways is one of the things that I and my friends at the mission do all the time," she told him as he scooped ice cream into his eager mouth.

"I didn't run away from New York," he answered with difficulty. "I was kidnapped."

"From your house?"

"House?" He laughed. "I don't know nobody that lives in a house." He shook his head.

"From a factory?"

"My mother died in a factory—far as I know."

He looked up, not at her, but at himself in the mirror across from where he sat at the counter. His reflection against the backdrop of drug-store splendor, a silver spoon full of ice cream suspended in front of his mouth, jerked him. What was he doing in this strange place with this woman who probably had the power to haul him into some institution? She could be a truant officer for all he knew.

He thought about throwing the spoon and the ice cream at her and running again, but the creamy sweetness cool against his tongue was just too hard to resist.

At least he could keep his trap shut. No more answers.

"Do you have brothers and sisters?"

He took another spoonful and shoved it into his mouth.

"How about your father? Where is he? Do you know?"

He studied the cut-glass ice cream dish, the tall glass of water clinking with ice beside it.

"Look," the woman said, again displaying the toughness that seemed to underlie her gentle demeanor, "let's not play games. I can call the police. I can call the truant officer. I can get a cabman to take you to the mission or even right back to that hotel. You're a vagrant and a foreigner ..."

"*You're* the foreigner!" he sputtered. But he knew she was right.

She tapped her fingers on the marble counter. For a while, that was the only sound in the place, which, Joe suddenly realized was deserted. Maybe it *was* too early for ice-cream!

"All right," he finally said. "I'll tell you about my family. If I got any brothers and sisters, which I doubt, I ain't never seen them. My mother died in a factory from breathing in dust. Dropped like a stone on the floor and they swept her body away with the dust she died from."

"That can't be true!"

"You want me to talk or not?"

She nodded and he went on.

"When my mother died, I went on the street. I tried selling papers but the bigger boys beat me up. I didn't want to beg. Too hard. So I did what my father did before he took off to play ragtime in Harlem with Billbone Benson."

"With whom?"

He considered trying to tell her about his father's Negro friend and their big plans to get rich playing fast piano music for colored people and white. Fat chance.

"With nobody."

They were both quiet for a minute.

"It must have been very difficult for you," she finally said.

Joe thought about that for a moment. "Sure," he said, "sure I got mad when my father took off. But he left me this—"

He pointed to the black bag.

"Your harp?"

"Yeah. So I play on the street. I make enough. I get along. And—"

Now he tapped on the counter, with a lot more emphasis than she had done. "I like New York just fine. I want to go back there. Right now! I never been out of my own city or away from my own people before. You say you can help boys and all that. Help me. Take me back to the train station and get me back on the train. I want to go home."

She put her hand on top of his, and he felt instantly calmer, though no less angry or homesick.

"You know," she said, "I'm at a loss to understand why a boy would prefer to work the streets of New York than to live with a rich relative."

"How do you know that old coot is my relative?" Joe asked.

Mattie laughed. "Why else would he have gone to such trouble to bring you here?"

"I told you. He didn't bring me here. That other guy kidnapped me."

She gave him a knowing look.

Okay, so it was the same thing. But obviously she knew nothing about Old Man Di Buonna.

"He's been after me since the day I was born," he said dramatically.

He saw Mattie try to hide a smile.

"It's *true*."

"He's a wealthy man," she said. "And he wants to share what he has with you, the way he's shared it with all those other boys."

"He isn't sharing anything," Joe said, his anger flaring up again. "Don't you know who those boys are? Don't you know why he's not in New York anymore? Why he had to go away a long time ago before I was born?"

"I—"

"Because them boys are his *slaves*."

"I don't think you know what you're talking about, Joe. I think …"

"No!" he insisted. "No. You're wrong. I know exactly what I'm saying. My father told me always to sleep with one eye open in case the old man came back to America."

"And can you do that?" Mattie asked, "—sleep with one eye open?"

"If I have to," Joe answered defensively. "And I *will* have to as long as I am in the same city with him."

"Joe," Mattie said, pushing aside the now empty ice-cream dish and signalling to the waiter, "tell me why you are so afraid."

The waiter brought a large glass of frothy milk and set it down in front of Joe, who eyed it as if it were poison.

"If I tell you about my great-grandfather, about that old man I saw this morning, will you help me get back to New York?"

"I can't promise to get you back to New York right away," she said. "But I will promise that if one bad thing happens to you in that hotel—if you are hurt or made to do things against your will or forced to work long hours or not fed or …"

"Shut up," Joe said, "you're scaring me."

Mattie touched his hand again. "I won't let you come to any harm here in this city. I promise."

"Okay," he said. "Here's how it is. Before I was born, when my father wasn't even as old as I am now, he lived with the old man in a house in New York City. There were two houses, really. One for little kid slaves and the other for grown-up women slaves. The kid building was full of monkeys. The boys and girls who lived there had to sleep with the monkeys and eat monkey food and some of them could even talk to the monkeys and make the monkeys talk back. All the monkeys and all the children could also sing, dance and play the harp— which they did on the street every day. The monkeys themselves didn't eat no monkey food, though. They ate something else."

"What?"

Joe thought about how his father used to tell this tale and he spoke carefully, wanting to tell it in exactly the same way.

"The monkeys ate kid-bits."

"What are you talking about? Surely …"

Joe drew out his words slowly. He was, after all, an entertainer. "The monkeys ate bits of disobedient children, ones that the old man cut up after he beat them until they died."

"Joe, I don't think you should talk like this. I—"

"The boys and girls had to practice singing and playing all night long. If a boy didn't want to play, if a girl got sick or went with a man—or even if somebody lost his harp or it got broken, Old Man Di Buonna would beat them up and if they died, he would feed them to the monkeys."

The woman sat silent, stunned.

"But one day everything changed. A thing was printed in the paper. A—"

"An article?"

"Yeah. And some Americans saw it and they complained to the police. They told the police exactly where the old man's houses were and that he was Italian and that he had slaves. The Americans just wanted to save the boys and girls," he said. "And it sort of worked because Old Man Di Buonna got in a boat and sailed it away—right up the Hudson River."

He paused. This was the first time he'd told this tale since sailing up the Hudson himself. The story of the old man really was an awesome tale when he came to think about it.

"Anyway," Joe went on, "the old man disappeared. Some people said he was in New England—whatever that is. And some people said he came back to New York in secret at night when nobody could see him. But my father told me what he really did."

"What did he do?" the woman asked. Her voice was barely above a whisper.

"He went to a foreign land," the boy said dramatically, "and he took as many boys and girls as he could fit on that Hudson-River boat with him. But ..."

"But?"

"But not everybody could fit. And some boys ran away. And my father—well, the funny thing about my father is that he kinda liked the old man and maybe he would have gone on that boat without being forced. Besides, he ..."

Joe stopped himself. There was one part of this story he had promised his father he would never tell. Maybe if his father had met someone like Mattie he would have told her everything. But Joe didn't want to take a chance.

"Besides what?"

"I forget. The important thing my father told me was that before he did the flit, the old man was hauled in by the police. And when he was in the police station, he swore revenge. He said that he knew every boy and girl that had ever lived in his house and that no one would get away from him. He said he would hunt them down unto the fourth generation."

He finished the story with a shudder. It was a flourish that he'd learned from his father's story-telling.

Mattie was staring at him, as if she couldn't think of a word. He pushed his dish away. The ice cream had melted into a puddle at the bottom. He was so full that his stomach hurt. He didn't see any reason to stick around. Promises were garbage, including her promise of helping him if he gave in and went to that hotel. "Thanks for the ice cream," he said. "Pleasure to meet you. I gotta go."

He took his hat and his bag and he slipped off the high stool. As he reached for the floor with the toe of his boot, his elbow hit the marble counter. Stinging pain shot through his arm. He drew in a sharp breath, stood unable to move for a second.

He saw his own pain mirrored in Mattie's face. Being noticed like that wasn't something he was used to.

"Are you all right?"

"Yeah."

He took a step away but she put her hand on his shoulder.

"Joe, those stories aren't true. They're tales your father made up to frighten you."

He was pretty furious with his father, had been since the man had taken off, but he didn't like someone else criticising Giuseppe.

"I don't get scared," he answered defensively. "I'm not a baby afraid of fairy tales."

"Look," Mattie said. "I know the Maestro personally. He's not what you think. He's done magnificent things in this city. If he's sent for you, you should be proud, not afraid."

Joe jerked out of her reach. "Leave me alone!" he yelled. "That old bastard sent you to get me, just like he sent the man who kidnapped me in New York." He balled his hand into a fist and shook it in her frowning face. "You leave me be and get out of my way."

He tried to get past her, but she was fast for a woman, and strong. She grabbed him. "Stop," she said. "Take it easy. Don't run. Running will get you nowhere."

"Leave me be."

"Come with me," she insisted, managing to pin his arms at his side. The tender spot on his elbow panged him again and he winced. "Ouch!"

She released her grip, but she still stood between him and the door.

"Come with me and I'll show you something that will change your mind about your family," she said. "Just give me an hour. Come with me for one hour and if that doesn't change everything you think about Maestro Di Buonna, I will personally put you on the train back to New York City."

He glanced at the door. The butler was ushering in more patrons now. Outside the day had grown gray. It looked like it was going to rain. In New York, all the street musicians had places to go when the weather turned too bad to lure customers into paying for a tune. The longer you'd been on the street, the more secure your shelter. Naturally. So where would he go now? Even if he decided to stay in this town and try to earn some money playing, he'd be the bottom boy. It would take a long time even to work his way back up to getting a decent ledge to cower under to get out of the rain.

He glanced back at Mattie. All his life he'd lived among con artists. Of course she was just one more.

But he was tired and his stomach hurt from the strange extravagance of too much ice-cream. He wished he could just sink down onto the black and white squares of this nice smooth floor and go back to sleep.

Instead, he nodded yes. "Okay," he said. "I'll go with you—for one hour."

"That's my boy," she declared with a triumphant smile.

I'm not anybody's boy! he wanted to shout at her.

But he was just too beat to bother.

CHAPTER 16

▼

Even though he knew that Mattie wanted him to walk beside her and not behind, Joe trudged along, unable to keep up. His harp was not big, and he was used to holding onto it all day long and all night, too. But it seemed to grow heavier with each passing hour. At least at home he had a place to hide it.

He kept his eye on her swishing white skirt and her high, laced shoes as he followed her through the crowded streets of the Ward until they turned a corner onto the large busy street with the tall buildings that he had been on before.

Darting between buggies, avoiding the leavings of horses, sprinting out of the path of a racing automobile, he ran behind when she crossed, but he had to stop for breath and she got quite a bit ahead of him.

Sudden panic gripped him. And then panic over the panic. He had never been afraid to be by himself on the street before.

Luckily, she stopped, and smiling, motioned for him to hurry.

By the time he caught up, she was standing in front of a great red-brick music hall. She was surrounded by a crowd of well-dressed swells and he could only pick her out of the throng because she was pointing up toward an iron balcony overhead.

He followed the direction of her finger. Did she realize that the sight of that balcony reminded him of home?

"Up there," she called to him, "the great Caruso stood and sang for the poor who could not afford tickets. Your people give the gift of music to so many others. You should be proud."

The Great Caruso! What did the famous tenor have to do with him?

"Come along, then," she said in her commanding but cheery voice.

Horses, buggies, more automobiles crammed the street in front of the hall. He'd seen places like this before. Some of the street boys dared to play for crowds like this, but not him. Among rich people, a street musician might be taken for a darling and showered with kisses and coins.

Or he might be spat at and kicked.

Joe didn't mind being kicked. Who cared? But he would not stand for being humiliated by people who considered themselves to be better than him.

Finally catching up to Mattie, he struggled with words. "Look, I can't stay here. I don't have any money to go in and I don't want to stand outside."

She didn't hear him. A woman in a dark blue silk dress was waving to Mattie, and Mattie was waving back. In an instant, a few more of the well-dressed crowd, including more than one gentleman, were at her side.

The crowd seemed to be growing, which should have given him the opportunity to escape, except that Mattie reached down, dug her slender fingers into his shoulder and held on until someone in her gang declared, "Show's on. Let's get inside."

He'd never seen a place like it. Row on row of red velvet seats trimmed in gold. Tiers of balconies with chairs upholstered in plush scarlet brocade. Curtains everywhere. Balconies, banisters, pillars—all gilded, curlicued carvings of wood. Once when he'd been really small, Joe had caught a glimpse of a circus wagon. This place was like the circus wagon of a king.

Though Mattie clearly wanted him to sit still and face forward, he couldn't resist squirming in his seat near the front and twisting back to fill his eyes with the sight of the electric lamps that lit the place and sparkled on the finery of the audience.

Nothing in the house, however, amazed him as much as what he saw when the show started.

A drum roll silenced the crowd. Slowly the curtain rose.

And there on the stage were a hundred child musicians just like the ones he'd seen walk down the stairs with Maestro Di Buonna outside the hotel.

Joe gawked at them. They were dressed in a style that even he recognized as having disappeared long before he was born. His father had a photograph of himself and his friends taken on the streets of New York by a famous photographer— one of the men who'd reported his great-grandfather to *The New York Times*. In that old picture, the Italian street boys had worn little black jackets and short pants and funny hats like the conical hat of a clown.

Here, decades later, in this city that surely was *not* New York, all these boys wore the same funny pants and jackets and hats.

Except that their outfits were new and clean and fit them perfectly.

"What the heck is this?" he whispered to Mattie, but she put her finger to her lip to shush him.

And then she winked.

He turned his attention back to the stage. The hundred boys all played at once, their fingers on the strings of hand-held harps and miniature violins moving in a blur. They were like dancers, four boys stepping forward in time to the music, strumming furiously, spinning on their heels without missing a beat, then effortlessly slipping back among the others.

Eight boys forward, fiddling at top speed. Eight boys back.

Then, too many boys to count, circling the stage, playing, bowing and smiling all at the same time.

When the bouncy, cheerful number ended, the audience broke into yips and yays and wild applause. "More," they shouted. "Bis." "Encore."

A hush fell over the house when a pretty little girl appeared, dressed in a long Alice-blue gown with a wreath of pale pink lilies nestled in her thick black curls. She began to sing a slow, sweet tune.

Joe sat higher in his seat, his attention riveted by the familiar melody and then by the well-known words. "The moon, the mountains and the sea ..."

He leaned toward Mattie to whisper again, to ask whether the Maestro had taught these children to sing all the songs Joe knew himself, as he had been taught on the streets of New York.

But when he saw tears running down Mattie's cheek, he decided not to interrupt her with his question.

It was the last time Joe's mind wandered during the entire show, which went on for two hours without intermission. He had always tried to imagine what happened every night in the grand theatres of which he'd only seen the outside. He never would have dreamed that the very songs *he* played could drive a well-heeled audience like this one into ecstasies of clapping and stomping.

The finale featured the little girl once more, this time singing a lament that she would never see Napoli again. Many of the thousand people in the hall wept openly, perhaps lamenting that they'd never seen Napoli in the first place.

Mattie dried her tears and smiled weakly. "Now," she said to Joe, "you can understand that these are your people. You belong with them." She reached for Joe's hand.

He pulled back. *I don't belong with them and I sure as hell don't belong to them.*

When the cheering ended and the audience began to vacate the hall, Joe frantically looked around. There were plenty of doors, but so many people clogged the aisles with their long skirts and their canes and capes …

His only choice was to keep following Mattie until he could escape.

She walked not toward the thickest crowd at the back, but toward the front. Joe walked a step or two behind.

When they got near the stage, Joe saw an opening in the crowd. And through it, he caught a quick glimpse of possible freedom. He'd spent enough time hanging around waiting for his father and Billbone Benson to recognize a backstage exit when he saw one.

He inched closer. Five or six of the performers were busy packing up instruments and props. In their fancy little outfits, they looked quite dandy.

Noticing Joe, who'd not changed his own shabby clothes in a good long while, they pointed and sniggered with obvious contempt.

Joe considered pounding the sissies—rich boys pretending to be poor boys! But he knew better than to try to fight six on one.

This was no way out.

He turned to follow Mattie again.

She was gone!

Much as he had wanted to be rid of her, he felt engulfed again by the feeling of panic he'd experienced earlier.

Confused, he spun around.

Then he felt strong fingers clasp his shoulder.

Relieved, he glanced up with a smile.

But it wasn't Mattie who held him.

It was Old Man Di Buonna.

CHAPTER 17

▼

Joe used all he had to get away. He flailed his arms, he squiggled his body. He kicked and he lashed out.

But the old man, though he looked frail, was remarkably strong. *Basta!* He hissed. "Enough, boy!"

You bet it's enough! Joe gave one, strong, final push with his head, shoulders and neck, and he felt the old man fall away.

He ran out the door and down the side street behind the hall. The sound of his own heart beating in his ears mixed with the sound of all those children playing in his memory. It was as if he *were* one of them.

He got to the end of the block before he remembered that he had no idea where he was.

He hesitated for a frantic second, balancing between turning left and right. Long years on the street had given him an innate sense of the way cities worked. He turned in the direction of that wide main street he'd now crossed a number of times.

He never reached it.

Just as he turned, he dropped his shabby black bag.

It opened, spilling his harp unto the brick sidewalk.

He saw the instrument as though it were suspended in air for an instant. He saw it bounce on the bricks. Then it came down hard again, and it shattered.

He knelt, the rough brick scraping at his knees, dove for the pieces of his harp, struggled to gather them in his hands, tried to stand up and stumbled.

He tried to stand again, but before he rose, he felt a heavy hand on the back of his neck, holding him down.

"Let him up."

He heard the voice and felt the hand release him, but he was too frightened to stand.

Because he knew the voice belonged to the old man. The man of the monkeys. His great-grandfather.

"Get up, *nipote*," the old man said. "Don't make an old man get down on his knees."

Joe didn't move. Or answer.

"*Per amore di Dio!*" the old man cried. "Get up! You been a long time on that train. I know this. And you are tired and afraid. Of course you are. Plus you don't like not to be in New York." The old man sighed dramatically. "From the day I leave America, I think always of New York. So I know how you feel. Get up and shake hand with your *bisnonno*."

Joe sniffled.

"He cry like a girl cry!" the old man spat out in disgust, taking a step away. "Leave him!"

Joe reached for the pieces of the harp and began to shove them into the bag. Tears blinded him, so that he didn't see that another hand was gathering the splintered shards.

"The old man knows what boys need," a familiar voice declared.

Startled, Joe looked up.

The thug who had kidnapped him in New York squatted in front of him on the sidewalk. The faded scar glowed faintly on his cheek, but he had a look on his face that made Joe think he wasn't as mean as he wanted Joe to think he was.

"You seen those kids on stage," the man said, handing Joe the last piece of his broken instrument. Joe shivered. It was the base of the harp, and his document was still inside it.

"They got good clothes, a place to sleep, more to eat that they want."

From behind him, Joe heard the old man shuffle toward them again. He mumbled something in Italian.

"He says give him the pieces you got there. He'll give you a brand new harp. How about it?"

"No!" Joe shouted. "Leave me alone. I'll fix my harp myself!"

"Boy," he heard Old Man Di Buonna growl, "you got a choice. Starve on the street or come with me." His shaky old finger pointed to Joe's young hand. "You bring that mess and I make sure personally that I get the best instrument maker in Canada to fix that harp for you."

Canada! What the heck was that?

If a person doesn't even know where they are, Joe thought, how are they ever going to get home?

He shoved the last remaining broken bit into his bag, drew its string, stood and followed the two men down the street.

Over the next little while, the old Maestro Di Buonna took Joe under his wing.

He was almost ninety years old, Joe learned, and he never went anywhere by himself.

Sometimes five or six of the boy musicians escorted him, carrying his hat, his cane and his cape, snapping to attention when those items were called for and receding into the old man's shadow when they were not. Despite the fact that they were always bowing and scraping and running around at the old guy's bidding, these boys were a cheerful bunch, which confused Joe. He decided to ask them a few questions if he got a chance.

Sometimes three or four really beautiful dames came along. Joe would have liked to question them, too, but the chances of getting anywhere near them were nil.

No matter who else might be with the Maestro, one person was never absent—the man with the scar. After a while, Joe realized that he, too, was an old man even if his hair was mostly black and his movements smooth and sure.

"You know who he is?" the Maestro asked Joe one day, catching him staring.

"No."

"That's my son, Ambrogio," the old man said. "*Il suo prozio*," your great-uncle. You know what that means?"

"Can't say."

The old man smiled. "Ambrogio is the brother of your grandfather who died in New York City before you were born."

"How do you know when I was born?"

Joe felt a sharp blow on the side of his head. He reeled, missed a step and nearly knocked the rickety old man to the ground. He turned and swung at Ambrogio. "What d'ya do that for?"

"Leave the kid alone," the old man said. "Ambrogio here had a brother, Giuseppe," the old man went on, "and Giuseppe had a son also called Giuseppe. He was—"

"My father—who ran off to Harlem to play ragtime with Billbone Benson."

"You're a bright boy," the old man said with a chuckle. "And you're gonna be happy you come up here. Just like we're all happy we come up here."

Over the next few weeks, Joe came to think of this city, which he learned was called Toronto, as one big feed bag. He ate mammoth crusty buns for breakfast, meatballs as big as his head for lunch, roasted chickens and massive slabs of beef that fell off the bone for supper.

He slept night after night in the Di Buonna hotel, the building he'd stood outside of that first day with Mattie. He didn't even have to share with other boys because, Ambrogio told him, he, Joe, was the *pronipote*, the great-grandson, *il sangue del mio sangue*, the blood of my blood.

Having nothing in particular to do for the first time in his life, Joe made friends with a few of the other children. He even told one or two of them the stories his father had told him about playing music on the street with trained monkeys. His audience responded with cries of "What bully fun!" and, encouraged, Joe went on to finish the monkey tale by relating how his great-grandfather—the Maestro himself—had been hauled off by the coppers in front of the very eyes of Joe's father and thrown into jail with criminals and killers.

Just as Joe got to the jail part of the story, he himself was hauled off by Ambrogio, who looked as if he wanted to hit the boy again, but who hadn't touched him since he'd been told off by the old man.

"The Maestro wants to go for a walk," Ambrogio said. "And you gotta bring the pieces of your harp."

Joe didn't like the sound of that, but he knew better than to argue.

The old man was waiting for him in the lobby of the hotel, a boy standing in front of his chair to give him a hand as he rose shakily from it.

As they walked down the grand front stairs, the old man kept his hand on Joe's shoulder for support. The boy felt a mixture of fear and pride. He knew it was usually Ambrogio who walked beside the old man and wondered whether Scarface had fallen a notch in the Maestro's esteem. *Too bad for him!*

Though they progressed slowly, it was only minutes before they were in the heart of the crowded streets that Joe had encountered during his first hours in Toronto. "This here," the old man said, "is called The Ward." He gestured toward the ramshackle houses that leaned in rows along the narrow alleys. "It don't look like much, but the thing you always gotta remember about property is that it don't ever go down."

"What?"

"Real estate."

"Oh." Joe had no idea what he was referring to, and was soon distracted from the old man's speech about the Ward because he felt someone following them. Glancing back, he saw a shabby little flower seller in a filthy white dress. A few straggly daisies were clutched in the girl's hand. Catching Joe's eye, she skipped forward and was soon walking beside him.

"Hey," she whispered, "don't you look grand. Who's the mark?" She nodded toward the Maestro.

Joe tried to ignore her, but he couldn't ignore the large drops of fresh blood wetting the front of her dirty dress. Just as he was noticing, she coughed, covered her mouth with her hand, rubbed her hand on her skirt and left another red smear.

"Get lost!" Ambrogio hissed at her.

Joe was shocked to see him raise his hand toward the little girl.

The Maestro caught the gesture, turned with difficulty and saw the girl standing behind him. A look that Joe couldn't read crossed the old man's wrinkled face. With shaking hands, he reached into the pocket of his fine trousers and pulled out a little leather purse. Carefully, he reached inside, found a large coin and handed it to the girl, careful not to touch the fingers that reached eagerly for the money. "Go away," he said softly. The little girl curtsied and fled.

Joe felt a stab of grief, the grief of one who is disloyal to his own in order to better himself.

"It's the White Plague," the old man said. "Rich people who get it have to sleep in a tent outside no matter what the weather. Poor people just die. You be careful, boy. You be careful."

Joe had heard of the White Plague. Who hadn't? Some people said TB came from sick cows, which was why he never drank milk, even from the open public troughs that were so easy to raid. The old man had a different theory.

"It comes from that bad star. The big one with the tail. Halley's Comet." The Maestro shook his head. "It will be the death of us all."

They walked in silence for a while, not that the streets were without noise. Musicians with tambourines, concertinas and little flutes gathered on corners. Women dressed in quaint peasant costumes offered to tell Joe's fortune. Men pulled various items from beneath tattered coats offering for sale knives and pens and jewellery that had been swiped from wealthy women. The old man ignored all this, and so did the boy. Nothing he saw here was unfamiliar to Joe.

"You know why I send for you?" the Maestro finally said.

Joe shook his head, but he felt that grip of fear again.

"I myself was once a great musician. But I decide that I be a teacher instead. I teach children to play."

"And monkeys?"

The old man stopped. He turned and studied Joe's face.

Joe waited for rage, for the old man to exercise the prerogative of his position and to do what he had forbidden Ambrogio to do. In other words, he expected to be hit and hit hard for his impertinence.

But that's not what happened.

Instead, a look of cunning came into the old eyes, the look of a smart man assessing an enemy who might just be smarter.

"I need a good harp player," the Maestro said in the tone of a man doing business. "I got a lot of ladies who'd pay top dollar to hear you. But you gotta have a proper instrument. You got that harp with you?"

"Yes."

"Give it here."

The Maestro signalled to Ambrogio who grabbed for Joe's black bag.

But not soon enough. Joe held on.

"Okay," the old man said, "Okay." To Ambrogio he said, "Let's go to Church."

"Church?" Joe said with alarm. "Forget Church! I ain't giving this harp to nobody. Even if he's a priest."

At this outburst, both his captors collapsed into laughter.

"Not *a* church, you fool," Ambrogio said. "Church *Street!*"

It made no difference. Joe still refused to hand over the broken harp, and when they reached Church Street and entered a remarkable shop where all manner of instruments were being made, cleaned and fixed, Joe insisted on remaining in the room with the master instrument maker, never taking his eye off the skilled hand of the man as he fingered the splintered white wood and made his pronouncement as to whether the harp was ever likely to make music again.

"I've not seen one like this in fifty years," the instrument maker said. He was a tall, thin man with big hands that touched the pathetic pieces of Joe's harp with a tenderness that even a twelve-year old could appreciate.

"My father gave it to me and his father gave it to him," Joe said. "Can you fix it?"

The thin man shrugged. "I don't know. Come back tomorrow and we'll see."

"Okay." Joe reached for the pieces, ready to scoop them back in the bag.

"He means you gotta leave it here overnight," Ambrogio said.

"No!" Joe shouted. "It's mine and it goes where I go. It doesn't stay any place over night!"

"Just put the damn thing down," Ambrogio insisted, lunging for the boy, who ducked, knocking into the workbench and causing a freshly varnished violin that had hung suspended over the workbench to fly into the air.

The instrument maker dove for the violin, catching it an instant before it hit the stone floor.

"I won't leave it!" Joe cried again. "You can't make me. It's mine!"

"*Abbastanza! Silencio. Andiamo pronto!*" The old man grabbed Joe by the neck of his shirt. Had it been his usual shirt, it would have ripped and Joe would have run. But he was wearing new clothes now, like every other boy who lived at the Di Buonna hotel. The fabric held. The old man was surprisingly strong. "You stop this minute. You are leaving the instrument to be fixed and you are coming home with me. *Oro.* Now!"

Joe struggled a little more, just because he hated to show that he had lost the battle.

On the way home, he kept quiet, thinking about escape but admitting to himself that getting away was becoming less attractive with every meal.

As they retraced their steps and walked once more through the Ward, Joe was surprised to see Mattie again.

He caught a glimpse of her teaching some children. Or at least that's what he guessed she was doing. They were passing some sort of store, a place with a wide window through which it was easy to see what was going on inside the small, clean building that stood out from the dingy buildings that surrounded it. Mattie moved among several children seated at desks. She seemed to be showing them something in a book. Joe pressed his face against the window to get a better look.

But Ambrogio yanked him away.

Joe expected to be punished for his outburst at the instrument shop, but when they got back to the hotel, all that happened was that he was forced to drink a large glass of terribly sweet yellow wine, in order, as the old man said, to calm him down.

Sent to bed, he lay down, his head spinning and his stomach lurching and heaving. Ambrogio sat outside his door, guarding it, but one look at the boy's face and he let Joe by, understanding without words what would happen next.

Which was that Joe ran out into the alley and vomited.

His head cleared instantly and, losing no time, he slipped out onto Chestnut Street, around the corner, and into another alley.

He dropped to his knees and began scraping away at the packed gravel of the alley, his fingers digging beneath the stone he'd used as a marker.

He found what he sought, and in the light from a streetlamp nearby, he carefully unfastened the little bundle wrapped in wax paper.

Yes, his document was still safe.

CHAPTER 18

▼

His harp got fixed—like new. And when Old Man Di Buonna gave it back to him, Joe couldn't keep his fingers off the strings. They felt new and sharp and bit his fingertips, but he liked the cutting sensation against his skin, as though the harp were fighting back, daring him to make it do things it had never done before.

With the Maestro watching, Joe ran a few trills across the strings and back. The instrument jumped to his will, making him remember what his father had told him about how the monkeys used to dance the minute they heard him play.

A ripple of strong, clear notes danced itself into a sweet melody of such piquant sorrow that the Maestro wiped away a tear.

It was a good act, that tear-wiping routine.

"I knew it!" the old man said.

Joe faltered in his playing.

Knew what? That Joe was hiding the very thing that the old man had sent Ambrogio all the way to New York to get? By now the Maestro knew the paper wasn't inside the harp anymore, didn't he?

"Play, son, play!" the old one shouted. "I knew you had it in you. You were born to play. Born to show the world once again what a Giuseppe Di Buonna can do!"

Bull!

But despite his opinion of the old man's overblown reaction to his playing, Joe had to admit that the new harp was magic. As if relieving it of the burden of that little piece of paper had allowed it to learn how to sing.

Apparently audiences agreed with the Maestro about Joe's playing. As the months flew by, Joe Di Buonna became the musical sensation of the season.

He started at Italian weddings, soon graduated to "Canadian" ones. He played at the finest department stores, where women dressed like the ones he'd seen at the concert the day he went with Mattie threw flowers at him, surrounded him when he tried to leave the auditorium, reached for him and stretched their gloved hands to touch his face, his hair, his hands.

He even played his own concert. With the hundred other boys coming on after the intermission and cooing behind him like a roof full of pigeons cooing behind a cat.

By night he played, by day he did what many of Maestro Di Buonna's children had to do. He dodged the wily truant officer.

The only child in the Ward that the truant officer wasn't interested in was the little flower seller. Joe saw her often because the pest wouldn't leave him alone.

"Quit following me," he told her one afternoon when he was taking a short cut back to the hotel and had to hide behind a row of ashcans in order to stay free.

"You don't gotta hide. The bastard truant officer's gone. He drove up Yonge Street."

"Drove?"

"Yeah. He gots a auto now. I wouldn't even mind goin' to school if I could get a ride in one of them."

Joe straightened up and brushed himself off. In the old days, when he had but a single suit of clothes to his name, he was completely indifferent about what happened to it, often sleeping in it without changing for months. But now that he had so many clothes that he couldn't wear them all at once, he had become fastidious.

"I don't think they'd let you in school," Joe said carefully, not wanting to hurt his little friend but not wanting her to have false hopes, either.

"They would if I could get to Wellington County," she answered.

"What the heck is that?"

"It isn't a what. It's a where." She sat down on the curb, and Joe, momentarily forgetting his fine trousers, sat beside her. "It's in the country. You can take a train there. I used to live in a big stone house with a red roof. There was a clock in a tower and on top, a thing that told you which way the wind was blowing."

"A mansion," Joe asked sceptically. Once or twice he'd ventured north on Fifth Avenue and seen the wondrous mansions there.

"Yes," the girl said, nodding. "And it had a name, too. The House of Industry and Refuge. It was in the middle of big fields of corn. My mother and father used to work in the fields and come in at night. And we all sat at a long table and ate and ..."

"And what?"

Unlike those of the Maestro, the tears of the flower seller seemed real to Joe. "Hey," he said, "don't go bawlin'. What the heck's the matter, anyways?"

"The place is run by a matron. Mrs. Grant," the little girl said. "When my folks decided to come to Toronto, Mrs. Grant told me I could come back to Wellington whenever I want. But my folks died and I don't got no way to go there never again."

Embarrassed, Joe stood and brushed himself off again. "Forget about that place," he said. "You live here now."

"You, too," the little girl answered.

No, I don't. I don't live here.

"I gotta go," he said to the girl. "Don't follow me."

"Okay." She sat still but stifled some sound as Joe walked away. Coughing or crying, he didn't know which.

As he made his way through the Ward toward the Di Buonna hotel, Joe remembered the day he'd seen Mattie through the window reading to children from a book. He calculated that the building must be nearby, and turning a couple of corners, he found it.

Mattie must be teaching the children to read! Much as he hated the idea of school, Joe had wanted to learn to read his whole life. Sometimes other boys read to him, but he was ashamed of his own inability and took elaborate pains to hide it.

Most of all, he wanted to read the small piece of paper that he had hidden away. Despite his success as a musician, despite the fact that Old Man Di Buonna never mentioned it, Joe was convinced that he had been kidnapped from New York because of that paper.

It took him a week to work up the courage to go back and reintroduce himself to Matttie.

"I'm glad you came here to the mission," Mattie said. "And so glad to see you again. I suppose you're aware that another famous musician is coming to town soon?

He didn't know what she was talking about.

"Yeah," he said, "sure ..."

"Well, you, yourself have done us proud. I heard you play at the concert hall!"

She reached over and tweaked his cheek. He rubbed it hard with his hand before he answered, "Ain't nothing. I just did what I always been doing."

"Not what I heard," Mattie said. "I heard you are a genius!"

Well, if he was such a genius, why did he have so much trouble learning to read? It took him five weeks before he could manage a few sentences on his own.

Each night, after playing in somebody's fine drawing room or in a theatre or the hall of a church, Joe would go back home, take out his secret paper, and try to puzzle out what the words meant. Being the great-grandson of the Maestro, he had the privilege of his own room, though he found it hard to sleep inside and alone. But the room was good for the privacy he needed to study his document.

One day he wandered into the restaurant on the ground floor of the hotel. It was a grand place with marble arches and fifty round tables always covered in white linen. Joe liked it best early in the morning when waiters in long aprons scurried around getting things ready for dinner, which was always served in the middle of the day.

On this particular day, he noticed that Signor Del Arte, the maitre d', was personally writing out the day's menu in his fine hand. Joe leaned over to see what the man was writing.

And he saw that the menu had two sides to it. One side was easy to read. He was thrilled to recognize a few words. Bread. Wine. Beef.

But the other side was incomprehensible.

Mattie had taught him to sound out words he couldn't get. So he sounded out a few words on that side of the menu. *Pane. Vino. Carne di Manzo.*

The truth hit him like a slap. He could read English but he couldn't read Italian. Yet, when he sounded out the Italian words on the menu, they made sense. He didn't need to study reading after all!

Excited by this discovery, he went back to his room and tried once again to read his document by sounding out the words.

But it didn't work! The words on the paper sounded Italian, but except for a few that were familiar, most were unrecognizable.

Unwilling to accept defeat, Joe made up his mind to go back to Mattie and to ask her whether he could learn to read Italian.

He set out through the streets.

But halfway there, he remembered how Mattie always insisted that each of her students should forget whatever language they had spoken before and only speak English. How could he convince her that he had to be able to read a language she would consider a waste of time?

There was only one way. He had to show her the paper.

He had never shown anybody before because he had promised his father.

Nor did he like to carry the paper anywhere without the protection of its being hidden in his harp. But since the day the harp had shattered, he'd never put the paper back inside it again.

He decided to put it into a small leather purse, like the one Old Man Di Buonna used for his coins. Only Joe was careful to tie the purse to a string and to put the string around his neck, underneath his shirt.

The way was not straight. Once more he thought about how like his home in Little Italy this part of Toronto was. But the Ward, with its street musicians, its peddlers, its denizens dressed in costumes more like those of the old world than the new, hadn't become his home. And it never would.

His nostalgic thinking distracted him, so it took him a few seconds to realize he was being followed.

All his street survival skills kicked in, the first being the knowledge that it's foolish to waste time glancing back to see who is following you.

Run, Joe, run.

He sped through the streets, easily skirting obstructions: wagons, carts, a horse, ashcans, boys and girls, a concertina player, a rag-and-bone man.

He'd been in Toronto enough months to know the back lanes and the places where rickety, hand-built wooden shacks overshot the corners, providing nooks to hide behind.

But he couldn't take the risk of hiding. Whoever was following him might know the Ward as well as Joe did—or better.

He careered around one corner, intending to take a sharp right and dash down the next street, when he heard a familiar voice shout, "Grab the little bastard."

Ambrogio, his nemesis, wasn't taking any chances! Too old to run after Joe himself, he had four or five younger, stronger men at his beck and call.

One of them lunged for Joe and caught him by the sleeve of his shirt.

He felt strong hands on his arms, his shoulders, his back. The more he squirmed, the stronger the hold of his tormentors.

He kicked out. And someone grabbed his ankle, pulling him hard to the ground. His elbow hit the rough cobblestone of the street and he yelped in pain.

His anguished cry only served to spur his enemies on. He felt the crunch of a bony fist against his jaw and the grip of a sharp-nailed hand clutching the back of his neck.

For a brief moment, he felt himself suspended in air, waiting for the inevitable fall to the hard earth.

As the ground rushed up to meet him, Joe instinctively reached for the leather purse around his neck.

And Ambrogio reached too.

It was that movement of Old Man Di Buonna's henchman that finally gave Joe the courage he needed.

"Get your damn hands off me, you thug!" Joe shouted, clawing at the rough hand that tried to tear the treasure from his neck.

The man's powerful fingers encircled the boy's throat, cutting off his breath, leaving him pulling hard on the smoky air, struggling to breathe, feeling the blood trapped beneath the skin of his face, making it feel about to burst or to bleed out of his eyes.

"What you've got belongs to me, you little bastard," Ambrogio shouted, shaking Joe violently. "I'm the old man's son, not you. You're nothing. You're nobody."

Choking, Joe kicked fiercely.

And he connected.

Ambrogio looked shocked. He loosed his hold and his hands shot down to the front of his trousers, finding and cradling his privates.

"You rotten son of a whore!"

Later Joe wondered what kind of cowards Ambrogio had brought with him because they crowded around the boss rather than going after Joe, but at the time, he didn't waste a second thinking about that. He just ran.

The blood was pounding in his ears powerfully, but the rushing sound of it was soon mixed with another sound.

From somewhere nearby came the unmistakable rhythms of a marching band! And not just any marching band.

There was not an American at home or abroad in the year 1910 who would have not have recognized the most famous musician in the world.

As he sped around one more corner, the thrilling melody of *The Stars and Stripes Forever* vibrated through Joe's whole body.

Ahead of him crowds lined a wide boulevard. He couldn't see the band at first.

In fact, over the heads of all those cheering people, all he could see was the Stars and Stripes themselves.

With a mixture of excitement, patriotism and opportunism, Joe realized what he had to do.

Worming his way through the crowd, he dashed out into the street in front of the band.

One or two musicians stepped aside, but nobody missed a beat.

And nobody followed Joe anymore either.

Because he had managed to separate himself from his enemies by putting the American flag, the width of University Avenue, thousands of admirers, a marching band, and John Phillip Sousa himself between them.

Once on the other side, he kept running until he couldn't hear the music anymore.

Crouching down, he opened the purse around his neck and examined what lay within—all he had left.

The document that was causing him so much grief, a document he still could not read.

And the fifty-dollar bill Old Man Di Buonna had given him the night of his triumph at the concert hall.

Joe figured the fifty could get him back to New York and he was right.

Once he got there, he never left New York or America again.

And he never thought about Canada again, either. Except twice.

The first time was when he had become a musician in his own right and finally had enough money to give some of it away. He sent a substantial check to the Wellington County House of Industry and Refuge. He was still a young man at that point, but he was sure that the little flower seller was long dead. He hoped his money could help someone else like that poor child.

More than eighty years later, he thought about Canada one last time.

The day the boy from Toronto came, the boy who was the blood of his father's blood.

CHAPTER 19

▼

The present.

"We want you to handle one more case …"

Mary Rose Cabrini fought to hide her feelings. Having been a lawyer for so many years, it was easier for her to conceal them than for most people. Anger, fear—those things were easy to hide. Disappointment was not.

"You're not pleased." The voice of Madam Hunt-Duval, the Chief Justice of Family Court, was smooth, her smile polished. Everything about Madam Justice was perfect: her Harvard law degree in its smart ebony frame, her priceless collection of original Hogarth prints, her sleek blonde hair, her air of uncontested power.

"Madam," Mary Rose answered, "naturally I'd assumed …"

Wrong word!

"Assumptions never serve us, do they, Counsel?"

"What I mean to say, Madam," Mary Rose tried again, "is that I was informed that I'd been appointed to the bench effective at once. Naturally I expected a period of orientation, but …"

The Chief Justice toyed with her Mont Blanc pen. It was a stout black piece that reminded Mary Rose of the stogies smoked by her old Italian uncles.

"I'd be glad to take on whatever additional case you have in mind, Madam," she conceded. "Provided that this is not some sort of test."

The Chief Justice bowed her head slightly in deference. "Of course we have no intention of testing you, Ms Cabrini. Your record is sterling. We have every confidence …"

Mary Rose forced a smile as Hunt-Duval opened the single file folder that sat on her shining mahogany desk. Her emotionless gray eyes scanned the top page.

"I've been asked to do a favor for the Orphan Advocate Office, and I've decided to elicit your help."

"My help?"

"Yes. I'm sure you've dealt with similar fact-finding assignments many times before. The case concerns a young man of about twelve years old. His name is Joseph Di Buonna."

Mary Rose started at the name and the Chief Justice asked why.

"It's nothing, Madam. It's just that we have Di Buonnas in our own family."

"Are you afraid of a conflict of interest?"

"Hardly. It's rather a cliché that all Italians—at least all the Italians in Toronto—are related."

"I hardly think racial clichés are appropriate to mention here. As I was saying, young Joseph Di Buonna was orphaned a few years ago. He seems to have adjusted remarkably well to his new circumstances. He comes from a very distinguished family. On his mother's side, he is Jewish. On his father's, Italian-American. Prior to recent generations, the Di Buonna family was noted for its exceptional musical talent. One of its members was a violin virtuoso who appeared on concert stages around the world."

"Romano Di Buonna—"

The Chief Justice glanced once more at the paper in her hand. "Correct," she said dryly.

An old memory stirred in Mary Rose. Her own grandfather pretending to play the violin like the legendary Romano, bending and weaving until he fell to the floor, sending her and her younger cousins into hysterics. Until this moment, she'd thought her grandfather had made Romano up.

"Joseph's paternal grandfather, called Joey Di Buonna, came to Toronto during the Vietnam War," the Chief Justice explained. "He eventually returned to the States, but his son, Joey Jr., Joseph's father, always lived here."

"Did they keep up the family's musical tradition?"

The Chief Justice frowned, as if the question were irrelevant.

Mary Rose's work with children had always depended on her knowing as much as possible about each child who came her way. These were not legal entities, they were people. And she intended to keep it that way, judgeship or no judgeship.

"The file states that both the child's parents died while attending to patients during the SARS epidemic."

"Tragic," Mary Rose commented, "but if the child is well-adjusted why is his file with the advocacy office?"

"We're concerned that a custody battle may be brewing," the Chief Justice answered. "Between the American grandparents and the Canadian grandparents." She hesitated for a moment as though framing her thoughts. "I've been advised that you have extensive experience with children of multi-ethnic backgrounds. You'd be ideal to handle this case. Plus, I need not mention, it will be a fine introduction to your new duties. As Judge of Orphans, you'll often be called upon to determine the fate of a child like this boy."

Mary Rose pushed aside a sudden jolt of that *Why me?* feeling that had plagued her since she'd been informed she'd been chosen for the judgeship. She'd never even applied for the position ...

"What exactly do you mean, Madam? Determine his fate in what way?"

The Chief Justice closed the file folder and crossed her hands on top of it. She had beautiful nails. On her left hand she wore no rings, but a large, very expensive-looking diamond and emerald combo sparkled on her right hand. A big piece that Mary Rose was willing to bet the justice had bought for herself to show she didn't need a man to provide jewelry.

"Mary Rose, I'm asking you a simple favor. All I want is for you to find out if this child is happy in his present situation."

"But why—"

"Please, just spend a little time on the case. Use your reputed people skills and your legal contacts. Check the child out. Make one or two simple observations. I promise you, it won't be a major undertaking. And as soon as you're done, we can begin plans for your elevation ceremony."

The woman looked at her steadily and suddenly Mary Rose finally understood what the real test was here.

"Yes, Madam," she said.

People in power, she realized, have to learn to obey, just like people without power.

She took the file.

She'd do as the Chief Justice asked. She'd find out whether little Joseph Di Buonna, orphan, was happy.

CHAPTER 20

▼

Mary Rose's office was on the sixth floor of the courthouse. The floor-to-ceiling windows looked north across a parking lot whose history she knew—unlike most of the two or three hundred other people who worked in the building.

It was nothing but an income-generating empty slab-of-concrete parking lot now, but once it had been the teeming center of The Ward, the section of Toronto that matched Manhattan's Lower East Side. Jews, Italians, Blacks and Chinese had lived cheek-by-jowl down there. Now their descendants—lawyers, clerks, cops, judges, worked together in the courthouse, never looking back toward the days when their ancestors had lived entirely different lives.

"You dreaming again?"

Mary Rose turned from the window at the voice of her secretary, Marlee Derson. The two women had worked together for more than a decade, so neither ever thought about the early days anymore. They'd met at Osgoode Hall Law School. Now one was a secretary and the other almost a judge.

"No, not dreaming," Mary Rose answered. "Just waiting. Where are the Steins? Have they phoned?"

Marlee glanced at the elaborate clock on the antique oak sideboard that served as one of Mary Rose's filing cabinets. "They were supposed to be here with the boy over half an hour ago," she said. "Shall I phone them?"

Mary Rose picked up the file folder that lay on her desk. "I haven't really had much of a chance to study this. Why don't we give them another fifteen minutes? In the meantime, I can glance at the reports …"

She was already reading by the time the secretary softly closed the door.

She'd seen much thicker files than this one, and many more depressing ones, too. This child was exemplary. No discipline problems in school. No drugs. The fact that he was only twelve didn't make much difference there. She'd had children five years old with substance abuse problems.

She read a report from the grief counsellor who had worked with the boy shortly after his parents' death. "Remarkably well adjusted," was the conclusion the counsellor had come to.

So what was this kid doing in the system?

She jumped when the door opened and Marlee stepped in.

"They've cancelled."

"Cancelled? What reason did they give?"

"The weather."

Again Mary Rose glanced out the window. A fine mist hung in the air. So it was raining, so what?

"I think the kid might have more problems than everybody is admitting," the secretary said carefully. "I heard screaming in the background on the phone."

"The child was screaming?"

"*A* child was screaming. Is he the only one in the home?"

"Yes."

"Well …"

"I think I'd better go over there."

Marlee shook her head. "Mary Rose, don't …"

Ignoring her secretary's warning, Mary Rose rifled through the few papers in the file and found the home number of the Steins. "I'll make an appointment to see them. Nobody can fault me for that."

"Yes they can," Marlee responded. "You should be calling the director. There's no way you'll be able to justify establishing personal contact with guardians who have failed to come in for an initial meeting."

Of course she was right, but Mary Rose didn't want to hear it. Everything about this case was irregular and she saw no reason why she should stick to protocol on the matter when nobody else had bothered to do so.

She picked up the phone.

But when she saw the look of concern—or was it disgust?—on her secretary's face, she hesitated.

Marlee smiled ruefully and shook her head. She was a woman of impeccable taste. Her black hair was smoothly straightened. Her dark skin flawless. She was a commanding person and sometimes Mary Rose felt a stab of guilt knowing that the things that had kept Marlee from finishing law school had had nothing to do with a lack of talent, intelligence or courage.

"Send the file back to the folks who sent it to you," Marlee said. "If you know what's good for you."

"Yeah, right."

But when the secretary left, Mary Rose opened the file again. There was a picture—not a new shot. The kid looked about five instead of twelve. Still, the photo showed a smart-looking boy with the intense look of an intelligent person strongly in control of his own feelings.

Every good lawyer is a detective.

That's what Mary Rose's mentor had told her. B. Sheldrake Tuppin had been ninety when he died, but even at that age, he'd had the sharpest legal mind Mary Rose had ever encountered.

What she needed was a way to speak to this child directly. It was going to be almost impossible, but that wouldn't have stopped Tuppin and it wouldn't stop her.

Start with what you know and use it to get to what you don't know.

Mary Rose locked her office door. Marlee hated that, but despite the inconvenience to her secretary, she didn't want to be interrupted. The first thing she needed to do was to find out whether the child had his own phone number or his own email. No one working on the file of a child was allowed access to such information. In fact, the law protecting the privacy of children was so strict, that should she or anyone in her office come across such information, they were legally bound to reveal it to their superiors and to turn the file over to them in order to have the private numbers officially expunged.

Fat chance.

Behind the locked door, Mary Rose went over every document in Joseph Di Buonna's file. She not only read every typed word, she also studied the notes from which the typed material had been prepared. Despite the careful work of the clerks in the Orphan Advocate Office—each of whom had to be cleared by police and bonded—errors still occurred. Sometimes a number or an address that had been expunged in the typed report remained in the handwritten notes.

But not this time. There were plenty of places where thick black marker had obscured information. Whoever had vetted this file had done a thorough job.

Always make use of the obvious.

Mary Rose reached for the phone book. She was surprised to see that the Steins, the grandparents in whose custody Joseph was, had a listed phone number and street address. She jotted those down.

There was an answering machine. A cultured male voice relayed a simple message from the Stein family. There was no reference to any other number or party on the same line. In the recent past, Mary Rose's clients often had a general message that led callers to other numbers for individual members of the family. Now that children were so vigorously protected, such messages had fallen out of use. She hung up.

She turned to her computer and searched Joseph's name on the internet.

Surprisingly she found a number of entries. The legal battle between the American and Canadian grandparents had generated a lot of paperwork, much of it matter of public record, court appearances and judgements.

A child at the center of this mess, Mary Rose reflected, was not well-adjusted, no matter what the Orphan Advocate Ofice might think.

There were also quite a number of references to the Di Buonna family. There were cheery family websites of distant relations with happy, holiday portraits. There were articles about the devotion to medicine of Joseph's parents and about their tragic deaths during the SARS epidemic.

And of course, there was the music. Mary Rose found references to the family's musical heritage that stretched back more than a century. She found an obituary of one Giuseppe Di Buonna who had owned a hotel that had once stood on the edge of the Ward—St. John's Ward—was the proper name. She scrolled among the pages of the site. She found a photograph from 1912 in which a group of children, mostly boys, were posed in front of the hotel. They held child-size musical instruments: violins, accordions and harps. They looked cherubic—dressed in sweet white suits, chubby-cheeked, grinning.

A loud knock sounded at her door. She ignored it.

She flashed through a number of other sites, but there was no hint of what she really needed to know—how to get in touch with Joseph Di Buonna without his family finding out.

The knock sounded again.

"What is it?" she shouted through the closed door.

The muffled response from Marlee was incomprehensible.

Mary Rose clicked off the web and went to the door.

"I need the file," Marlee announced.

"What?"

"I need to return the file to the safe."

"The safe?"

"Yes. It's restricted. You *are* finished with it, aren't you?"

Mary Rose hated it when Marlee pulled her routine of scrupulous efficiency. She also hated herself for hating it.

"Yes," she said. "I'll get it."

"Thank you."

"You're welcome."

Sometimes her mixed feelings toward her secretary made her wish she could fire Marlee, but there was no way. Anyway, everything was about to change. As soon as Mary Rose became a judge, she'd certainly have a new office, possibly have a new secretary and likely have a new attitude.

There was no way a judge would do what she was about to do.

CHAPTER 21

▼

The Stein's home was perhaps the loveliest in its neighborhood, an antique-rose brick Georgian with a wide front lawn, bordered by a garden that must have been lush in summer, but now, in November, seemed a somber gathering of late-blooming mums in rusty shades of orange and purple. A high flight of stone steps, flanked by juniper bushes, led to a double wooden door, richly varnished and seeming to glow in the late afternoon light.

As she approached the front door, Mary Rose heard someone practicing the violin. It sounded good, and the lilting melody made the big, cold house seem friendly. Should she just knock?

Maybe not.

For starters, the Steins, in cancelling their appointment without proper notice were probably letting her know that they were hostile.

Secondly, as she had considered before, she had no appointment to speak to the child, and therefore was out of bounds in approaching anyone connected to him.

Finally, at houses like this, it was not the owners, but the servants who answered the door. How would she explain what she was doing there?

As she stood in front of the door, ridiculously exposed, her attention was caught by the sudden cessation of the music and a slight movement of curtains at the very top of the house. Someone was watching.

Mary Rose felt embarrassed. In fact, she felt ashamed.

Was she out of her mind?

She was acting like a stalker. And for what? To find out if some spoiled child was happy? How preposterous!

She turned on her heels, eager to get back to her car.

The next morning, she asked Marlee to draft a memo for her, explaining to Madam Justice Hunt-Duval that she had checked out the home environment of Joseph Di Buonna and had found nothing amiss in his circumstances.

"You went to his *home* yesterday?" the secretary asked.

"Yes."

"And you checked it out—"

"That's what I'm saying in the memo, then, isn't it?"

"Did you get inside? Did you speak to the Steins in person?"

"Marlee, just do the memo, okay? If I decide that it doesn't reflect what I've done on the case thus far, I'll adjust it and get you to run it through the computer again."

The secretary did a little huffy thing with her shoulders and flounced out of the room.

Mary Rose thought about the fact that Marlee, always tense, had been acting especially picky and contemptuous lately. Was she envious because of the impending judicial appointment?

Mary Rose hoped not. She felt guilty about her mixed feelings for Marlee. But it wasn't entirely her fault. Sometimes Marlee was wonderful. A lot of times, she wasn't.

Mary Rose intended to follow up the memo with a phone call to Madam Hunt-Duval's office. She wanted to know exactly when her elevation to the bench would take place. In a way, she was glad that the Steins and their grandson seemed so inaccessible behind the stone walls of their mansion. On reflection, she realized she didn't want to talk to them in person, didn't want to become directly involved in the life of yet another needy child. In her new life she'd be dealing with principles and policies rather than the messy lives of individuals. Maybe it was about time.

But that evening, she reconsidered. She thought about the memo she'd not yet sent to the Chief Justice. Marlee had been right. It wasn't proper procedure to report on a child's case with no real attempt at contacting that child's guardian.

On her way home, she approached the Stein residence again. The moment she stepped on the flagstone path that led to the front door, a row of ultra-bright lights flicked on, flooding the garden. She stumbled on the uneven path, her heel catching in the space between two stones. Her arms flailed wildly.

The door swung open and in the soft light of the foyer, a slight woman with beautiful dark skin, intense eyes and amazing long black hair stood studying Mary Rose as intently as she studied the girl.

The nanny ...

"Sorry," the girl said. "Nobody home. Come back again."

In the background, Mary Rose could hear music—the violin. And voices. "I think you must be mistaken. I'll just ..."

Before she could finish her sentence, the door was torn out of the hand of the nanny and a furious, red-faced, elderly woman was standing in front of Mary Rose looking ready for battle in a slim black Simon Chang jacket over black cigarette slacks, a red silk blouse, gold Chanel earrings and a silver-gray upswept hairdo.

"Excuse me, Mrs. Stein. I'm sorry to bother you," Mary Rose began, clearing her throat and calling upon her best lawyerly voice. "I imagine that you are rather surprised that I've taken the liberty of coming to your home—and in the evening at that."

The polite words had no effect on Mrs. Stein. Having dealt with litigants for years, Mary Rose was sensitive to their needs, their frustration. She struggled to remain professional, to remind herself that this woman's negativity and defensiveness were probably not regular components of her personality.

"I realize that you must be very upset over the difficulties you're experiencing with reference to the custody of your grandson. Perhaps that's why you cancelled your meeting with my office ..."

"What does anybody at your office know about my grandson?" she demanded. "How dare you come here and harass me? I'll report you to the law society!"

"Please, Mrs. Stein," Mary Rose said, raising her hand in a gesture of conciliation.

"Don't you dare raise your hand against me! And don't you assume you know *anything* about our Joseph."

At the sound of the boy's name, Mary Rose suddenly realized that the child himself might be listening.

The thought made her cringe. She was well aware of the damage done to children who were forced to listen to endless disputes between parents and grandparents over their custody. It was a trite, sad fact that such children always blamed themselves for what they were hearing.

"Mrs. Stein," she said, "once again, I beg to apologize. Of course, you're right. Of course you know what's best for your family. But the court has asked me to take a look at Joseph's file and I'm concerned about him."

"Apologize all you want," the woman sputtered. "It makes no difference to me. I've had countless calls from the Orphan Advocate Office. I didn't speak to them and I have no intention of speaking to you."

"Mrs. Stein," Mary Rose persisted, "let me ask you just a few routine questions. Once I'm assured that Joseph is alright, I can write a report that will ensure that you'll not be visited again."

"I've heard that before, Miss," the woman said. "In fact, I've heard all I care to hear about the government's concern for our child. Get out! Just get out of here and stay away. I'll call the Attorney-General! I'll call the police!"

There was a sudden ear-splitting screech. Mary Rose couldn't tell whether it was Mrs. Stein yelling or a violin bow being violently drawn across the strings.

She didn't stick around to find out.

CHAPTER 22

▼

"You were right."

Mary Rose plunked a package down on Marlee's desk.

"What's this?"

"A forgive-me gift."

Marlee inspected the present with its gold foil wrap and yellow silk ribbon tied with a sprig of copper-colored taffeta maple leaves.

"Why, what did you do wrong?" She shook the box. "Chocolates?"

Mary Rose nodded. "You were right that I shouldn't be submitting any report about a client without making every reasonable attempt to see that client in person first."

The secretary began to unwrap her gift with careful, beautifully manicured fingers.

"So you saw him in person—the client, I mean?"

"Not exactly," Mary Rose admitted. "He was guarded by a dragon."

"You met Mrs. Stein in person, then."

"Yes."

Marlee extracted a small, perfectly round candy dusted with a tiny bit of powdered white sugar. "Champagne truffles," she said with a broad grin. "You spoil me. You ought to do wrong things more often." She popped the delicacy into her mouth.

"Yeah. I ought," Mary Rose answered absently.

The secretary glanced at her. "So you want that report printed, or what?" she asked.

"Bring it up on the computer and I'll add a sentence or two," Mary Rose answered.

When Marlee had printed the final draft of her report, Mary Rose walked down the block to Osgoode Hall intending to deliver it by hand before stopping off at the law library in the same building. Fully expecting to be asked to leave the report at reception, she was surprised when the receptionist told her that the Chief Justice wished to see her.

Madam Hunt-Duval's door was ajar. Her Ladyship was intent on her reading, slowly turning the pages of a big book bound in red leather. She didn't look up.

Mary Rose felt like a child called into the principal's office. She fought the urge to clear her throat to draw attention to her presence.

After what seemed an eternity, the justice raised her eyes. "Well," she said, "I understand you have a report for me."

Mary Rose held out the two stapled pages.

The Chief Justice scowled at it as if to say "Is that all?"

But she actually said nothing, just motioned for Mary Rose to sit.

"So," the Chief Justice said when she'd finished reading the report, "this is succinct."

Mary Rose nodded. "There's not a lot to say."

"Suppose you elaborate a little. Give me your overall impressions of this situation."

Once more Mary Rose felt mystified. What was so special about this boy? True his parents had died under tragic circumstances. Was there an orphan whose parent's hadn't?

"As I've said, my attempts to gain permission from the guardians to speak directly to the boy have been unsuccessful. I have, however, done a home visit." She hoped that standing on the front porch being yelled at by a hysterical grandmother counted as a home visit.

"And?"

"And though the guardian appears to have something of a minor anger management problem, the home is certainly well maintained. In fact, it's luxurious. I see no reason to interfere with this family. I understand that a custody case is before the courts, but from what I've seen, I feel the family is in a position to take care of the legal challenges that face its members."

"Do you have a recommendation, then?" the justice enquired. She picked up the report again. Gingerly, as if it were a dirty scrap of paper from off the street.

"Madame Justice," she finally said, "I do have a recommendation. In fact, I have two. The first is that you leave this family alone. They have problems, true, but they have ample resources with which to address whatever confronts them. I don't feel we need to compound the issue by adding the intervention of the court to their woes."

"You perceive the work of the court as adding to the *woe* of our constituents?" the Chief Justice said in disapproving shock.

At these arch words, Mary Rose's own anger management problem kicked in.

"Yes. Yes I do. It would be dishonest to say otherwise. If I could help this child personally, I would. But there is no way. And, I'm quite convinced, no need. As for my own involvement here, I did as I was requested. I checked out the boy's circumstances. I found them satisfactory. However, I find it distinctly unsatisfactory that I am being put to a test like this. May I remind you, Madame Chief Justice, that my appointment to the bench is not conditional. My appointment has already been announced. I do not except any further delays in being informed of the exact date on which I will be invested. My second recommendation is that you inform me of that date at your earliest convenience."

It took Mary Rose a few seconds to calm down after this passionate speech. A few seconds were long enough for her to realize what she'd done. What was she thinking, speaking to the Chief Justice in so disrespectful a manner?

She lowered her eyes and kept them down until she heard the Chief Justice respond.

"Very well."

Not sure what she'd heard, Mary Rose said, "I beg your pardon?"

"Fine. I accept this report. Consider yourself off the Joseph Di Buonna case. You may go."

CHAPTER 23

▼

Over the years. Mary Rose, preoccupied with her work, had never got around to buying a house or—despite several offers—marrying either.

For a long time she lived in a spectacular downtown condo, a three-bedroom facing south and southwest with a wrap-around balcony from which she could watch the sun rise over the houses and highrises of the city at dawn and set over the lake at dusk. This she used for entertaining, including the occasional male dates, most of whom never made it past the living room.

One day she decided to sell the place and move back to what remained of the Little Italy downtown—the neighborhood where she'd been born. She now had three book-lined rooms above a row of stores. She loved it there and it was there she headed when she came home the night of the meeting in which she'd shot off her mouth and got booted off the Joseph Di Buonna case.

She opened the door, dumped her purse and briefcase and made straight for the phone, surprised to see the message light flashing. She'd cleared everything on her way up. Someone had called since she'd reached the top of the stairs?

On the line she heard nothing but some prankster banging away at the piano—a jerky, off-rhythm rendition of two-finger "Chopsticks". Irritated, her own finger slid toward "delete".

But in the split second before she depressed the key, she heard the recorded melody change.

Once again, this time in a simple, almost awkward piano version, came the mysterious tune she realized she'd heard both times she'd been at the Steins'.

Without erasing the message, she slammed down the receiver.

Was she stalking Joseph Di Buonna or was he stalking her?

She pulled from her purse the tiny recorder she used for note-taking and held it up to the phone. When she was finished, she dialled a familiar number.

"*Maria! Ciao Bella! Come stai? Che fa?*"

"*Ciao, Luigi. Sto bene. Grazie. Lavoro molto. Et tu?*"

Mary Rose responded mechanically to the usual string of personal queries that would have sounded polite coming from anyone other than Dr. Luigi Giordano. On the tongue of the Italian professor, a suave, energetic, cherubic little man who had pursued Mary Rose since she'd reached puberty, the questions sounded invasive, provocative, even lascivious.

"*Io anche. Sto bene,*" he answered. "Like you I'm fine—and hard at work. Always. What can I do for you *mia cara Maria*?"

"I need your help to figure out …"

"My help? Anything. Any time. Tell me where you want to meet and I'll be there. *Pronto!*"

"I don't think we need to do this in person," Mary Rose hurried to say. "I just need you to listen to something and to tell me what it means."

She pressed play. "What do think that tune is?" she asked after a few seconds. "Have you ever heard it before?"

"Um … Maybe. But I could know better if you came over here. I have my collection of tapes and discs in my home office. Come now. I'll wait for you."

Before she could reply, he was off the phone.

Half an hour later, he met her at the door of his cliché of a college professor's lair—all scuffed leather chairs, glass-fronted bookcases, brass lamps with green glass shades. An impressive array of framed diplomas covered one wall. Paintings, drawings and photos of Italy graced another.

Beside the oak refectory table that served as his desk, a marble-topped cabinet held a tray with two cut-crystal goblets and a matching decanter of golden wine—the sweet muscatel that Mary Rose had been offered by him every time they'd met since she'd been a teenager. As always, she refused the drink.

He shrugged as he poured a drink for himself. "Such a beautiful woman," he said sadly. "She doesn't drink. She doesn't marry. What else doesn't she do?"

Mary Rose smiled despite herself. "The ones I like never like me. That's why I don't marry."

He moved closer and the rich smell of distilled summer grapes met her nostrils. "You could have married me."

"You! You've been married four times. If you wanted a wife so much, why didn't you keep one of the ones you had?"

He laughed good-naturedly, took a sip of his drink, pulled a chair a little too close to the one he offered her.

"Let me hear that song," he said.

He listened to it only once.

"Laurenzana."

"Laurenzana?" Mary Rose repeated. "What's that?"

"It's not a *what*," the professor answered. "It's a *where*."

He stood and from a shelf behind him, pulled down an atlas and opened it to a multi-colored map of Italy. He pointed at a place south of Rome.

"For generations," he began, "right up until World War One, the people of Laurenzana sent their children abroad to make their fortune playing music on the street. Every one of those kids—or so the legend went—was a musical genius. And some of them, according the same legend, held the secret to immense wealth."

"Wealth? How could child street musicians be wealthy?"

"Who knows? There were a million such stories. Always are in the folk lore of poor people. Some said there was a jewel that the family had long ago stolen from a king and had hidden in one of the instruments the children played. Or maybe it was a map of a treasure or a paper that proved that a boy who seemed nothing but a dirty urchin was really a prince." He shook his head. "Pathetic, really."

"Yes."

"Anyway, these children managed to make their way onto the streets of most of the major cities of the western world. They might start in Naples, then Rome. Paris, London, New York. Some made it all the way to Buenos Aires. And then back to Naples."

"You mean the same child might travel all over the world?"

"Yes."

"But how?"

"By ship, of course."

"That's not what I meant."

The professor pulled his chair closer and sat. Mary Rose fought the urge to pull her chair away. "Maria," he said softly, leaning toward her, "are you sure nobody ever told you these things before?"

His intensity surprised her. "No. Why should they?"

"Non importante," he responded. "Anyway, the children were able to travel under the tutelage of a *padrone*, a boss who made all the arrangements. Some of these men were benevolent, some tyrannical. Most were both, depending on what the circumstances demanded. They fed, clothed and housed the children.

Sometimes they fed them garbage from the streets and clothed them in rags they stole from the Jewish ragmen. Sometimes they treated the little ones like royalty. But they never failed to reap whatever profit they could from the labors of those children. Profit, then, like now, came first."

"I've done child labor cases," Mary Rose said thoughtfully. "They are few and far between now. Thank God." She thought about Joseph Di Buonna. A violinist? Was he a child held captive for the value of his labor? The thought was too ridiculous to contemplate.

"A good part of the economy of the world runs on child labor," Dr. Giordano answered. "People don't want to think about it, but it's a practice as old as time."

"But what does all this have to do with the tune?" Mary Rose asked.

The professor went to one of his bookcases and took out a binder of compact discs. He selected one and slipped it into a player on his desk.

Immediately the song from Laurenzana, the tragic, pining melody, filled the room. Within seconds, a mellow voice joined the instrumental music. On the disc someone was singing lyrics to the piece.

Mary Rose listened carefully.

"I can't understand a word," she said after the professor had played it for her three times. "It sounds like Italian, but I just can't catch it."

"It's dialect. Nineteenth-century. Could be *Molisano*."

"So this song is from Molise? I thought you said Laurezana."

"Could be from Molise brought to Laurenzana."

"And then brought to Toronto? But when? Must have been a long time ago."

The professor reached past Mary Rose to retrieve his wine. His arm came near to brushing the front of her blouse. She didn't allow herself to react.

"A lot of what came to Toronto from Italy in the nineteenth and twentieth centuries," he said, "came indirectly."

"Indirectly?"

"Yes."

He reached across to put his drink back down, and this time he was careful not to touch her. He clicked the disc on again. "This version of the song," he said, "is not from the hills of Molise or the villages of Laurenzana. It's a little item from the hit parade of 1910. Listen again."

He pressed a button and the disc skipped to a different track. Now the words were in English. "The moon, the mountains, the wild sea. Can't they bring you back to me?"

"Yeah," he said. "This was a big hit back then. Fresh from the streets of old New York." He gave her a look that she couldn't read. Sneaky.

"What?" she asked him.

"Nothing. I was just thinking that it is not impossible that some relative of yours sang this song here in Toronto—or in New York, or even in Italy."

"No way," she replied. "I don't come from street urchins."

"Nobody knows who they come from," the professor said, once again shaking his head. He reached out and touched her hand. "Have a late dinner with me tonight," he begged.

Mary Rose laughed. "I may not know where I come from, but I know where I'm going. Thanks but no thanks. I'm out of here."

CHAPTER 24

▼

"Looks like news! Let me …"

Mary Rose snatched a pile of mail from the hands of her secretary before the woman could get through the door.

"Slow down. Can't you wait until I open and date-stamp it?"

"Sorry." Mary Rose ripped open an envelope from the Attorney-General's office and scanned the contents. "It's about time!"

"What? Have they finally told you the date of your elevation?"

"Well," Mary Rose answered, "I think we can safely assume I'm in." She held out a fan of papers. "Here's a request for me to make an appointment to be measured for a judge's robe and an invitation to the reception that follows the induction—with my name printed on the list of honorees. They also want to know how I would like my name printed on my new judicial stationery."

"It ain't over until it's over," the secretary responded tartly, shaking her head.

"You know, if I didn't know you better, Marlee, I'd think you were envious of me."

"You may not know me as well you think. Stop prancing around imagining yourself in that new judge's robe. There's other mail you've got to see."

She nodded toward the remaining items, then reached for the coffee carafe, before heading in the direction of the kitchen Mary Rose shared with several other lawyers in the courthouse branch of the Orphan Advocate Office.

"Hey," Mary Rose called after her, "*I* was going to get the coffee."

Marlee shrugged but she didn't turn.

Fine. Be in a snit.

Mary Rose shuffled through the flyers, bills, legal notices and magazines that had come in. At the very bottom of the day's mail, she found a white envelope with a double red stripe along the bottom edge and two black and red stickers plastered across the flap. One sticker was the seal of the official courier used by the director of the orphan office. The other was the seal of the director himself.

Both stickers presented problems. Marlee had been right. Official mail needed to be duly processed. The courier sticker had a detachable portion that had to be date-stamped and received back by the sender within twelve hours. Otherwise, security guards from the courier company would hound Marlee, even pulling her out of bed if necessary, for proof that the letter had been duly received.

As for the seal of the director, unless Mary Rose's own personal legal seal was affixed to it before she opened the envelope, she faced criminal charges under the Protection of Secured Information Act.

So she waited until Marlee came into her office with two steaming mugs of coffee and an "I told you so" look on her face. With a little too much pomp and ceremony, Marlee unlocked the cabinet in which the date stamp and the legal seal were kept.

When the prescribed procedures had been performed, Mary Rose slit open the envelope.

It contained a single sheet of paper covered on both sides with lines of exceptionally neat, small but perfectly legible handwriting.

It took her a minute to realize she should not have opened the envelope after all.

The paper she held appeared to be a hand-written report submitted by a social worker who had interviewed Joseph Di Buonna in connection with his custody matter. Significantly, the report seemed not to have been typed into a computer. Could this mean that it was too confidential even to be transcribed? Across the top in red ink, in a different hand, were scrawled the words, "Highly confidential."

Why? Mary Rose had seen hundreds—perhaps thousands of such reports. What made this one so secret?

Obviously whoever had sent this document was as yet unaware that Mary Rose had been removed from the boy's case.

She had no legal authority to see this paper. Even if she had been authorized, she was not supposed to read it in the confines of her office without a witness. And there was a protocol for papers received in error. She was supposed to call in her secretary, to get Marlee to reseal the envelope in her presence. Then the two were supposed to initial it and together deposit it in the secure out-box that was emptied by the OPP, the Ontario Provincial Police, once a day.

No.

Who would know if she glanced at this report it before she dispatched it back to where it belonged? It *had* been sent to her, after all, hadn't it? With determined curiosity, she unfolded the paper, closing her office door as she began to read. She dared not lock it. Marlee might hear the sound of the bolt and become suspicious.

Joseph Di Buonna is a twelve-year-old Caucasian male, a Canadian citizen and the orphaned son of Shona Di Buonna (nee Stein, b. Toronto, 1974) and Joseph (Joey, Jr.) Di Buonna (b. Toronto, 1969). The child is of above-average intelligence, well-adjusted and generally competent.

Blah. Blah. Of course Mary Rose already knew all this. Disappointed, she refolded the report to shove it back into its envelope.

She changed her mind when her eye fell on the first sentence of the second paragraph.

I was called to the home of the subject at six a.m. in order to assess erratic behavior that had persisted for upwards of fourteen hours. Medical personnel had already seen the child and sent him home with a prescription for tranquillizers, and he was calm, but he refused to stop obsessively talking about an incident that had happened on the afternoon of the previous day.

The family had hired a new cleaning service. The new employees had not been told that the child's room was off-limits. Joseph Di Buonna is exceptionally particular about his personal belongings and cleans his room himself. When he discovered that the room had been entered by others, he spent five hours checking to make sure that nothing was missing.

At first, all seemed in order. At about four p.m., though, the boy discovered that a drawer in which he keeps his most prized possessions appeared to have been tampered with. Though nothing was missing, the thought of another having touched these items sent the boy into a trance-like state.

He began to "relate" an incident that could not possibly have really taken place. He persisted in repeating this tale over the course of several hours. In my capacity as social worker assigned to him, I, myself heard the tale and record it here.

Joseph Di Buonna said, "I went to New York City. I talked to my grandfather's grandfather. He was an old man—at least one hundred. He told me I am special. He told me I am the blood of my family. He told me that no matter what happens, a boy has to be loyal to his family, and he made me promise I would always be faithful and that I would never do anything against our blood. He was too old to walk himself. He told me to walk to the window and to look out. I had to stand on my tip-toes because the window was so high. I didn't think I would see anything. But the buildings were so big that I could see the tops of lots of them.

"The old man told me that someday I would be rich. He said the richest people are those who own the country they live in. He asked me what country I lived in, but I didn't know. He asked me if I could keep a secret and I said I could.

"Then he said that secrets come in many shapes. He said some secrets are words and some are things. He told me that he would give me a secret and that no matter what happened, I couldn't give the secret to anybody else until I became a man. He asked me if I could remember that, and I said yes.

"He gave me the secret. Today, somebody saw the secret. I broke my promise."

The boy then broke into uncontrollable sobs.

This behavior continued for about one hour after my arrival on the scene. Then, for no reason apparent to me, the child pulled himself together. He insisted he was now all right. Despite the protestations of his grandmother and myself, he was determined to attend school that morning, and he was allowed to do so.

No further incidents of this type of behavior have occurred during the forty-eight hours between the time I was called to the home and the time at which I submit this report.

Mary Rose knew of a two-year-old who'd saved her mother's life by pressing redial when the woman collapsed during a phone call to a friend.

She knew a twelve-year-old with a B.A. and more than one child whose net worth, earned from after-school self-employment, was higher than her own.

So why should it be so hard to believe that Joseph Di Buonna might have been given or told some secret thing by his ... She thought about it for a minute. By his great-great-grandfather? She did a rough calculation. Suppose the old man was in his nineties and the kid three or four? Could it have happened? She needed to know more about the genealogy of the family.

Slipping the report back into its official envelope, she stepped to the door. Marlee was getting ready to leave on some errand.

"Did the OPP empty the out-box yet?"

"No, why?" The secretary frowned at Mary Rose's empty hands. "You got something we should deposit before I go?"

"No. I was just wondering whether Joseph Di Buonna's file was in there."

"Why wouldn't it be? We signed it off yesterday." She made an annoying shaking motion with her head, as if she thought Mary Rose was losing it. "Don't tell me you forgot?"

"Sorry," Mary Rose said absently. "I guess I got too much on my mind." She glanced at the grandfather clock that stood beside the door to her office. "How long do you plan to be gone?"

The secretary shot her a look of surprised anger. Mary Rose realized it was probably the first time she'd ever questioned how her secretary used her time.

"I'll be back when I'm back," Marlee said. Then, her face softened, "You're not concerned about being here alone, are you?"

It was an odd question, but Mary Rose didn't give it much thought. Being alone was exactly what she wanted. If Marlee left, she'd have a chance to reread the Joseph Di Buonna file, but she needed time. Nobody knew the combination to the outbox except the OPP, and they might be here any minute.

Mercifully, the secretary didn't dawdle.

The only clue Mary Rose had as to the combination was her vague memory of what she had seen the countless times she'd absently watched the OPP officers key in the code of the box.

She approached the smooth steel cube with its digital number pad. She stood in front of it and forced her mind to picture the two officers and the motions of their fingers. She had a good memory. She was able to "see" the two cops, to decipher, or so she thought, the remembered movements of their imagined hands.

She moved closer to the cube. At one corner of the keypad was a small steady white light. The minute her fingers touched the keys, that light turned green. She remembered the officers joking that they could unlock any box before the green light turned yellow. This meant there were only two chances to open the box. If that light turned red, the police would be there within seconds.

Mary Rose concentrated, her fingers poised over the keys. She closed her eyes.

Two.

That had to be the first number. Close to the edge of the top of the pad. She pressed. The light stayed green.

She pictured the officers again, willing her mind's eye to see their fingers.

Five.

The number directly beneath two.

No!

The light blinked from green to yellow.

Mary Rose suddenly recalled that when any alarm light in the office, for example the alarms on the safe and on the secure filing cabinets, went to yellow, the door of the office automatically locked. It would not unlock until proper procedures were applied to get the light back to green by keying in the whole correct combination.

Her fingers hesitated over the numbers. She had to get it right now or risk setting off the next and last level of the alarm.

If it isn't five, then it must be eight.

Her finger came down on the number.

The light remained yellow. The cube remained secure. The office door remained locked. The next number had to be correct or the light would go to red.

Her fingers hovered.

And as she stood there trying to figure out the last number, the unimaginable happened.

The number pad picked up the heat of her nervous hand and all ten numbers lit up at once!

She jumped back, waiting for all the alarms in the place to go off simultaneously.

Instead, there was a small click. The light near the number pad turned back to white. A door in the box slid open.

The Di Buonna file was the only thing inside.

Rapidly she shuffled through the papers in the file. She jotted down names, dates. There was no complete record of the generations of Di Buonnas who had gone to the United States from Italy and then come to Canada, but there were names of people and places that Mary Rose knew she could look up on the internet.

Roughly she sketched a time-line, based to some extent on the generations of her own Italian family.

Joseph had been born twelve years ago. And his father, both the file and the social worker's report indicated, had been born in 1969. Such a person's own father had probably been born in the 1940's. His father, that was, Joseph's great-grandfather could have been born around 1920. And *his* father, the "old, old man" of Joseph's story, would probably have been born at the turn of the last century.

It fit. The grandfather of Joseph's grandfather could easily have been in his nineties when Joseph was three or four.

And a child of Joseph's intelligence could remember meeting him, could recall an unusual conversation between them. The boy could make a promise and keep it.

Why would nobody believe his story?

And more importantly, what was the secret?

Before she could ponder this, Mary Rose heard voices in the outer office. The OPP had arrived.

She listened for Marlee's greeting. There was none.

Quickly she returned all the papers to the file, composed herself and stepped through her door.

"You guys better get your act together," she declared, waving the file in their faces. "That stupid thing is malfunctioning. I had to rescue this file and take it into my own office in order to avoid breaching confidentiality. I'll let you take it, but on condition that you sign it off—and that you get that outbox fixed at once."

The stunned officers took the file and promised they'd look into the matter right away.

They resealed the outbox, nodded to Marlee as they crossed her returning to her desk, and disappeared down the hall.

"What's going on?"

"The outbox wasn't working," Mary Rose answered.

She didn't hear Marlee's reply. She was too busy figuring out a way to get to meet with Joseph Di Buonna.

Alone.

"Why don't you just call that kid and ask him to lunch?" Marlee said sarcastically.

CHAPTER 25

▼

The King George Hotel!

Mary Rose checked out the lobby looking for Mrs. Stein and her grandson. She was used to meeting child clients in neutral locations: popular restaurants, the public library, a community center. Never an expensive place like this.

"Can I help you, madam?"

"I have reservations for lunch in the Café Windsor," she said. "The name is Cabrini."

"This way, please."

As soon as she was seated, Mary Rose caught sight of Mrs. Stein standing in the doorway, decked out in head-to-toe Chanel. Beside her, holding the woman's hand as if he were embarrassed to death to do so, was a beautiful twelve-year-old boy.

He seemed too small and slender for his age. His skin was pale for an Italian. His eyes were downcast, showing the length of his thick black lashes. Even in repose, his face shone with intelligence.

Mrs. Stein stopped about ten feet from where Mary Rose sat staring at the two of them. The older woman nodded and gave the boy a gentle push.

He didn't move.

"Go ahead. I'll be waiting for you in the lobby, Joseph."

With a little brush of her hand against the young man's thick, well-cut dark hair, she turned to go.

Then she turned back. "Remember," she said, "you don't have to be here if you don't want to."

The boy remained perfectly still

But when Mary Rose nodded and smiled at him, he approached, and pulling out the chair opposite her, took a seat.

"Good afternoon," he said. "I'd like an Earl Gray tea with cream, not milk. I take sweetener. It can't be aspartame. I'd like a buttered scone with raspberry jam."

"Sure."

"And if you wish to take notes of our conversation, I will require a copy."

"No problem. But I don't normally take notes. I just listen. That is—if you feel there's something you want to tell me."

The boy made brief eye contact, glanced away.

"I asked you to come here today," Mary Rose said, "because I think you're trying to tell me something. I think you called and left a message on my answering machine."

He looked up, smiling slightly. "You figured out that it was me. Cool. That's why I agreed to meet you today." He hesitated, "Besides, I'm an orphan. You're the Judge of Orphans."

"How do you know that?"

"I saw you in Nathan Phillips Square."

She remembered his challenge to the mayor, his strange intensity. When the time came, she'd ask him about that, but not now.

"But I don't want you to judge me."

"What *do* you want? Aside from scones and tea, that is."

"Not scones. One scone."

"One scone."

"I want you to know about my family."

To a child advocate, such a statement was as fragile as a soap bubble and as likely to disappear with the slightest jarring motion.

When a waiter came to take their order, Mary Rose feared that the moment had been destroyed, the opportunity for Joseph to open up irrevocably lost.

But she was wrong.

"My grandparents are very good to me. They send me to a great school. They encourage my music without being on my back all the time. They live in a neat house and I appreciate it."

"But—"

"Did I say but?"

"No."

"My parents died helping sick people."

"I know, Joseph."

"And I miss them, but I'm working on that."

"In what ways?"

He glanced around the room before he said, "Do you like this place? It's pretty isn't it? Old-fashioned. Like in a movie or something. Or like an old theatre. Did the social workers tell you that everybody in my father's family except him was a musician?"

"Joseph," Mary Rose said carefully, "I have to be fair to you. I have to explain that I can't talk to social workers about you. I'm not here as a social worker or a lawyer or ..."

"You'll get in trouble if you talk to me?"

"Not if I have your grandmother's permission and if she is in the building."

"Otherwise?"

"Joseph, tell me why you need to talk to me."

He seemed to study the floor-to-ceiling window. He reached out and touched the deep green velvet drape that brushed the table near where he sat.

"Before my parents died we were a family. Everything we did was together. My mother was Jewish. My father was Catholic. But even that was okay. Now my grandparents are having a war. America versus Canada. The territory they're fighting over is me."

"And you think I can help in this battle?"

"No. I don't care about the battle. I only care that I betrayed my family."

"Joseph," Mary Rose said, wishing she could reach out and touch him but very careful not to, "often when a parent dies, a child blames himself. It might seem like a betrayal but it's not."

A sarcastic smile curved the boy's lips. "No kidding? Look, I've had grief counselling. I know all that stuff."

"Then ..."

"When I was four years old," he said, "my father told me that I had an American family as well as a Canadian family and that it was time to meet them."

"Yes?"

"My father said that now I was old enough to remember things that I saw. So he—not my mother—just my father ... He took me to New York City. We flew. And I remember every minute of the trip. It was cloudy when we left Toronto, but when we got to New York, you could see it from the air. What I remember most is the bridges. They looked like toys. Even the Brooklyn Bridge. Have you ever seen that?"

He leaned across the table, jarring it a little and causing the crystal salt shaker to teeter. Instinctively, Mary Rose reached for it. As she steadied the object, she lifted her gaze. The intensity of Joseph's eyes as they met hers jolted her. "Have I seen the Brooklyn Bridge?" she asked absurdly.

"Don't answer a question with a question," the boy warned.

Startled, Mary Rose struggled to remember what he had just asked her. After a moment she replied, "Yes. Yes, I've seen the Brooklyn Bridge. And the Manhattan Bridge and the Williamsburg and ..."

"My father's family lives in Manhattan," Joseph said, continuing his narrative in a monotone. "The time we went, I saw my grandfather. No big deal. His name is Joey and he used to live in Canada and he comes here lots.

"Anyway, while I was there, Joey and my father started watching this thing on TV. A football game or something. I got thirsty and I went to look for my grandmother. Except she wasn't there. So I decided to try and find the kitchen and grab a cola or whatever. The place they live in, it's a pretty big apartment. I always lived in a house, so I don't know much about apartments. It had a long hall, and I just wandered down it."

He stopped for a minute. The waiter had silently delivered his scone and jam, but it sat untouched in front of the boy. Mary Rose risked taking a sip of her tea, not wanting to interrupt the telling of the tale.

"I walked down the hall and all the doors were closed. I just wanted to find the kitchen, so I opened one of the doors. I could see right away that it wasn't a kitchen but some sort of bedroom. And it didn't smell like a kitchen, either."

The boy wrinkled his nose. "It smelled old and like piss. Or maybe it smelled like old piss."

Mary Rose set down her tea.

"Anyway, it was sort of disgusting. So I shut the door right away. That's when I first heard the voice."

"The voice?" Mary Rose was beginning to get a feeling she hated. There was, in her opinion, always an overly dramatic quality to the evidence of children who were lying. Young people describing the truth often told tales without color, without detail. But children who were fabricating used story-telling techniques familiar to them from television and from listening to adults read children's books. "What voice?"

"A voice calling me into the room. An old voice. The voice of a man much older than my grandfather—or anybody else. I opened the door and peeked in. And I saw this old guy like a mummy. He was scrunched down in this chair that looked way too big for him. He was sitting by a window but the shade was down and there was only this one dim light in the room. I wasn't sure what I was seeing.

"But he could see me and he even knew who I was. He said my name. He said, 'You're Joseph. I am waiting for you.'"

The boy seemed to shiver. And so did Mary Rose. With impatience. What was the kid up to?

"I felt scared at first," he continued. "But there was something about the old man that made me stay in the room. For one thing, even though he was so old, he looked a little like my grandfather. I told him that. And he told me something really amazing."

"What, Joseph, what did this old man tell you?"

"He said he was the grandfather of my grandfather and that he was almost a hundred years old and that he had a secret and he was waiting to give it to me. He said he'd carried the secret from America to a far-away place—hidden in his father's harp. I told him I didn't know what a harp was. And he laughed and said he didn't know anymore, either. Then he told me to go to a certain place in the room …"

The boy stopped. He picked up the scone. Put it back on the plate. He shook his head. "That's the one thing I just can't remember. Where in that smelly room he told me to go. But wherever it was, there was a piece of paper there—hidden, maybe in a book or a drawer. He told me to bring the piece of paper to him."

"What did you do?"

"I did what he said. The thing was completely ancient, just the kind of document a really old guy like him would have. He said I had to take it, that I had to put the paper in a secret place, never tell anybody about it, never let anybody else see it until I got a sign that I was showing it to the right person. But now I think the cleaning lady saw it. I think I failed. All the old guy said to do was to not let anybody else see—and I failed!"

"Joseph. Joseph! You can't …"

The boy didn't hear her.

"He said that the paper belonged to our family. When I asked him whether that meant it belonged to me, he didn't answer. I thought he couldn't say anything else. So I took the paper and just put it in my pocket. I started to walk out the door. Then, he called me back. He put his hand on my hand. It felt just like the paper—old and dry and creepy.

"'Someday,' the old guy said, 'you will know who the paper belongs to, and you will do what you have to do.'

"I told him I didn't even live in America, but he didn't answer. It almost looked like he fell asleep. I didn't want to touch him again or try to wake him up. I stood there without knowing what I was supposed to do. Then, I heard my father calling me. So I just walked out. I never saw that old guy again. I don't know if he was really the grandfather of my grandfather or just some crazy freak."

Mary Rose asked gently, "whatever happened to that piece of paper?"

No answer.

"Joseph," she said, "I think you can understand why I might have questions about a four year old carrying on a meaningful conversation with a very elderly man and then remembering the gist of it for eight years. Nonetheless, I want you to know that I believe children are capable of remarkable feats."

The boy shrugged in apparent indifference, but he didn't rise from the table.

"I have a friend," Mary Rose continued, "an Italian professor. To tell the truth, he's a pain. But he knows a great deal about the history of children. He told me, for example, that as recently as a hundred years ago, there were whole armies of children who lived without parents, supporting themselves by selling things on the street and by doing odd jobs for people."

"No parents?" Joseph said.

"Right. These children lived in all the great cities of the world: Rome, London, Paris, New York. Some of them were born in America and Canada. But others were born in Europe and crossed the ocean several times before they were fourteen years old. The same child might work in Paris one year, London the next, New York or even Toronto the next."

"How did they cross—in ships?"

"Yes. In the holds—the most crowded, dirty and frightening voyages imaginable." She shuddered. "I think it must have been worse for a child used to living outdoors to be on one of those ships than for someone more used to being confined in a building all the time."

"What did they do on the street?"

Encouraged by his interest, Mary Rose said, "They were well organized. Different groups of children had different trades, depending on their age and their background. For example, a number of boys, perhaps especially African Americans—they were called 'Negroes' then—worked as bootblacks, shining the leather shoes of men on the street. Another group were newsboys. They may have been the largest and most recognized by society. There were hostels for them to sleep in. There was a smaller group of boys who sold white plaster statues. They carried them on a sort of platter over their heads."

"What about girls?"

"The girls sold ribbons and flowers."

"What about musicians?"

"Ah," Mary Rose said with a smile, "that's a different story."

"Why?"

"Because a musician needs talent and skill. And he needs an instrument."

"I'm not sure how they could keep an instrument," Joseph commented. "Street people get their stuff stolen all the time. My grandmother does a thing called 'Out of the Cold'. Do you know what that is?"

"Yes. It's a program in which religious institutions and other groups give the homeless a meal and a place to sleep."

"Right. And my grandmother says that the homeless are always afraid that somebody is going to steal what they've got. So they have to sleep on their shoes, like a pillow."

"Regrettably, that's true."

"And I see homeless kids all the time. I don't think they have any possessions. Except ferrets and rats." .

Mary Rose couldn't help but laugh. "Joseph, I see those homeless teens all the time, too. I don't really think they need to worry about having their rats stolen."

"But they do!" For the first time, the boy was animated. "They have to keep other street kids from stealing the rats."

"Yeah. How do you think they do that?"

"With a rat leash," Joseph joked. But then he became serious again. "One way to keep anything safe is to tie it to you with a leash."

"What?"

Without warning, the boy reached up and undid the top two buttons of the shirt he was wearing.

Alarmed, Mary Rose reached across the table to stop him. What was he doing? "Joseph. Don't ..."

"I keep this tied to me," he said.

Despite all she knew about the necessity of never appearing to engage in intimacy with a child, Mary Rose leaned closer to Joseph.

It was the size and shape of a bullet and it glinted like one in the low light of the tearoom.

"What *is* that?"

The boy lifted the chain slightly so that Mary Rose could get a better look. "It's a flash key—a portable hard drive," he answered. "You've never seen one before?"

"Not one that looks like ammo!"

"I take it with me everywhere. Nobody can access it but me. The information on this drive is top secret." The boy swung the chain a little, causing Mary Rose to suppress a smile. Was he trying to hypnotize her?

"Why are you showing me this, Joseph?"

"Because you came when I called."

"Huh?"

"The day I saw you give a speech," he answered. "I was on some dumb field trip to City Hall. There were people talking. Blah. Blah. And a cornerstone with some stupid fake cement. But there was one good thing on that trip and it was you."

Mary Rose's mind raced back to the day of the ground-breaking of the new courthouse. She remembered the officious speech of the mayor, the vaguely threatening presence of Antonio Di Marino Bianco, the real estate developer.

And she remembered the piercing eyes of the boy who had sat staring up at her as if entranced by her every word. *Somewhere in this city there is a child in need of rescue.*

"You were there."

"Yeah. And I figured you were somebody I could maybe show this to."

"This?"

Again the boy gently swung the chain.

"Okay," Mary Rose said carefully, "tell me what you want me to do for you."

Joseph shook his head. "Not here. There are too many people around. We have to be alone. Just the two of us ..."

"Alone?" Mary Rose repeated in alarm. "This is as alone as I'd ever be allowed to be with you. You understand that, don't you?"

"I don't talk in public," he said, his voice as assertive as that of an adult. "In order for me to show you what's on this drive, I need to be alone with you—the way the old man was alone with me."

Mary Rose thought she knew every manipulative technique a child was capable of pulling. She'd seen this one plenty of times before and hadn't fallen for it yet, though lots of others—teachers and lawyers—had. And they'd ended up with lawsuits when they were lucky and criminal charges when they were not.

"I can't be anywhere alone with you Joseph. I suspect you know that as well as I do."

"Please," he said softly, in the voice not of an adult but a child.

Mary Rose glanced across the table. The boy's dark hair, his fine skin, his remarkable eyes touched her with something she almost never felt, regret that she herself was childless. "Joseph," she said, "find a way for us to meet in a public place with access to a computer, and I promise you, I'll look at what you want to show me and ..." She reached across the table, though she knew she could not touch his hand, "and I'll do everything in my power to help you with whatever it is that you're so worried about."

"Forget it!" the boy cried harshly.

Then he tore away from the table and fled from the room.

CHAPTER 26

▼

"It serves you right. You're not supposed to be talking to that boy and you know it. You want to go sneaking around and meeting with people you're not supposed to see and jeopardizing something you think is already in the bag? Fine. But count me out. I'm not making any phone calls to that family."

"All right, Marlee, all right." Mary Rose left her secretary stewing and went back to her own office.

But within a minute, Marlee was standing in her doorway with that I-told-you-so look on her face.

"Okay," she said. "I called."

"And—?"

"And Mrs. Stein said if you don't stop harassing her family, she's going to call the police."

"Are you serious?"

Marlee nodded.

"Damn!"

The secretary came around behind Mary Rose's desk and looked over her shoulder. It bothered Mary Rose that Marlee always seemed to be watching her, but for the sake of maintaining peace, she didn't comment on the secretary's nosiness.

"How are you coming with that speech?"

"My judicial induction speech is supposed to do three things," Mary Rose said. "It's supposed to sum up my accomplishments so far ..."

"Easy," Marlee said softly. "You're the top children's advocate in this country and ..."

"Thanks," Mary Rose said, "I've got a copy of my CV right here."

"Okay. So what's the problem?"

"The second part of the speech is supposed to delineate my vision of what the Judge of Orphans will be doing for children. I don't have a problem with that, either. But ..."

"But what?"

In her mind's eye Mary Rose saw Joseph's back, his shoulders rigid, his head held high as he stomped away from her, furious at what he saw as her unwillingness to help him.

"The problem is this, Marlee. It's easy to spout platitudes. It's hard to convince people that everything I am about to do affects not only the law and the court but individual boys and girls. I hold their fate in my hands."

"Take it easy, boss," Marlee said. After a moment of silence, she added, "What about the third part of that speech?"

"I have to thank my family and friends. I don't have any family except my brother in the States. And I don't have any friend except you."

"This is getting nauseating," Marlee responded. "I'm going for coffee."

Another couple of hours' work didn't do much for Mary Rose's speech. In frustration, she decided to call it a day.

Later, at home, she thought she heard a light tap on her door.

There were only four apartments in the building, and the door that led up to them opened directly onto busy College Street. Once in a while a homeless person found his or her way into the front hall, and once a crazed drug dealer shot a customer who wouldn't pay, and the poor client nearly bled to death on the sidewalk in front of the building, but for the most part, Mary Rose and her neighbors didn't take extraordinary precautions when it came to security.

Still, she never opened the door to her apartment unless she was sure she knew who was on the other side.

She squinted out the peephole.

Nothing!

But the light tap sounded again, and this time she could tell the knock came from low on the door—near the middle.

Puzzled, she glanced out again.

At first, she still saw nothing.

Then an image slowly formed in the lens of the peephole.

Against the opposite wall of the hallway, stood Joseph Di Buonna. He was holding up the little bullet-like object, swinging it as he had done before.

The gesture was clearly threatening.

As if he understood full well that by showing up alone at Mary Rose's home, he held the power to ruin her legal career for good.

"Joseph," Mary Rose called out without opening the door. "What are you doing here?"

No answer.

"Are you by yourself?"

Still no answer.

"You're with your grandmother, right? I can't open this door unless I know you are with an adult."

This time there was an answer. Another series of light taps.

Exasperated, Mary Rose threw caution to the wind and opened the door. "Look, you know I can't be alone with you. There's a lot at stake here, Joseph. I respect you, but you have to return that respect. If you are here alone, you have to leave right now."

In answer, Joseph pushed past her, slammed the door and left her standing in the hallway.

Stunned, she did the only thing she could think of, which was the same thing he had done. She knocked on the door.

"I need to talk to you without my grandmother—without anybody," came the voice from behind the door. "You have to listen to me."

"Joseph, if I'm found alone with you in my home, I'll be fired from my job and I might even face criminal charges. Do you know what that means?"

"Please. Please, Ms Cabrini. I have to show you something. Now."

An idea occurred to her. It wasn't the best solution but it was certainly better than being with him in her home.

"Joseph, listen to me. You are going to open that door and you are going to walk out here in the hallway. When you come out, I'll go back in. I'll get my coat and we'll go downstairs to Starbucks. You can have a hot chocolate and I'll have a coffee and we'll talk. How about it?"

"Forget it," came the voice.

"Joseph open that door or I am going to get the super ..."

The door opened, but the boy didn't come out.

Mary Rose was beginning to lose her temper. Despite years of working with children, she was no more immune to their wiles than anybody else. She pushed on the door and stormed in.

Joseph jumped back. "I need your computer," he said. "I need it now."

"All right," she conceded. But before she closed the door, she put a book in it so that it had to stay open. It was the smallest, but also the only, thing she could do to protect herself. If someone came by and found her alone with the child, at least they could witness the fact that she was not trying to keep their meeting a secret.

"The computer is in my study down the hall," Mary Rose said. "Let's go. And let's make this quick. The sooner you get out of here, the better."

Without a moment's hesitation, Joseph dove for the machine and turned it on. He pulled the bullet-like object off the chain around his neck, fiddled with it for a second and bent down to plug it into the back of the computer. He pressed a couple of keys.

Nothing happened.

"What …?"

He ignored Mary Rose and kept at it.

"I don't know what you intend. I think …"

Before she could finish her sentence, the screen sprang to life.

A faded document floated there like a sepia ghost. A message in ink that had once been black but was now golden brown, scrawled its way across the small paper in the graceful hand of another era. It seemed to have been written at two different times, though by the same person. The writing in the first paragraph was strong and large. The writing in the other paragraph was shakier, cramped and slightly darker, as if it had been added at a later date.

"Joseph, what is this? Is this what the old man gave you?"

"Yes, but there's more …"

"More what?"

"More to my story. After I met that old man—a long time after—I went to a geneology site on the internet. I checked him out. And I learned the name of my great, great, great, great grandfather—or something like that."

"That's nice, Joseph, but …"

"He was a big boss, a *padrone*, a guy that got kicked out of town by *The New York Times*."

"What?"

"He got in trouble in New York is what I found out. So he came here, made it big, got rich, had children and grandchildren, all ancestors of mine and …"

"Look, Joseph, you took math in school. You must know that even if what you say is true, a man who was your great, great …"

"Whatever."

"Right. That man would have hundreds of descendants by now. And whatever money he might have had a hundred years ago—Well, who knows what would have happened to that?"

"Listen," Joseph said, suddenly angry, "I'm not stupid. Of course I'm aware that propagation is exponential."

"I'm sorry. I—"

"But I have something nobody else in family has. I have that."

He pointed to the image on the screen.

"I figured out something else from the internet," Joseph said. "I figured out the exact street where they all lived in New York."

"How did you do that?"

"I plugged in my last name and after a while, I got a shock. I found some websites about child labor. On one of them, I found out that in 1873, the *Times* published an article about children working in New York. Then I went to the public library where they have those old reels of film that you can put in a machine and read, just like you were reading the paper. I found the articles. One said that people living at a certain house on Crosby Street had put other articles in the paper saying that children had run away and that their anxious relatives were looking for them. I even found those articles. They were fakes, of course. The runaways weren't relatives. They were children who had escaped."

"Joseph," Mary Rose had said carefully. "Do you have proof of any of this?"

The boy smiled. "I have a log of every website, a notebook that lists the dates and pages of the newspaper. I have copies of photographs showing Italian kids in funny hats playing accordions and harps. And even dancing with monkeys that had little funny hats of their own."

"What is it that you *don't* have, Joseph?"

"Huh?"

"What is it that you want from me?"

Joseph hit a key and the document disappeared from the screen. For a moment, Mary Rose wondered whether the whole thing hadn't been some sort of trick. A boy capable of making up a story such as she'd just heard would also be capable of creating a fake nineteenth-century document. All he'd need was good photo-manipulation software.

"I need you to find out what this piece of paper has to do with my family."

She couldn't make any promises. She didn't make any. She called a cab and sent him home.

Then she called Professor Luigi Giordano. And he told her that everything she was saying about the *padrone* and *The New York Times* and Crosby Street made sense.

"Book me a flight to New York," she told her secretary the next morning.

"What?" You can't leave town. The Chief Justice's assistant wants that speech right now. And you haven't gone for the gown measurement, either. Plus you've got to give me your list of people to send invitations to for the reception following the induction ..."

"La Guardia is fine. Try for first thing tomorrow morning. See if you can get that flight that leaves about 8 a.m. And get the airport limo to pick me up at 5. I'll need plenty of time to get through security and customs."

CHAPTER 27

▼

Fifty-one Crosby was an empty lot. It was the first thing Mary Rose saw as she walked south on the east side of Crosby, and it alarmed her. What if the whole street had been changed beyond recognition? It had been over a hundred thirty years since the events that Joseph Di Buonna had described.

But there *was* a building next door. Across two lots, stretched a rather handsome structure of seven or eight stories. It was painted a fashionable shade of gray-green. Classic 1890's New York. The height alone made it extremely unlikely that the building would have stood in 1873. If the occupants of this site had been the people Joseph thought they'd been, the bunch of them, monkeys, boys and slave-drivers would have had to use the stairs in 1873. In 1890, there were elevators.

She needed more information. It was Sunday. All the libraries and archives would be closed. She gave up and walked a few blocks east toward Mulberry Street.

Once Little Italy had been a thriving segment of the Lower East Side, alive with vendors and street musicians, redolent with the aromas of the immigrant Italian cooking that would eclipse all other Italian cuisines in America for all time.

There were but three blocks left of that old Little Italy, Mulberry Street between Kenmare and Grand. On Sundays it was blocked off, and for a few hours each week, became again the pedestrian thoroughfare it had once been. White-aproned waiters stood outside Italian restaurants beckoning prospective customers. Storefronts that hadn't changed much in a hundred years offered bargains in clothing and handbags. And street vendors with new wagons made to look old hawked souvenirs and CD's, tee-shirts and flags.

Mary Rose was several generations removed from her Italian roots, but she nonetheless considered herself one of the "Children of the Bend," the descendants of the Italians who had originally come to New York and settled near the place where Mulberry Street curved at its southern end. It had eventually become such a bad slum that it had been wiped out and a park put in its place. Still, to come back to Mulberry Street, and especially to sit on the patio of her favorite Italian café—even on a cold day—was a treat that Mary Rose gave herself at least a couple of times a year.

She carried her double-long espresso to a table on the sidewalk and sat down, thinking about the past week she'd spent in New York. She'd made no progress in figuring out what Joseph's document might be. Even the New York Public Library hadn't been able to help.

She was startled out of her solitary thoughts by the sudden and unlikely appearance of Professor Luigi Giordano from Toronto in the company of another professor-type. He bid his friend goodbye and made for Mary Rose.

"*Accidente! Cara Bella!* How can it be that we meet?"

She hid her irritation behind an expression of semi-fake surprise. "What are *you* doing here?"

"When you called me last week," the professor said, settling comfortably beside her and winking at a waitress who scurried inside to get him an espresso, "I was worried. You sounded—I don't know—maybe frightened."

"Why would you think I'd be frightened? The questions I asked you related to something that happened more than a hundred years ago."

Luigi Giordano smiled. There was an edge to that smile that Mary Rose hadn't noticed before. "Time," he said cryptically, "is four-dimensional."

"What?"

He reached across the table as though he were about to touch her hand, but his fingers stopped a fraction of an inch from hers.

"Look around you," he said, gesturing to the street where the people—every one of them an ordinary twenty-first-century American—chatted with each other, relaxed and happy. "Maybe you see today. Maybe you see people like you and me. Me, I see something else."

"What?"

"Everywhere I am, I am here and now, which is two dimensions. But I am also here and then. That is two more dimensions. This little boy with his story of long ago—why does he come to you?"

"I don't know," she answered truthfully. "That's one of the things I can't figure out."

"I will tell you," the professor said. "For him, you are here and now. Where his home is, his computer, his information that he has found out. But you are also somehow for him in the past."

"Because I'm older?"

"That surely is part of it, but there is something else. For him, you are part of the past that he so much needs to connect with. For him, you live back where all these things that happened long ago are somehow still happening."

She looked hard at Luigi. He was often incomprehensible, but this time he was reaching a new low. What was he talking about?

"Why me?" Mary Rose ventured. "Why would that child think I had any connection to the things he's told me? Except, of course that he *has* told me?"

"Perhaps he knows something about you that you do not know about yourself."

"Are you kidding? That's ridiculous! What could anybody know about me that I don't know?"

"Well, for one thing, *Cara*, you have never known how beautiful you are!"

"Get off it, Luigi, I've had enough."

"Come with me," he said. "Let's go over to Crosby and I will show you how to answer some of the questions you asked me last week."

She stalled until they'd both finished their coffees. Then she gave in.

"Of all the things in this world that are traceable," he told her, "the ownership of real estate in Manhattan is surely one of the most traceable. If you want to know every building that has ever stood on any lot on Crosby from the time the Dutch settlers came to New York, you can do that with a single hour's work. You can find every owner, every transaction in which the property changed hands."

Suddenly a thought came to her.

"What does a deed look like exactly?" she asked.

He seemed a little startled by the question. "What deed?"

"Oh, I don't know. A deed in general. Say, for example, the deed to this building here." She gestured toward the lovely 1890's building she'd noticed before.

"Well," Luigi answered, "depends on when the deed was made, and where. Every deed has certain things: a description of the property, the people who are exchanging the real estate, the consideration—usually money, but not always. Could be other real estate, other business interests, token amounts, like when someone sells something to somebody else for a dollar ..."

"Is there any such thing as a bearer deed?"

Luigi wrinkled his forehead and ran his fingers through his graying curly hair. "I don't know what you mean."

"I mean like bearer bonds. You know, they signify that whoever holds the paper can claim whatever the bond represents. Maybe there's a bearer deed. Whoever holds the deed, can claim the property."

"You've seen such a thing?" Luigi asked. His interest was as keen as usual. He practically jumped in front of her as they strolled down Crosby. "You've seen a deed such as you describe?"

"Not that I'm aware of and even if I have, how would I know what it was? I'm not a real estate lawyer. I don't know anything about deeds. Or about historic Italian land deals. That's why I'm asking you."

"Right. Right. If you see something like that deed," Luigi said, "you call me. You show me. I'll find out for you, okay?"

"Yeah, sure, thanks."

"Don't forget!"

"No, no. I won't forget."

But by the time she got back to her hotel on 51st Street, she'd forgotten about Luigi already.

As she entered her room, she saw the red light on the phone flashing. Two messages.

The first startled her. Marlee: "You better call the Chief Justice's office first thing tomorrow morning, They've been phoning for you for days. You never sent the measurements for your robe—or that invitation list. Their office was pretty abrupt. They can't understand how you could leave the country without making adequate preparations for your swearing-in."

How did the Chief Justice's office know that she'd left the country? And why was Hunt-Duval so eager to elevate her to the judgeship after she'd attempted to stall by giving Mary Rose the Joseph Di Buonna file? These things didn't add up.

And when Mary Rose factored in her escape to New York with no real reason except the effect of having seen that strange old document, her own actions didn't seem to add up, either.

Marlee was right. She had to get back home. In fact, she had to get a life.

She was about to call the airline to confirm her return ticket, when she remembered there was a second message. She pressed the pick-up key.

"To be with you was a pleasure I never expected. You were so beautiful today. So like a student who wants to learn all she can. I want to see you for breakfast tomorrow. Call me now. I have so much more to tell you—about history, about New York. Here are my numbers—my hotel, my two cell phones, my ..."

At first, Mary Rose struggled with the cheap plastic pen and the small pad of white paper that the hotel had left beside the phone.

Then she thought better of it.

Luigi had followed her to New York. Why? Even his usual ridiculous ardor couldn't account for that.

If she needed to find out more about history, about deeds, about Joseph Di Buonna, she was going to have to do it on her own.

Being on Crosby Street, even if the original building wasn't there anymore, had filled her with a new resolve. Like millions of other Italians, her own ancestors had begun their North American life on the Lower East Side. Maybe there *was* some way in which her own history reached back to touch the history of the boy who had sought her help.

She sat down and made a list of all she needed to know and to do.

At the top of that list was the document. If it had been Italian, she would have had no problem. But the document appeared to have been written in some obscure and archaic dialect. She spent several more frustrating hours in the library, poring over dictionaries, studying letters and journals, scanning catalogues of items in the library's collection pertaining to Italian immigration to America.

But she never cracked the code of the little piece of paper that she carried with her in the form of a photocopy that she carefully kept from the wandering eyes of other researchers in the library.

On the evening of the third day, she took off the white gloves researchers were obliged to wear, retrieved her personal belongings from library security and headed up Fifth Avenue toward the lobby bar in the Algonquin Hotel for a light meal.

As she sat, she reviewed her notes. They seemed completely useless. Nothing she'd found seemed capable of making that dialect give up its old secrets. Nor did those two paragraphs in two versions of the same hand tell her anything she needed to know.

But wait a minute. Suppose she took another tack? What if she considered the document itself rather than what it said as the focal point of her search for its meaning?

Thinking about the papers she'd seen over the past few days, she began to scribble new notes, listing three categories of documents.

First: deeds. She'd already considered that the "Joseph document" as she now began to think of it, might be a deed—to property on Crosby? What had Luigi said about the ease with which title could be traced in Manhattan?

Then there were labor agreements, including agreements between Italian bosses in America and the laborers they had sent for in Italy, arranging passage in payment for promises of work. She had even seen two agreements between padroni and the parents of child musicians sent to play on the streets of New York during the nineteenth century.

Then there was the third category—personal letters.

The Joseph document was not a personal letter. Some things were the same in any language. Letters had salutations, addresses, complimentary closes. They were written once and that was it. Nobody kept a letter without sending it, then added something to it years later in the same hand, did they?

She needed someone who could answer questions about papers as papers. About documents as objects rather than as messages.

CHAPTER 28

▼

When she got back to the hotel, she discovered the phone light flashing again.

"Mary Rose, I really think you'd better let the Chief Justice know when you plan on returning to Toronto. Call me now and give me a flight number."

She called Air Canada to book her return flight.

But the line was busy and she was put on hold.

The same thing happened the next time she tried. And the next. She hung up, grabbed the yellow pages, made a list, headed out into the streets. *One more day is all I need.*

She soon learned that finding experts in old papers was not easy and getting them to talk to her was impossible.

The first place she went seemed to be some sort of mistake. Though listed as a dealer, the swank building on 59th Street near Second Avenue was not a store, but an apartment building. And when she asked the concierge, he said she had the right address but that she was mistaken than any dealers operated there.

She had more luck with the next address. It was a storefront also on 59th, but farther west, close to Lexington Avenue.

She peered in the window. It was full of charming framed pictures of famous people, each photo accompanied by an autographed document. A movie contract signed by the Marx Brothers. Two tickets to baseball games, one signed by Babe Ruth and the other by Mickey Mantle. A matchbook cover signed by Frank Sinatra.

When the proprietor came out onto the sidewalk to invite her in, Mary Rose was a little surprised to feel intimidated.

"Looking for something in particular?" he asked. She had the ridiculous feeling that he was expecting her to answer in code or to offer some password.

Instead, she moved on.

The next place was a worn-out third-floor walkup in a run-down office building off 66th Street. She felt a surge of hope when the door opened to her knock.

But the grimy man who answered said he couldn't talk to anybody he didn't personally know and that he didn't know nothing about no papers or autographs.

This despite the fact that there was a letter with Thomas Jefferson's signature on it hanging in a battered wooden frame on a nail by the door.

By the time she got to the fourth address, an apartment building on Madison Avenue, she was beginning to suspect that the trade in valuable papers was for insiders only.

She dared to enter the lobby. Very near the door, behind a small marble stand, a woman in a cream silk Dior suit sat eyeing her. "Can I be of assistance, Madam?" she asked Mary Rose in chilling tones.

Mary Rose took a quick glance around. There was a Monet on the wall. And it wasn't a reproduction. There were pale yellow Turkish rugs and white orchids with deep golden centers cascading from vases of crystal and gold. None of that was fake, either.

Mary Rose laughed lightly. "Good heavens!" she said, as if accidentally wandering into luxury lobbies was a careless little peccadillo of hers. "Looks like I've got the wrong address again. So very sorry ..."

She walked out gracefully, but she didn't waste any time. The woman at the door was wearing a very fine Gucci belt accessorized with a little antique, pearl-handled 22.

All the more determined now to pick the brains of one of these expert dealers, Mary Rose quickly realized that she needed an appointment—or some other "in."

She checked the yellow pages again. Just because she had not been successful at getting into any of those dealers, didn't mean that the info in the phone book was wrong. In fact, all the addresses had been right.

Which could mean that the phone numbers were correct, too. All she had to do was to figure out the right thing to say to get them to talk to her.

She decided to go straight to the top, the Madison Avenue place with the Monet.

And she decided to get in by describing exactly what she had before she mentioned her name, her credentials, or how she had come to have what she had.

She dialled the number.

The phone rang several times with no answer. Then there was a click and the line seemed to go dead.

Just as Mary Rose was about to replace the receiver, she heard a deep, husky, masculine voice with the sort of "Mid-Atlantic" accent that rich North Americans acquire by right or by affectation.

"Marsh, here," was all the voice said.

But it sent a shiver through her.

She took a breath, rallied, gathered her thoughts and spoke.

"I have a document I think you want to see. Nineteenth-century. Rare Italian dialect. A deed. Possibly a bearer's deed."

It was a long-shot, that last phrase. Luigi had never answered her question about the existence of such a thing.

"Who is this?"

"You don't know me, Mr. Marsh. But I know you through a mutual acquaintance." *Yeah. Mr. Manhattan Yellow Pages.* "I'm a legal official in a foreign country."

"Canada."

"How did you know?"

He laughed. "You sound like a fake American."

"Nothing about me is fake," Mary Rose retorted, but she felt that shiver again.

"If you have what you say you have," the dusky voice ordered, "bring it now. The original."

He hung up.

Later, she wondered how she could have been so rash, but in that moment, she felt flushed with excitement.

She went down to the front desk of her hotel, asked for the envelope she'd left in the hotel safe, zipped it into the safety pocket of her black raincoat, grabbed a cab and headed for Madison.

It was dark, rainy. A perfect cliché of a New York night—all reflected neon, unexpected bravery, silly hope.

The sort of night that's a trap for tourists and other naïve people.

The neighborhood seemed to have changed since night had fallen.

In the afternoon, the sixties blocks on Madison had been bustling and all the store windows had been glittering with fine merchandise: jewelry, clothes, collectors' objects like books and prints.

Now the area was deserted. Whoever lived in these fine buildings obviously thought it unsafe to be outside at night.

And the store windows were completely dark.

As the cab sped off, Mary Rose felt the urge to call it back—to get away.

But it was too late.

She took a step toward the building. A man jumped in front of her, blocking her path.

She nearly screamed.

But before she could move a muscle, a second man appeared from nowhere and with a few fast, harsh words, chased the first man away.

Breathless, Mary Rose stood shaking on the sidewalk.

"Calm down," the second man told her. "I'm Mr. Marsh's bodyguard. He sent me down to wait for you."

She glanced up at the man. He was young. Beneath his suit, which struck Mary Rose as very fine for a mere guard, she could see the outline of the powerful muscles of his arms and shoulders.

"I'm not sure I ..." she stammered, still contemplating the possibility of fleeing.

Except the street was so dark and so empty.

"You're safe with me," the young man said in a voice that was emotionless, but nonetheless somehow reassuring. "In fact, you've been safe with me all day."

"What?"

"Mr. Marsh realized that a foreign woman was seeking either to buy or sell a document that he might be interested in. So he sent me to, uh, watch over you."

"But how did he know I—?"

"He doesn't like to wait, Mam. I think we better go up."

Without questioning the guard further, she followed as he entered the exquisite lobby she'd seen earlier. The woman in Dior must have finished her shift. She'd been replaced by a man a little older and even more powerful looking than the one who was escorting Mary Rose. As they passed the concierge, Mary Rose noticed two things: that a mere nod from her escort assured her entry into the building, and that both her escort and the concierge were armed. Not with cute little 22's but with semi-automatic pistols.

Not daring to turn back now, she allowed herself to be ushered into an elevator paneled in pale golden oak inset with white-framed mirrors.

She caught a glimpse of her reflection. She looked terrified.

As the elevator rose, she suddenly remembered the first man who'd accosted her outside the building. Had he bumped her?

Every warning she'd ever received about pickpockets seemed to shoot through her mind. Frantically, she searched the pocket of her coat. It was zipped.

But it was empty.

"Is this what you're looking for?"

In front of her nose, the young man flicked his powerful fingers as if he were doing some sort of magic trick.

She saw nothing in his hand. Then, in an instant, she saw the small plastic bag with its precious cargo. Of course, she lunged for the document.

He pulled it away, and she staggered.

She lunged again and grabbed the thing.

"You really gotta be more careful with your personal belongings," the young man taunted.

She had a retort for his smart remark, but it was wiped out of her mind when the door to the elevator slid open on a scene that took away all words.

Thirty stories below, but as close as if she could reach out over the East River and touch it, stood the 59th Street Bridge—the Queensborough. The delicate tracery of its wrought-iron towers was vaguely discernible against the shimmering water. The lights on the bridge, that string of diamonds linking Manhattan and Queens, sparkled in suspension over the shining white and black waters. Beyond lay a matrix of scattered jewels, Queens itself. And far beyond that, the sea.

But the view was nothing compared to the splendor of the apartment. A room that appeared to take up the whole width of the building stretched before her. Works by the great masters adorned the walls. Her eye fell first on a Rembrandt, then a bank of Turners, a Caravaggio, a Monet even more evanescent than the one downstairs.

From somewhere behind her, came the sound of a Beethoven piano sonata. She thought it must be an extremely fine recording but knew she was mistaken when the music disintegrated into a careless run of notes.

Startled, she turned.

She saw him rise from the grand piano and knew at once that this was the man she had come to see.

Slender. She judged him to be at least ten years older than herself.

He wore a hand-tailored gray silk suit. His hair looked like gray silk, too, smooth and shining softly in the room's low light.

"I don't do business with Canadians," he said, without greeting or introduction. "You are complex and troublesome people." He moved closer and she could see the sensuous curves of his face, the strong brow, the lips a little too thick, the jaw square and determined. "You are soft on the outside, but hard within." He looked at her mouth. "Like a ripe cherry. Like the olive that breaks one's tooth."

"What the hell are you talking about?"

Surprise flashed across his features. He was still for an instant. Then he smiled.

"What you have brought to show me isn't what you think it is."

"How do you know that?"

He didn't answer. "Can I offer you a drink?"

"I don't think so."

"Then at least let me offer you a place to sit."

Realizing her extreme vulnerability in the quarters of this stranger, Mary Rose glanced helplessly around. The guard had disappeared. So, it seemed, had the elevator. At least, she couldn't see where it had opened. The wall was seamless. A wave of claustrophobia swept over her and she swayed.

"Yes," she said, "I think I would like to sit down."

The man reached out a hand and she took it, surprised at the warmth of his fingers.

"You've come to me about a document," he began, his voice low, almost soothing. "You haven't had it for long. You're not sure who it belongs to. You have no idea what it's worth. But you are going to tell me how you acquired it and why you've come all this way to find out what it means."

"If you know so much," she said, "why should I bother talking at all?"

He dipped his head slightly—a nod of assent? A gesture of contempt? "As I said. Difficult people with whom to do business. Show me what you have."

There was no real reason to trust him, and yet, Mary Rose reached into her pocket, which this time was *not* empty and retrieved the document. She carefully slipped it from the plastic bag.

"A boy lent it to me," she said. "He pursued me."

"What?"

"I should explain," she said nervously. "For a number of years, I've been an advocate for the legal rights of children. During the course of this work, I've often been asked by young people to assist them in matters that fall outside the scope of my regular duties. I've been approached by a young man who claims to have been given this paper by a distant relative here in New York. At first the boy only showed me a computerized image of the paper, but then, when he learned I was willing to go to New York, he produced the document itself. I knew I was taking a risk in accepting it, but ..."

"But you found it irresistible?"

It wasn't a word Mary Rose would have chosen to describe the attraction of a piece of paper, but now that he had said it, she realized it was right.

"Yes."

"May I?"

She handed him the paper.

He seemed to take a very long time examining it, though he did not touch it except to let it lie in his palm exactly where Mary Rose had placed it.

As he studied the document, she studied him. His body was lean, his posture perfect, but there was a disarming innocence about the way he gazed at the object in his hand. She had expected scepticism. Instead, she saw reverence.

There was such a long silence, that she had to force herself to keep quiet. She'd spent a lot of years facing judges and soon she'd be one. It was best to let the experts think in silence.

"Tell me all you already know about this," he finally said.

"I know the boy claims it has been in his family for generations. I know from my research in the library that there are probably thousands of extant documents relating to the immigration history of Italian Americans, documents that have been catalogued and are in archival collections—and a whole lot more in people's basements. In fact, I seem to remember a box that sat in our own basement for most of my childhood."

The man did not smile at this charming recollection. "And?" he said impatiently.

"And," she went on, "I know it's written in a dialect of Italian, though I have no idea which dialect. I'm also aware that it's not difficult to trace land registration in New York and that there is a possibility that this might be a deed of some sort ..."

"What land?"

She told him about Crosby Street, about some of things Luigi Giordano had told her concerning deeds and titles, though she was careful not to mention the professor's name.

She also told him about her adventures among the other dealers in documents, but she could tell he wasn't interested in that. She remembered the guard's puzzling claim to have been with her all day.

"I came to you because I understand you're the top man."

Apparently he wasn't interested in hearing that, either. He ignored the comment. "If this is a deed," he said, "and if it is for property such as what you describe on Crosby Street, it would be title to real estate that was worth more than ten thousand dollars at the turn of the twentieth century."

"Ten thousand—more than a hundred years ago? Today it would be worth what—twenty million?"

"A large lot in Lower Manhattan could easily sell for twenty million. And if it did, and if you had, say, a ten per cent interest in this deal ..."

He looked at her. She looked away. The money hadn't even occurred to her, but nobody would believe that, especially nobody as sophisticated as this.

"If you had a ten per cent interest," he repeated, "you'd be looking at two million dollars. Not bad payment for a quick trip to the city."

"True."

"But maybe you're not in it for money. Maybe you're an unusual lawyer as well as a beautiful one."

She shot a glance at him. *Yeah, I'm a regular ripe cherry.* "Could we get to the point, Mr. Marsh?"

"Rudi."

"Rudi."

"The point is," he said, "I don't help people unless I know what's in it for me."

Mary Rose was taken aback at his frankness, but of course, a man with a wall full of Turners and, she now realized, a Turkish carpet as big as a New York block, didn't do anything for free.

"Mr. Marsh—Rudi—anybody smart enough to let a perfect stranger from a foreign—oh yeah, and *difficult*—country into his personal art gallery because he can smell a twenty-million dollar real estate deal is smart enough to figure out what he can get out of it without being told."

He laughed with delight, handing her back the precious paper with a connoisseur's care.

"A difficult and stubborn race," he said. "But never mind. Can you come back tomorrow, Canada?'

She said sure.

Then she remembered that she was supposed to be on her way back home.

Again he offered her a drink. Again she refused.

Since she had imbibed nothing the whole time she'd been in his apartment, there was no explanation for her light-headedness when the elevator magically reappeared and smoothly carried her, unescorted, to the first floor.

She was surprised to see that the elegant lobby was empty.

Stepping out onto Madison, she took a deep breath of the cold air, hoping to clear her head.

She thought about his demand to know what was in it for him if he got further involved in what she was beginning to think about as "her case".

The idea of monetary gain, so thoroughly absent before she'd met him, now loomed disturbingly large. Instinctively, she reached into her pocket to make sure she still had the precious document.

She felt it, but, still unsatisfied, she reached in and pulled the package out.

In that moment, a large, rough-looking male hand appeared out of nowhere and grabbed her wrist, trying to jerk the small plastic bag free of her grasp.

She pushed hard and the hand fell away.

It was only then that she remembered the man who had accosted her before she'd been rescued by Rudi Marsh's bodyguard.

"Get away from me!" she hissed.

The man fell back, and Mary Rose gave him another strong shove. Helplessly she glanced up Madison. She saw two or three cabs, but all of them were too far away. If she ran, the man would chase her.

She turned back toward the door she'd just exited, but a single glance told her it was bolted.

Terrified, she realized her only hope was to stare the man down, to somehow talk him into leaving her alone, to distract him until someone else showed up.

"I don't carry cash," she said, rather absurdly.

"Look," the man said, "I'm not after money and you know it."

His voice was shaky and he made no further attempt to come closer. Mary Rose took a second to study him. He was well-dressed. Not Rudi Marsh well-dressed, but not shabby, either. He looked sort of old-fashioned Ivy League.

"Get lost before I scream," she said. But she knew she didn't sound very convincing. Because her curiosity was overtaking her fear.

"I didn't mean to scare you. I'm sorry," the man said. "I shouldn't have rushed you or grabbed. I'm, I'm not normally so rude. I've tried to contact you a number of times, but ..."

"Contact me? What are you talking about? Who are you?"

"I'm a person who wants to reclaim what rightly belongs to my own people. If I could have spoken to you before you spoke to this, this ..." He shook his fist at the building behind them—"this exploiter—I could have made you understand that it's not right to sell what you have."

Years spent in criminal and civil courts had taught Mary Rose the difference between a dangerous man and one who was merely desperate. She looked around. Across Madison, an event of some sort had apparently emptied out. Suddenly there were people on the street. And the cabs she'd seen a few moments before had been joined by others. The momentary lull in the business of the street had given way to frenzied activity.

It would take about half an hour to walk to her hotel and she could do it mostly along Lexington, which would be even more crowded than this street. The night was cold, but she felt in need of fresh air. She glanced again at the man standing beside her. He looked familiar. She started to walk. And when he began to walk beside her, she let him.

Because she realized he was the man she'd seen with Professor Giordano on Mulberry Street.

"Like the young man you represent," the stranger began, in a voice as educated and cultured as Mary Rose's own, "I am a direct descendant of Giuseppe Di Buonna, the Maestro of Orphans."

"The what?"

"The Maestro, a man who brought a hundred child musicians to Toronto so many generations ago—the man who made them legit. I'm a descendant of one of his children, and that makes my claim to the family inheritance as strong as the claims of anybody in Canada."

Mary Rose thought about that for a minute.

"First," she finally said, "I don't *represent* anybody. Whatever Luigi Giordano told you, you're mistaken if you think I'm involved in some sort of civil suit over an inheritance."

"But—"

"Second," she persisted, "I know nothing about any such inheritance."

"But—"

"Finally, my understanding is that seven or eight generations have passed since the Maestro, as you call him, left America. He would have hundreds of descendants by now …"

"What I'm trying to tell you is that you're holding something that has belonged to the wrong people for over a century."

Mary Rose stopped. "Who *are* you?" she demanded.

"My name is Bob Fortuna, Dr. Robert L. Fortuna, and I—"

"How can you claim to be a descendant of the male line of the Di Buonna's if your name isn't even Di Buonna?"

"Not the males, the females. Look," the man said, standing in front of her, desperate to explain his position. "It's all too complicated. I can email you something. I can …"

"I think you better leave me alone."

"No, wait. I'm not a dealer. I'm a history professor. Despite the monetary interest that a greedy capitalist like Rudi Marsh might have in that document you carry, I'm convinced it has no monetary value."

She laughed. "Oh, yeah? Then why are you so interested in the piece of paper? And why now? It was written more than a century ago. And it's been lost for nearly the same amount of time."

They'd reached Lexington and turned the corner near a coffee shop that Mary Rose frequented. The light here was good and she could clearly see how expensively the man was dressed. Also, he was very attractive—a little younger than her, stocky but not fat, dark-haired and intense.

"You want to go inside for a coffee?" she asked impulsively.

The man smiled. "Sure."

When they'd sat down with frothy large cappuccinos, Robert Fortuna continued to set his case out for Mary Rose. "Every family," he said, "especially every Italian family, has some story that passes down from generation to generation."

"Yes," she agreed. "Seems to me those tales are always about murder or money—or both."

He nodded. "From time to time," he said, "someone in the family seeks professional help to determine whether the story is true. Invariably they discover that it is, at best, true in a way, or true in part. But there is never the genuine possibility of regaining some great fortune or of righting some great wrong."

"No," Mary Rose agreed, "not really."

"So the story is buried again," he went on, "but as the years go by, it slowly makes its way back to the surface."

He knew what he was talking about, and so did she. There were stories in her own family that she'd been told as a child. She'd dismissed them long ago and doubted she could even remember the gist of them now. But for the second time, she remembered the box in her parents' basement and made a mental note to call her brother and ask him about it.

"This is all very well," she said to the man sitting across from her, "but it doesn't explain your interest in the matter."

"Well," he answered, "it's not money and it's not murder." He laughed but pleasant as it was, the sound of his laughter unnerved Mary Rose. She moved her chair a little away from the table. If he noticed, he didn't show it.

"Not directly about money or murder anyway," he said. "The fact is, the piece of paper that everyone seems so interested in impacts on my career. I'm sure there are few people who care about this aspect of the case, but I do care. You see, that piece of paper is not about moral or legal vindication. Nor is it about the transfer of a parcel of land worth millions of dollars. Land down on the Lower East Side is indeed worth millions, but the document is about something else."

"What?" she asked, excited. "What's it about?"

He glanced up at her. There was suspicion in his eyes. Up until now, she'd been the suspicious one.

"How much do you know about the Di Buonna family, anyway?" he asked.

"More than I'm willing to tell a perfect stranger who practically assaulted me," she said, remembering that he'd as much as attacked her not once but twice outside Rudi Marsh's building. What had she been thinking about letting a man she didn't know walk with her on the street? She was out of her mind.

"I've had enough of this conversation," she said, standing abruptly. "If you want more information about the Di Buonna's, ask your friend Professor Giordano. I'm sure he'll be happy to fill you in. As for me, I've said all I'm going to say. And," she added, "I think it would be a good idea if you stayed away from me."

"Wait, don't go yet!"

One final time, the man's fingers shot out to grab her wrist.

Before she could pull away, he pressed a card into her hand. She didn't waste time looking at it. She shoved it into her coat pocket and fled.

She pretty much ran all the way to her hotel, bumping into people on the crowded sidewalks, embarrassed but reluctant to slow down except to occasionally glance behind her, sure he would follow.

Apparently, he didn't.

With relief, she rounded the corner of 3rd Avenue and 51st Street, only half a block from her destination. Her heart was pounding painfully and she could hardly breathe.

But the scent of roses, musky and sweet against the cold damp of the November night hit her nostrils as she passed the banked blooms of a sidewalk flower stall. She slowed and caught her breath.

Ahead she could see the canopy that covered the entrance to her hotel.

And beneath the canopy, lurking near the door, lounged the silhouette of a familiar and unwelcome visitor.

Luigi Giordano!

For a moment, she considered turning away, but it was already too late. He saw her and came running with the clumsy gait of a spaniel or an awkward child.

"Thank God I've found you!" he cried, as if she'd been lost. "There's trouble!"

The sight of the professor on the verge of hysterics was somehow relaxing to Mary Rose. His habitual frantic overreaction to minor matters was part of the reason she had never taken his protestations of love for her seriously.

"What trouble?"

The professor fell in beside her as she continued her short walk to the hotel, but he hopped and swayed and swung around her as though in his extreme agitation, he was having a hard time keeping his body down on the sidewalk.

"You have to return to Toronto this minute," he insisted. "Not tomorrow. Tonight. You have to be there in the morning before court opens."

"Court?" She stopped dead. "What are you talking about?"

Luigi Giordano jerked his wristwatch toward his nose and studied it. "Our plane leaves in less than an hour. La Guardia. You have to take your things and leave right now."

"Calm down," she warned him. "You're working yourself into a spasm. What could possibly be so important that ...?"

"I'll brief you in the cab," he interrupted, as if he were some sort of top government official instead of an Italian teacher. "Please hurry because you are already late."

"Stop, Luigi," she demanded. "You stop this nonsense at once. I am *not* flying off to Canada tonight. There is nothing so urgent that I have to pick up and go without ..."

"Mary Rose, listen to me and do what I say. You have more urgent matters to take care of than you dream of. This is not a game."

She stared at him. Her whole life she'd considered him nothing but a quaint little object of humor. But there was something different about him now. For the first time it occurred to her to remember that he was the head of a major department at a university with international significance. Until that moment, she'd never seen his power.

Now she did.

"All right, I'll pack. I'll check out of the hotel and meet you in the lobby."

"You are already packed and checked out. Freshen up. We leave in five minutes. Don't dally. Being home before court opens tomorrow is your only hope."

CHAPTER 29

▼

Rarely can a cab speed in mid-town Manhattan, but every couple of blocks, their driver managed a wild burst of power that enabled Mary Rose and the professor to jut ahead of a couple of other vehicles.

"There is a warrant out for your arrest in Toronto," he told her.

"What?"

"You are wanted."

"Luigi, if this is some sick joke, I'm going to kill you."

"Mary Rose, I think from now on, you're going to have to watch every word you say. Including to me. It's not a good idea to utter threats—even as a joke."

Though it was night, the streets were so alive with light that Mary Rose could clearly read the expression on his face. It was deep concern.

"Okay," she said weakly, "okay. But please, tell me what this is all about."

He drew in a breath. "Unless we are extremely lucky, when you arrive in Toronto, you are going to be arrested for child molestation."

"Child molestation! Luigi, in all these years I've never even touched a child!"

"Did you go to the home of Joseph Di Buonna and stand outside his house observing it without permission?"

She was enough of a lawyer not to answer that question except in her own mind. Of course she had.

"And did he arrive at your home without adult accompaniment? Apparently, the grandparents of this child have learned he has been in your home. Apparently, they've reported it to the police." He shook his head. "It's said you stalked the boy, lured him and eventually confined him."

- 154 -

Stunned, Mary Rose sat silently for a long minute as the cab made its way over the 59th Street Bridge. Vaguely aware of her surroundings, she remembered the brief moments in the apartment of the autograph dealer. While she'd been wasting her time trying to verify Joseph Di Buonna's foolish notions, the boy had been busy at home destroying her career!

Distraught as she was, by the time the taxi screeched to a halt at the Air Canada departure deck, she'd already begun her mental list.

The most immediate thing she had to fear was to be arrested right there in the United States. Nothing could be worse. Not only would she have to arrange a defense long-distance, she'd also end up spending time in a New York City jail and probably have to face a complex extradition hearing.

But even more importantly, having an arrest warrant on her record could cost her the judgeship.

And her legal practice.

Her head reeled, but she managed to get out of the car, to retrieve her suitcase and briefcase and to follow the professor into the terminal.

"*Pray* that you get through security here in New York without trouble," Luigi uttered in a stage whisper just audible over the ambient noise of the busy terminal. "Be smart. Silently hand them your passport. Don't utter a single word unless they ask you a question."

She really didn't need his melodramatic advice. Who did he think he was, anyway? And, she suddenly wondered, why had this bad news come through him and not to her directly?

Occupied by this thought, she absently put her bags on the x-ray belt. When the security officer *did* ask a question, she missed it.

Fear gripped her. She hesitated even to ask the officer what he had just said.

"Well, Madam?" he insisted.

She looked up at him. He looked bored. "Pardon?"

"I asked you whether you are travelling alone?"

"No, I'm …" She looked around.

Luigi was gone.

Her hands trembled as she fastened her seatbelt. First class. She hadn't had time to ask the professor how he'd managed to obtain her plane ticket—and how much she owed him for it.

She sank back into her seat with a deep sigh of relief. Getting on the plane had been easy.

Getting off might be a different story.

Would the police be waiting for her in Toronto?

Over the intercom came the unwelcome news that they would be in the air for forty-three minutes.

Not much time in which to plan actions that would affect Mary Rose for the rest of her life!

Whatever happened at Customs in Toronto, the first thing she'd have to do would be to phone a top-notch criminal defense lawyer. Then she would have to turn herself in and get out on bail. *No, not bail.* With the right lawyer, she might be able to get a release on her own recognizance, on her own promise to appear. Luigi didn't know as much as he thought he did. She wouldn't have to go to jail or to court, either. At least not right away.

She flicked through the addresses in her electronic data organizer. As soon as the plane landed, even if she were arrested, she could call Marlee and give her secretary instructions as to which lawyer to contact.

Once that decision had been made, she felt better. About a quarter hour remained before landing. Fifteen minutes in which to think about what to say to the lawyer. Of course, she would say nothing to the police in the event of her arrest. That was her right and she would exercise it totally.

She needed to find out what Joseph had said about her. She shuddered to think that whatever the charges against her, the whole case would be nothing but his word against hers. There had once been a time when no child would have been believed over the word of an adult, but that time was long past. For better or for worse.

She tried to go over in her mind everything they had talked about the time they'd met in the hotel tea room and the time he had come to her apartment.

All she could remember them discussing was the document.

The document!

She had completely forgotten about it.

She grabbed her purse and began rifling through the contents. She hadn't thought about the handbag and what was in it since she'd jumped into the cab with the professor. She'd been so upset that she hadn't even been watching the security personnel inspecting her belongings before she'd boarded the plane.

Normally her purse was tidy, but now it was a mess. She found her wallet, intact and full of small American bills. She found the little leather folder in which she kept her credit cards.

Her compact was open; the pressed powder had cracked and spilled. Instinctively, she blew, and a fine cloud settled over the front of her clothes.

She ignored it, digging deeper into the bag.

The seatbelt sign clicked on.

She ignored that, too.

Then came the warning that the plane was about to land.

Mary Rose dumped the entire chaotic, powder-covered contents of her purse onto her lap.

There, on top of the sloppy heap was the little plastic bag with its contents visible inside.

"Madam," she heard over her shoulder, jumping at the sound of the steward's voice, "we're about to land. Please put your personal belongings away."

Mary Rose struggled to jam everything back into her handbag. She managed to zip the plastic bag containing the document into an inner pocket of her purse.

Then she tried in vain to wipe away the pale powdery mess that stained the front of her dark coat.

Moments later, as if embarrassed for her, a Canadian Customs official waved her through after a cursory glance at her passport.

Was she home safe?

Or was her ordeal only about to begin?

CHAPTER 30

▼

"You should have returned my calls last week instead of running around New York and ignoring your obligations up here. You're lucky you're not in jail or worse. I got your message at midnight, and I called the lawyers first thing this morning. Serves you right if you had a sleepless night. I've got you an appointment in two hours—at 11:15. You've got piles of paperwork here, but I think you better stay put for a bit, then take a cab down to Welton, Welton, Rich and Clarton. Welton, Senior will see you. Bring an overnight bag just in case."

"Thanks, Marlee, I don't know what I'd do without you!"

Mary Rose's secretary ignored that remark. She sounded furious. As if Mary Rose's failure to keep in touch with her were the criminal offense that she was charged with.

"Did you get the package?"

Mary Rose glanced around. She'd picked up the week's worth of mail that had lain on the floor near the door. "What package?"

"Something came from your brother in Montreal. It looked personal. Foolishly thinking your return was imminent, I sent it by courier to your apartment," Marlee said frostily. Then she relented, and her voice warmed a little. "Maybe they took it for you downstairs in the store."

Exhausted from her travels and anxious to see the lawyer, Mary Rose tried to get a few minutes' rest before calling the cab, but she found she couldn't sit still. She grabbed her keys and headed down to the street level to see if the convenience store owner on the first floor had indeed intercepted her package. She had called her brother about it only two days before and was amazed that it might have reached her so soon.

"Right here," the store owner told her. He didn't speak much English, but he was helpful and kind. Mary Rose always "remembered" him at Christmas. As she took the parcel from his outstretched hand, she was grateful for his trustworthiness.

She carried the box upstairs. It was almost two feet square, but it wasn't very heavy.

She set it down on the rug in the living room and, with a knife from the kitchen, slit open the top of the box.

She found a package within the package and on top of that, a handwritten note from her brother.

Dear M.R.

This has been in our basement here in Montreal for as long as I can remember. It's stuff Dad's mother used to cart around. Didn't have time to open it since I moved here. I think it's old letters. Enjoy!

G.

Putting aside the note, she lifted the inner package. It was wrapped in dusty brown paper with writing on it that Mary Rose recognized as her grandmother's. The old lady had been dead for twenty years or so, and all that remained of her meagre personal belongings were a few items of gold jewellery that Mary Rose had been left in her own parents' will.

The handwriting on the box was perfectly legible, but all it said was, "Papers, etc. Don't Throw This Out."

Mary Rose carefully undid the old tape, which came unstuck without much effort. Unwrapping the box and opening it, she found a modern-looking white envelope. She tipped it, and out slipped black and white and faded color photographs of people in clothes from the nineteen-sixties and seventies. She recognized a few of the faces—her grandmother and her grandmother's friends.

Beneath that, Mary Rose found another, older envelope. She lifted its fragile flap. Inside were dozens of letters with Italian postmarks and colorful but faded stamps. She unfolded one of the letters. It was written in old-fashioned script. Incomprehensible because of the handwriting, but also because it was in Italian dialect.

She glanced at the clock. It was still too early to call the cab that would take her to the lawyer.

But she had no desire to try and decipher these old letters now. She began to slip them back into the envelope. Doing so, she noticed that among the letters were some old receipts from businesses that must have been in the neighborhood of her relatives and their relatives. Her eye fell on a printed heading. There, as clear as when it had been printed almost a hundred years before, was a picture of a stately building, and under that building was its name: The Di Buonna Hotel.

Astonished, Mary Rose held the paper closer. She saw that a few words had been scrawled across the bottom in ink, ink much more faded than that of the heading, but still readable—and in English. It said, "Thank you for your patronage. We will be closing later this month." Beneath was a date penned in the ornate numerals of another century. It looked like "7/15". Did that mean July 15th?

Her hand shook. Of course it was not at all unusual for her own immigrant forbears to settle where other Italians had settled. It was just that she'd never before connected herself, her own personal past, to the story that both Joseph Di Buonna and Luigi Giordano seemed to think was true.

But that wasn't all.

There was a third layer, separated from the others by crushed newspaper. Mary Rose lifted the first piece of newspaper. Her eye fell on the date. 1979.

Her grandmother must have been cleaning house, packing up, storing things she didn't want lost, just a little while before she had died. What else had she saved besides these old pictures and older letters?

Mary Rose lifted another piece of newsprint.

And beneath it, she found a package about a foot square wrapped in white tissue that was still crisp.

She took the package from the box. It was neither heavy nor light. About the weight of an old photograph in a wooden frame with glass in it.

She sat on a chair and put the package in her lap.

Slowly she began to remove the tissue, fully expecting to find a portrait of her grandparents.

Instead, as she pushed away the last piece of paper, she saw a small white harp.

The wood was battered. The paint was chipped. The strings were rough, and two of them were broken, curling around Mary Rose's fingers as she touched them.

Clearly it had been made by someone who loved music, wood, religion and the feel of the knife in his hand. For the little instrument was beautifully carved. Wreathes of flowers decked the post, the body of an angel formed the other two sides. Its outspread wing was the top, its head and flowing robe the third, slanted side.

Marvelling at the intricacy of the carved folds of cloth, Mary Rose turned the harp over so that she was looking at its bottom.

And there she saw a tiny slot closed by what appeared to be a sliding door.

Almost afraid to touch it, she nevertheless slid it open.

Despite the decades—perhaps the centuries—that had passed since it had been made, the little door moved smoothly to reveal a small chamber in the base of the harp.

She peeked inside.

The chamber was empty, but it was big enough to hold the document in her purse.

The document she had planned, until this moment, to hand over to her lawyer.

The lawyer!

She looked at the clock.

It was time to get the cab.

Quickly, she re-wrapped the harp, put everything back into the box, resealed it. There was no time to figure out what its presence meant, what she should do with it.

She hurried downstairs and hailed a taxi on the street.

CHAPTER 31

▼

It should have been the most humiliating day of her life.

Humiliating to become a client of a law firm so prestigious that she, herself, had never had a hope of working there.

Humiliating to be accompanied to a police station by Welton, Senior, a fatherly man with a wild mane of white hair, a bushy mustache, and a reputation for winning cases for people widely considered to be lost causes.

Humiliating to be released on a promise that she would attend court in the near future to answer to the charges of child molestation that had been laid against her.

Humiliating to sit with Welton afterward and have to listen to him expound on things she well knew without his hammering them home.

"Either this young man has lied to his family, Ms Cabrini, or else his grandparents have put him up to laying these charges in order to use him as a pawn in the family custody battle—or both. It will be my job to find out whether this boy is your enemy or is himself a victim. I need not warn you that the worst thing you can possibly do now is to attempt any further contact with this child. I trust that's clear?"

Of course it was clear.

But Mary Rose intended to ignore this advice.

Because she was *not* humiliated at what was happening to her.

The sight of the little harp had changed everything.

This was no longer Joseph's battle. It was her own.

Mary Rose now saw that this whole bizarre adventure was not a case, not business. It was personal. It was about her.

There could be only two explanations for the presence of a little white harp with a secret compartment being among the belongings of her own family.

The first explanation was that hiding valuables, including deeds, in their instruments, might have been a regular practice among Italian street musicians and that her family, like other Italian immigrant families, had had a child musician among its antecedents. Like almost every grandmother she'd ever met, hers had saved the things she found most valuable in the hopes of passing them on to someone who cared as much as she had. Well, Grandma's box had finally found the right recipient.

The second explanation was simpler, but it had shattering implications.

It was that this was the very harp that had belonged to the Di Buonna who had fled from America more than a century before. And that the vague recollections Mary Rose had about her family might harbor a truth she had yet to discover.

Either way, even the shame of what she was going through that day seemed a small price to pay to get to the bottom of this mystery.

She saw now that there was only one way to set things right, and that was to prove beyond any doubt that the document she still held was the real thing.

Though exactly *what* real thing, she still didn't know.

She had to get back to New York. She had to do better than she'd done the first time.

And she had to get back into that Madison Avenue penthouse and talk again to the powerful man who knew the value of rare papers.

But she couldn't help thinking about Joseph. Maybe he was trying to ensnare her. Maybe not. Either way, she decided she couldn't abandon him entirely. Anonymously she phoned the hot line of the orphan advocacy office and convinced them to send someone to the house to check on him.

She stopped by her own office, cleaned up what she could. She sent her measurements and her invitation list to the Chief Justice's office. Maybe that was an exercise in futility. She didn't hang around to find out. She headed back to New York.

Wanting to get away at once, and wanting to avoid the record-keeping that would result if she flew, she took the subway to the bus station. It would take her twelve hours to get to Port Authority Bus Terminal in the heart of Manhattan, but the security would be far less rigorous. The Americans might already have a record of her outstanding criminal charges. She'd have to take her chances.

At the last moment, she saw it was raining, so she grabbed her raincoat.

She felt something in the pocket.

She reached in and pulled out a creased business card. She was shocked to see that it bore the insignia of a major New York university!

Then she remembered Dr. Fortuna, the man who had stalked her in New York, the man she'd left in the coffee shop on Lexington Avenue. She remembered, too, that he'd said he needed the document because it impacted on his career.

Mary Rose called him right from the bus.

"I'm sorry I ran off last week," she began, "I should have looked at the card you gave me."

"Yes," he said, his voice curt, "you should have."

"If it's not too late," she went on, trying to sound as conciliatory as she could, "I'd like to get together with you again. I'd like to hear what you have to say about the Di Buonna family."

"About *my* family," he said, still sounding distant and edgy.

"*Your* family."

"All right," he said after a pause. But he sounded uncertain. As if all the eagerness he'd shown before had disappeared.

Nonetheless, he offered Mary Rose an appointment to see him the next afternoon. She jumped at it.

Partly because that gave her the morning free, and she intended to use it to get back into the penthouse on Madison Avenue.

CHAPTER 32

▼

He sent a car for her. The minute he heard her voice on the phone he said he would send it, and he did.

She had never had a car sent for her before. And when the unpretentious dark gray Bentley arrived, and the driver got out and stood on 51st as if he had all time in world, and she slid into the back seat, and the driver took off without needing a word of instruction, she felt like somebody who had suffered a great loss. For it suddenly hit her hard that her chances to be a big-wig were gone. Had she become a judge, she would have had plenty of chances to ride in a private limo. And were she to end up a criminal, she'd have plenty of chances to be driven around, too. Police cruisers. Paddy wagons.

How could she have been so foolish? How could she have been so tricked by a child after having been so careful for so long?

She wished she could turn back. Not just back to her hotel or back to Canada. She wished she could turn back to that day she'd stood beside Mayor Franklin in Nathan Phillips Square, the day she'd been a dignitary at the cornerstone-laying for the new courthouse.

For everything seemed to have been different with her from that day on.

She remembered the false smiles of the officials on the platform with her, the leering gaze of Bianco, the property developer.

She remembered the gist of the speech she had given about children in need.

And she remembered the little boy who had stared at her so intently that she'd lost track of herself.

She now realized why Joseph Di Buonna had been there. He had already targeted her.

And so, she thought, had other people.

Why else had she been sent Joseph's file? Why else had this strange odyssey unfolded?

The new courthouse, the courthouse she now had lost hope of working in, was already rising on the site of the building that had long ago replaced the old Land Titles Office. What had happened to all the records that the Land Titles Office had held? Had there been a record of the closure of the Di Buonna hotel?

"Madam, we've arrived," the chauffeur's voice interrupted her thoughts.

He opened the door for her and stood guard while she stepped out onto the sidewalk. But she wasn't alone for a second. Another uniformed man escorted her to the elevator and once again, disappeared as soon as she'd entered Rudi Marsh's magnificent apartment.

"How was your return to Toronto?" he greeted her, slipping her coat off her shoulders, which surprised her. Didn't he have a maid for that?

"How do you know I returned to Toronto?"

"Because I called for you at your hotel and found you missing."

He was wearing a dark suit today, charcoal wool with darker stripes that looked like silk. A bit of gold glinted here and there. His finger, his cuffs, his wrist. His neck? No. Mary Rose didn't see him as the sort of man to wear gold chains around his neck.

"Thanks for agreeing to ..."

Before she could finish her sentence, he reached out and took her elbow. It was a simple gesture, but it unnerved Mary Rose. She stumbled.

"You're tired from your trip," he said softly. "Come and sit down. I'll have some tea brought up. You Canadians love tea. Or would you prefer sherry?"

"It's ten o'clock in the morning," she said lightly. Then her eye fell on a golden mantel clock surrounded by porcelain figurines with slender arms that seemed to embrace the face of the clock, which was mother-of-pearl inlaid with more gold. Of course he knew what time it was!

"Sit down and relax," he invited again, "before you tell me what I can do for you. "Or would you like me to show you around a bit?"

"Okay," she said, trying not to sound as curious about him as she truly was, "show me around."

As he nodded in acknowledgement of her interest, she caught his scent. *Blenheim Bouquet*—one of the costliest. Rumor had it that it was the choice of the Prince of Wales.

He led her first to a bookcase with bevelled glass doors ten feet tall and shelves made of polished mahogany. "These are not my rarest," he said as he reached in and chose a small volume bound in aged green leather. "I have what some consider the most significant private collection of incunabula in the world, but I don't keep them here." He caught her gaze. "You *do* know what incunabula are?"

"Books printed between the invention of the moveable type press and the year 1500," she said.

"Yes!"

He selected a volume. "The books in this cabinet are my personal favorites from sixteenth and seventeenth-century England. Here, look at this one."

Casually, he handed her the book. She was almost afraid to touch it, but he took her hands and firmly placed the book into them.

"Books are tougher than they look," he said, "like some people."

She smiled and turned the book over. She saw that there was a faded green ribbon marking a page.

She opened the book at that page.

"It's a Bible," she said.

"A very famous one," he answered. "What do you see on that page?"

"The ten commandments, but ..."

He laughed at her surprise. "But what?"

"But one of them says, 'Thou *shall* commit adultery! Clearly something is missing!"

"Yes. This is an original copy of what has come to be known as 'The Adultery Bible'. It was printed in 1631 and very few copies have survived. There is one, by the way, in Toronto."

"Is this some sort of typographical error?"

"Some think so. It's a well-known fact among editors that typographical errors are very common in any text that has to do with the topic of sex. For centuries, bibliophiles have debated as to whether The Adultery Bible was the result of error or of sabotage."

"Which do you think?"

He moved away from her a little, and she realized just how close he had been standing. She moved, too.

"I don't need to think about what I can know for sure, Ms Cabrini. Let me show you something else."

Near the bookcase was a small table on top of which sat an ornate lamp. Her host flicked it on, and, from a drawer in the table, extracted a small green leather box. Unlike the binding of the book and the faded ribbon, this green was bright and new.

When he removed the lid, Mary Rose saw that the box was lined with pearl-gray satin.

And lying on top of the satin were three tiny objects.

Pieces of lead type. An *n*. An *o*. A *t*.

"Sabotage, right?" she breathed.

Softly he answered. "For sure." Looking up at her, he added, "I'm a man who deals in things other men cannot have and facts other men cannot know. My work covers the centuries and it covers the globe. The world is full of secrets. But it is not full of people strong enough to figure those secrets out. Generally, however, secret-hunters know each other."

His eyes in the glow of the lamp, in the shadows that daylight did not dispel, his eyes were the same color as the pearl silk.

"Show me more."

He showed her an original score of *The Stars and Stripes Forever* in the hand of John Philip Sousa.

He showed her a letter that Heloise had written to Abelard.

He showed her things that no-one knew existed. "Do you know the story of Beethoven's *Immortal Beloved*?" he asked.

Mary Rose thought about it for a second. "She was a woman that Beethoven loved but nobody knows who she was."

"Yes. Among Beethoven's possessions was found a letter that he wrote to her declaring his love, but not mentioning her name."

"And you have that letter?" Mary Rose asked in astonishment.

"No. I have something better."

From within a small safe, he took a metal box. Inside the box were white cotton gloves that he slid over his long, slender fingers. He used his gloved hand to open a second metal box, and from that box he pulled an envelope far older than the ones Mary Rose now had in her apartment.

She leaned closer, eager to see what this envelope might hold.

"When you learned about Beethoven's letter, did it ever occur to you to find it strange that the letter was in *his* possession?"

"I just assumed he had never sent it."

"Do you do much assuming in your job?" he asked with a smile. "As a lawyer, I mean?"

"Never!" Mary Rose insisted.

"Nor do I," he said. "There are many reasons why a letter might remain in the possession of the man who wrote it. It might, for instance, have been returned by the person to whom it was written …"

As he spoke, he opened the old envelope and carefully slipped out a piece of paper nearly as old-looking, but covered with writing that was still clear.

Mary Rose leaned closer. "It's in German!" she said with disappointment.

"Of course it is," the man said. "Do you want to know what it says?"

"Yes."

He read the few words. "Herr Beethoven, do not write again. My husband knows. I return this lest he find it."

"Who wrote it? Is the woman the Immortal Beloved?"

"Of course she is," he answered. With his gloved fingers he traced the woman's name, slowly pronouncing it in unhalting German.

"Who is she?"

"I can tell you her history. And I can also tell you that she is not among any of the women that scholars have speculated about all these years."

"Does this mean that you are the only person who knows who the Immortal Beloved is?"

He laughed again. "Not quite. Now you know, too."

"How much is this letter worth?"

With almost a lover's reverence, he folded the letter and put it away. He took so long to answer that Mary Rose thought he wasn't going to bother. Had she been rude?

"One of the things I love about the business of collecting rarities is that the assumed value of an object—I mean what the uninitiated think it is worth—very seldom matches its value on the market and almost never matches its intrinsic value."

"What do you mean?"

"Some things seem to be worth a great deal of money, but are actually quite easy to come by. Autographs of famous people, for example. Other things are worth a great deal of money because they were created in a moment of central significance in the life of a person. That day you went to the shop on 59th street, you probably saw such items. I myself have held the contract signed by Marilyn Monroe to indicate that she was converting to Judaism. And the first movie contract she signed."

"Wow!"

"But there is another category altogether. The category of items that have not to do merely with a famous person or a significant event. There is a class of objects that are intimately connected with the fate of a nation and its people. With the birth of a science. With the death of an old way of life."

"Show me!" she said. "Show me more!"

He reached out and touched her face. The intimacy of the gesture shocked her.

But even so, it felt right for him to touch her that way.

She raised her hand and touched her cheek where he had touched it, though she couldn't say why.

"Your enthusiasm is beautiful," he said, "but even I'm limited by what I can keep in premises as unsecure as these." He gestured toward the apartment with its amazing treasures, and Mary Rose's eyes followed his hand. The East River glinted in the sun. Beyond, a light covering of snow made Queens look like the magical kingdom she had dreamed of as a girl. Queens!

"What do you have that you can't keep here?"

He told her about the great library at Alexandria, how any scholar who went there had his books taken from him and was given a handwritten copy of the confiscated volume in return. The library had been destroyed more than a thousand years ago, but those copies remained among the very most valuable books of all time. "I have," he said, "a copy of the work of Euclid."

"Worth more than this apartment?" she asked.

He smiled. "Things that are priceless cannot be compared even to things worth tens of millions."

He told her about a letter that Columbus had written in 1493 to the Royal Treasurer of Spain.

"About America?" Mary Rose asked.

"About America."

They might have gone on like that forever, he listing the amazing things that he owned, she becoming more intrigued by the man than the belongings.

But finally, she pulled herself together and forced herself to pay attention to the reason that she'd come in the first place.

She reached into her purse and pulled out the plastic bag that held Joseph Di Buonna's paper. She felt embarrassed to be carting it around as if it were a sandwich, especially with Rudi Marsh standing so close to her that she could catch his scent, vetivert and lime?

"I've learned about the family of the man who wrote this, about Crosby Street where they lived, about the Di Buonna Hotel, which they owned. And I've done a lot of work trying to translate it, but I had no luck." Without looking up at him, she added, "I need you. I need your expert opinion as to what this paper means."

She opened the bag, took out the paper and handed it to him.

"Wait," he said, before he took it into his hand. From the pocket of his fine jacket he pulled out another pair of white gloves. And something else. Mary Rose watched as he fingered a small black case, gave it a flick, and was suddenly holding a powerful magnifying glass.

There were several minutes of silence. He seemed not even to breathe as he gazed intently at the object. After what seemed an eternity, he said, "What I'm about to tell you is based on a cursory examination without benefit of the lab. Under ordinary circumstances, I never give a report without thorough scientific analysis, but I'll make a small exception in your case."

"Why?"

He lifted his gray eyes from the document and caught her gaze. His face was serious, but some emotion played at the corners of those lips that seemed too full and sensuous for his strong jaw.

"Because I don't think you came here to have this piece of paper appraised for the trade," he said simply.

After another pause, he said, "This paper—I mean the paper itself—looks to me to be American from about the middle of the nineteenth century. The ink looks to be about the same vintage. That would mean the document was probably originally created in the course of everyday business. Paper was not always as easy to come by as it is today, and even now, old papers are sometimes put aside and kept for special documents. But when a person uses contemporary paper and ink, it generally means that they attach no ceremonial importance to the document they are creating. But," he added, "that doesn't mean that the document is unimportant."

"What does it say?" she asked.

He shook his head. "I don't know. I can tell you that the two paragraphs it appears to contain were not written at the same time, though you may have already figured that out."

She nodded. "The bottom part looks more recent—as if the person who wrote it was older perhaps?"

"Yes," he said. "The second paragraph was written a short time later by the same person who wrote the first paragraph. But the ink is so close that I don't think a long period transpired between the writing of the two segments. Perhaps the second part was written in haste or even ..." He held the magnifying glass over the document again, "in fear."

"Fear of what?"

"Without being able to read the document," he answered, "we can't know what."

"Could this document be a deed to land here in New York that would now be worth millions of dollars?"

"I doubt it. The document doesn't appear to be in the expected form of a deed. Besides, land transactions in Manhattan are among the least likely to be questionable in the world. Every piece of this island has been kept track of since the Dutch acquired it from the Indians. There's a story to this paper all right, but it's not a story about New York City real estate."

She longed to ask him more, but he handed back her document in a way that made it clear he had finished talking about it.

Frustrated, she decided the hour had come to leave. It was late in the morning, and she needed time to get uptown for her appointment with Dr. Fortuna.

She looked around for her coat.

"Not yet," her host said.

"What?"

"I have something else to show you," he said softly. "Don't leave just yet."

The room, despite the huge windows on all sides, despite the feeling that the apartment gave of being held aloft over the entire city, the room still seemed bathed not in light but in shadow.

"Come here and look at one last thing."

She followed as he led her across the expanse of carpet toward a tall room-divider, a screen covered in antique rose damask.

Mary Rose stopped, unsure where she was supposed to go next.

With a smile, he took her hand and led her around to the other side of the screen.

Here, daylight fell fully, but the bright light in no way diminished the mystery of the glowing painting that hung on the other side of the screen. She had seen one in the same style, the same size—presumably by the same legendary artist—a hundred times on Fifth Avenue at the Met.

"How can this be?" was all she could think to ask.

"You know the companion piece," he said.

"The Picasso Gertrude Stein," she answered. "One of the most famous portraits in America. But I never knew that there was another."

She studied the picture. The dark, intense eyes of Alice B. Toklas stared back at her. If it was indeed a companion piece, it would have to have been painted a hundred years ago. But Alice's expression—her subservience combined with defiance, her American Jewishness combined with European élan, her love combined with scepticism, flowed out of her vibrant face as if the picture had been painted yesterday.

"This may have been made for Gertrude's eyes alone," Rudolph whispered. "Almost no one in the world has seen it. Almost no one is worthy of seeing it."

"Why me?"

"Because," he answered, "I want you to know what I have."

She had no idea what he meant. And she was rapidly losing any idea of why she was there. She struggled to find some way to ask him why he was detaining her. It should have been an easy query for a lawyer to make. But anything she said now would sound personal, and she still considered this a business meeting. Or did she?

Into the silence of her hesitation came the melodious chimes of the pearl-faced clock. Then it struck the hour. Each of the twelve strokes seemed to match a beat of Mary Rose's heart—the way the deep throb of the bell at Old City Hall courthouse in Toronto used to sometimes call her out from court and into Nathan Phillips Square at lunch.

Where am I? What am I doing?

"I have to go."

"No. It's time for lunch."

Somehow her coat was in his hand.

Somehow the elevator had reappeared and the bodyguard and a driver for his personal car. A Rolls. *Of course a Rolls!*

And of course a private club on Fifth Avenue that overlooked Central Park where skaters whirled beneath trees festooned with what looked like diamonds but were really crystals of ice sparkling in the afternoon sun.

He talked of art and real estate, of America and Canada, of value and the lack of value. His gray eyes were always still, no matter how animated his conversation. His wide lips always seemed to hover on the verge of a smile, which amazed Mary Rose. How could so obviously powerful a man be so relaxed, so happy?

As if he had guessed her thoughts, he said, "I am never more at ease, more at home, than when I have just discovered something of astonishing rarity and remarkable beauty, something that has been making its way toward me without its knowledge for its whole existence."

When lunch was finished, he took her to the Met to see Gertrude once again.

And then he took her to the Yacht Club on 44th Street for cocktails.

And to dinner.

And when she said it was time to go back to her hotel, though time had long since lost its meaning, he told her it was too late to go out into the streets.

And somehow she believed him and spent the night.

And in the morning, he took her to breakfast in the newly renovated Palm Court at the Plaza Hotel, though he insisted on sitting in a private corner where they could see without being seen.

And in all that time, they talked and talked, as if there weren't words enough in the world to discuss the things they suddenly found in common.

Except for one thing.

He never mentioned Joseph Di Buonna's document again until, late on the second afternoon when they were riding through the park in his car on the way back to his place from a side trip to Tiffany, Mary Rose took courage and brought up the subject of the piece of paper herself.

"There's a bit more to this than I've mentioned before," she admitted.

"More to what?"

"More to the story of the document. I wasn't born yesterday. I know that stories of people holding old papers worth millions are nothing knew. Even in my own family there was a story like that, though I can't recall much detail."

"A story of a document?" he asked with interest.

"Not a document exceptional in itself. Before my own generation, my family went back and forth between Italy and Canada often—sometimes a generation would go back to Europe, then their children would come back to Canada. Naturally the family lost track of a lot of things. Apparently there was a family story that we once held a deed to a building in the Ward in Toronto. That would be sort of like owning a building on the Lower East Side—except on a smaller scale. The story goes that one night there was a card game and the deed was gambled away. It didn't matter though."

"Why?"

"We were told, even as children, that the City 'stole' the land. Eventually I came to the conclusion that a great deal of the land that belonged to Italians in the Ward was expropriated for public buildings. Two courthouses. City Hall. The Land Titles Office …"

No. That was there before.

"Courthouses?" he asked.

Without warning tears sprang to her eyes, and though she tried at first to hide them, then to brush them away, she failed.

The man beside her gently took her hand as if to wait patiently for her to compose herself.

"Mary Rose, my Canada," he said, "the case against you is fraudulent. You're a lawyer; you know that there's no problem that proper legal counsel can't solve."

She glanced up at him. The sun was beginning to sink behind the tall buildings that lined the avenue. Once again she noticed how he seemed always partly in shadow. But there was such comfort to his slight touch, such warmth in his deep voice with its sophisticated, rich-man's way of savoring every word, never in a hurry, never pressed, always the one hurried for, never the one hurrying.

"I will make sure you have the best legal counsel that money can buy," he told her.

She caught her breath. "Why?" she asked him. "Why would you do that for me?"

"Because I'm falling in love with you."

"But you don't even know me!"

He drew his finger along her cheek as he had done once before. It seemed as if a very long time had passed since the first time he'd touched her, but it had only been a day. "I have spent my whole life learning how to identify the rare, the valuable and the nearly unattainable. I know that the man who cannot see what he wants at once, loses it."

CHAPTER 33

▼

On the way back to his place, he told her that she had to leave New York right away, that she had to gather all the information she would need for his lawyers to tackle her legal troubles and to get her charges withdrawn. As his driver neared the apartment, he ordered a limo for her and said that the limo would meet them at the front door on Madison Avenue in a few minutes. He told her that by the time the limo had taken her back to her hotel, her flight arrangements would be complete. For the second time in the same week, she would be packing in a hurry and rushing out of town.

She agreed to all of it.

And before he slipped out of his car and into hers, he kissed her.

Swiftly, strongly. Leaving her shaking.

It was only minutes to her hotel, and not much longer to pack and check out. As Mary Rose left, she saw three limos parked in a row outside the hotel's front entrance on 51st Street. At first all the drivers looked the same in their peaked caps and dark suits, but then a door opened and the driver who had brought her stepped out onto the sidewalk.

Mary Rose took a step toward him.

But just then, another driver approached him. They exchanged a few words, and the first driver got back into his limo and began to move up the street. When the second driver signalled to Mary Rose to get into *his* car, she shrugged her shoulders. He smiled, nodded and made a small gesture that gave her the impression that the two drivers were working together. She got into the second car.

Then, out of the rear window, she saw her own driver jump out of his car and wave frantically.

At the same moment, she realized she wasn't alone in the back seat of the car.

"Well, this is a surprise. You're about twenty-four hours late, aren't you? You really ought to keep your appointments." The voice at her ear was sinister—angry with an edge of vindictiveness and threat. It was also familiar.

Suddenly Mary Rose's lost hours came crashing down on her. What had she been thinking? Her meeting with Dr. Fortuna had slipped her mind. While she had been having lunch over Central Park, he had been waiting for her. How had she so completely forgotten her whole reason for coming to New York? Rather than knowing more about the document she carried, in some respects, she felt she knew less. The list of the things that it *wasn't* was growing.

"I'll deal with her," came a second voice. And this time, Mary Rose was truly shocked.

"Luigi," she hissed at the Italian professor. "This is an outrage. What are you doing here? What sort of cat-and-mouse game is this, anyway?"

"I told you before, Mary Rose, you are in a precarious position."

She had never heard him sound so determined, so sure of himself. For the first time in all her years of knowing him, she felt afraid.

She lunged for the door.

But though she was sitting nearest it, Luigi Giordano managed to grab her arm hard, keeping her from reaching the handle.

At the same time, the driver peeled away from the curb, hit the gas, and sped the wrong way for half a block, narrowly missing three pedestrians as he spurted onto Second Avenue, headed downtown.

Terrified, Mary Rose fought the urge to scream and struggle. She'd never been held captive before. She was in good shape, but she was no athlete. Even if she could get the door open, she couldn't jump out of the cab. To land in the middle of Second Avenue would be fatal. New York cabs had only two speeds. Stopped. Full steam ahead. The traffic on Second was moving. She'd be dead in a New York minute if she jumped.

She sat back and shot a glance at her kidnappers.

They certainly weren't run-of-the-mill abductors.

For one thing, they appeared to have hired a very expensive limo and driver.

For another, they had marvellous credentials—the two of them. Both distinguished professors. Why in heaven's name would professors kidnap anybody?

They were staring back at her as if waiting for her to tell them what to do next.

"Are you armed and dangerous?" she asked.

She wasn't surprised when they looked more scared than she was.

"Look, Luigi, you're pretty good at warning me about my legal liability. What about yours? You think you can just snatch a person and divert them from their lawful activities?"

"And as for you ..." She turned on the man next to her with a ferocity that she later regretted as being a little too much. The man appeared to cower. "So I missed an appointment? So what? You must have students who miss seminars all the time. What do you do to them? Abduct them? Prevent them from exercising their right to be where they want to be?"

The two men glanced at each other as though they needed to have a meeting in order to decide what to say.

"Driver," Mary Rose instructed, "Turn, get onto a street that goes uptown, get onto the 59th Street bridge and head to La Guardia this instant."

She didn't know her own power. The cab screeched around one corner, then another. Then another. First she was nearly in the lap of the professor from New York. Then he was nearly in hers. Then she was nearly in his. When all that was straightened out and she was confident that they were indeed headed for the airport, she demanded that they tell her what they were up to.

After a brief silence in which everyone, including Mary Rose, appeared to collect themselves, Luigi began with a rather formal introduction of his colleague. "I believe you met Dr. Fortuna."

"I've had the pleasure," Mary Rose replied sarcastically.

"Robert and I have been working together on a ground-breaking study on the mechanics of trans-Atlantic mid nineteenth-century southern Italian child indenturement," Luigi explained.

"What's that supposed to mean?"

"We've been collecting letters of indenture to and from American *padroni*, men who trafficked in children from Italy."

"Trafficked in children?"

"Yes. They gathered young boys—and sometimes girls—and arranged for them to work all over the world. We have completed a good deal of this work," Luigi added, "but our funding is running out."

"And you intend to raise money by kidnapping *me*?"

Stuck in traffic, the cab eased along Northern Boulevard in Queens. It occurred to Mary Rose that she had no idea what airline she was flying on. She had no ticket, no boarding pass. Now that she was with the wrong driver, how would she even know where to get out of the limo?

"Look," she said to the two scholars, "I don't know what you think I have to do with all of this, but I'm ..."

"You're in a hurry. You're in trouble. You're in the middle of something that you don't even understand."

"Thanks for that, Luigi," she said. "Any other news?"

"Look, we're not kidnapping you. We're just asking for your help," the other professor butted in. "We need you to give us that document."

"Are you crazy?" Mary Rose shot back. "Why would I do a stupid thing like that? I don't know *you*. And besides, the document is not mine to give."

"We only need it long enough to have it authenticated. We would need exclusive use of it for only a few days."

"What does it have to do with your funding?"

The two men exchanged a secretive glance.

"We would promise to return it to you in the same condition that it was in when we borrowed it."

"You've got to do better than that, Luigi," she replied. "Why can't you just use a copy? I might consider giving you a copy when I get back to Toronto."

"Anybody can alter copies these days," the other professor said. "But if we have the original, we can submit it as part of our funding application. Once it's authenticated by the funding body, they'll return it. It's standard practice for materials of this sort."

Mary Rose stared first at one man, then at the other. "I'll make a deal with you," she finally said. "I'll grant you a period of time with the document. But you have to tell me the whole story about this piece of paper. Give me everything you've got on it. Tell me what it really means and what it's really worth."

"Fine," Luigi answered. "Give us the paper and ..."

"Not so fast. I need several things from you two before I turn it over."

"We have no time to waste," Luigi said angrily. "You've thrown away enough of our time as it is—running back and forth to New York, spending endless hours with that shyster paper peddler. Rudolph Marsh ..." He spit the name out as though it soured his tongue.

"We can't wait. We need that document right now. Before you board your plane," the other scholar added.

At that moment, Mary Rose caught sight of something through the window.

The driver that Rudi had originally provided had tailed them! His limo was two cars behind. Up ahead there were signs for La Guardia. Time was running out.

Mary Rose was glad she had only a small suitcase with her.

Because at the next red light, she bolted.

She left the door of their limo and the mouths of the two professors wide open as she darted through traffic and into the car that Rudi had meant for her.

CHAPTER 34

▼

Back in Toronto, everything was a mess.

"They cancelled the order for the robe," Marlee told her. She didn't add, "And it serves you right," though together, those two small statements said everything about her legal career and the shambles it was in.

Of course she had lost contact with Joseph.

And her lawyer wasn't taking her calls. It didn't matter. All he could tell her was to show up for her first court date. The shame of being formally arraigned on the child molestation charges was something Mary Rose couldn't bear to think about.

But none of that was the worst of it.

The worst of it was that she did a little research in the spare time she now had for the first time in her life and discovered a portrait of Alice B. Toklas fitting the description of the one she'd seen in Rudi Marsh's apartment on a list of works that had disappeared during the Second World War, never to be seen again.

Looted Nazi art treasure!

She wished she could tell somebody how she felt about all this, but she couldn't.

She'd never been close to her brother. And even if she could talk to him, she'd have to tell him about the harp. It was as much his as hers. But now wasn't the time to get into all this with him.

And she couldn't tell Marlee anything else, either. She didn't need more of the secretary's judgemental comments.

Thinking about the harp, Mary Rose went into her bedroom and dug the box from out of the bottom of her closet. She wasn't sure why she'd hidden it. After all, it wasn't as though anybody but her was ever in the apartment.

Once more she carefully unfolded the tissue and lifted the ancient treasure out of its protective wrap. Forgetting all about white gloves, she touched the strings of the little instrument. They felt rough, not at all the way she would have expected the strings of a musical instrument to feel. And when she plucked one of them, it made no music, only a dull thud.

But even though it was no longer capable of making music, the heft of the harp, the worn smoothness of its wood, even the smell of it—musky, almost spicy, drew from Mary Rose something she'd long forgotten, a song her grandmother used to sing to her when she was a child. She knew it only in Italian, had never heard it translated, but now she recognized quite a few of its words. The word for *sky*. For *azure*. For *lover*. For *gone*.

She sang the song softly to herself.

On impulse, she picked up the phone and called the one number she had the least reason in the world to dial.

"Mrs. Stein, please don't hang up. I need to talk to you about something that has nothing to do with Joseph. I need to ask you about a painting, I mean about things stolen during the War ..."

"Who is this?" the voice on the other end asked shakily.

"It's Mary Rose Cabrini. I need to talk to someone, and I think you're the only person who can help me get the information I need."

"Oh, Ms Cabrini, Joseph's been asking for you," the woman said pleasantly. "He was afraid he might have upset you. He's been wondering why you haven't called."

What?

"Mrs. Stein," Mary Rose said carefully, "I'm a little confused. Surely you didn't think I'd be allowed to talk to Joseph after the charges were laid."

"Charges?"

There was a long pause on the other end of the line. Mary Rose struggled to assess what she was hearing. Was Mrs. Stein on some sort of medication?

"I don't know anything about charges. Do you mean criminal charges? Against my little Joseph?"

"Oh, no, good heaven's no!" Mary Rose hastened to answer. She didn't want to add that the charges were against *her*. Not yet anyway.

"Would you like to talk to Joseph right now?" the woman asked.

And even though she knew it was something that could land her in a great deal of trouble, Mary Rose said yes.

There was another pause as the phone was passed to the boy. He didn't sound friendly. In fact, he didn't even say hello.

"Where's my paper?"

"It's safe, Joseph. I took it to the bank and put it into a safety deposit box."

"Did you find out what it means?"

"No. Not yet. But if you help me, I might be able to find out soon."

"You want me to meet you again?" he said. She thought he sounded frightened.

"No. We can't do that just now. But what we can do is talk a little about your great-great grandfather. The old man who gave you the paper."

There was such a long pause that Mary Rose feared that Joseph was about to hang up. Maybe she should get him to give the phone back to his grandmother instead. "Joseph?" she said. "Are you still there?"

"He hardly said anything."

"What?"

"The old man. He hardly said anything. It was like he couldn't talk because he was so old and his voice was squeaky, like he had to squeeze it out or something."

Carefully Mary Rose formed the next question in her mind before she actually asked it. "Joseph," she finally said, "do you remember any of his actual words?"

"I don't think so. Not really. Except I remember that he said he was waiting for me to come back from Canada. He said the paper belonged to the one in Canada."

"What does that mean?"

"I don't know," Joseph said. "I can't remember anything else. Except he told me never to show anybody. I shouldn't have showed you. I need it back."

The child was right. Whatever the paper had once meant, whatever it meant now, it was his by color of right. It was not Mary Rose's just because she had temporary possession of it. The right thing would be to get it from the bank and to return it by courier to Joseph Di Buonna.

It might be too late to salvage her elevation to the bench, too late, too, to save her legal career.

But there was still time to save her sanity.

"Okay, Joseph," she said, "I'll send it back to you tomorrow."

Before she left for the bank to retrieve the paper, she checked her email.

Ms Cabrini:

I apologize for frightening you during both your recent trips to New York. I feel I never had the opportunity to explain myself, and I would like to do so now.

As you know, I am a professor of Italian-American heritage here in the City, but I am also a person with a strong, legitimate connection to the Di Buonna's. I believe that the boy in Toronto who entrusted the old document to you is also a scion of the family—on his father's side. As for me, my mother is a descendant of one of the daughters of the original padrone. *The story of his disappearance from New York has long been a legend among us. My mother's grandmother often told the tale of a man who trained monkeys and little boys and who kept a magical piece of paper in a golden box. He thought the paper would keep him safe from the police, the fear of whom permeates immigrant society.*

In any event, I had no understanding of what this magical paper might be until I began my own studies. I have located quite a number of distant Di Buonna relatives, including direct and indirect descendants of Giuseppe Di Buonna, known as the Maestro of Orphans. Because he had only two sons and each of them left only one son, the male descendants are limited. But there are many descendants on the female side.

To make the story short, nothing any Di Buonna owned in nineteenth-century New York was of significant or lasting monetary value. It's easy to trace the house they lived in on Crosby. It was a rental property at the time the Di Buonna's lived there. The value of the paper you have lies mainly in its historical interest as documentary evidence of my mother's family's struggle to get to America and to become established here.

I realize that you are not American yourself, so perhaps you fail to understand the importance to us of artifacts from the struggle of Italians to become assimilated into American life. Professor Giordano and I agree that the document is most likely a certificate of indenture, an authorization for the old maestro to hire the boys in his care and to sub-contract their services to others. He no doubt believed that such a contract would exempt him from the laws of New York State, thus making him innocent of breaching child labor legislation.

To be honest, since new efforts have been made to retrieve and preserve such documents, they have become worth money in themselves. I first became aware of the existence of papers like yours in a catalogue of items offered for auction by Rudolph Marsh. I can therefore understand your hesitation in allowing access to the original paper.

Can I convince you to simply send me a certified copy?

Mary Rose thought about this email as she set out for the bank.

Who was Rudi Marsh? She tried to put aside the memories she had of their brief time together in Manhattan. Everything that had happened between them had been so like a dream that it should have been easy for her to dismiss it.

A dream or a show?

If she had been the sort of woman to have lots of girlfriends to confide in, she would have been able to ask *them* what she should make of an exotic, handsome, rich man who was claiming to have fallen instantly in love with her.

Just as she was locking her door, the phone rang, startling her out of her deep thoughts.

"*Cara!* You're home. I was afraid I would never see you again. How can you run off like you do—as if you were a deer? A bird, even?"

"Cut the bull, Luigi. You scared me witless in that cab. What were you trying to prove, anyway?"

"*Bella*, come have coffee with me and we can discuss this in a mature manner."

"You tried to kidnap me!"

"No. No, you are mistaken." The flirtatious silliness was suddenly absent from Dr. Giordano's tone. "We had come to talk to you. We saw you from a distance as we neared your hotel. We instructed our driver to wait until you had concluded your business at the hotel. We were as surprised as you were to find ourselves together with you in the back seat of that car."

"I find that hard to believe, I—"

"Listen," he interrupted, "you've lost perspective entirely. I'm amazed that you would create such havoc over a document that you can't even read."

"How do *you* know whether I can read it or not, Luigi?"

"Because if you could read it, you might not have run to New York. I assume you received the email from my colleague?"

"Yes. And I'll consider sending a copy of the paper." She paused. "Does that mean that you know what it says?"

"No. Do you understand any words from the Neopolitan dialect, Maria?"

"A few. But that didn't help me one bit when I was trying to decipher the paper."

"Of course not. Because village dialect from 1860 or so is not going to be the same as urban dialect of the twenty-first century. Professor Fortuna is an expert on archaic rural dialects of the Bourbon diaspora ..."

"What?"

"Mary Rose," he said, "you've risked everything and you don't even know why, do you?"

She couldn't answer that question.

"So end it now. Take that document out from wherever you've hidden it. Get a certified copy and send that copy to me by courier as soon as you can. I guarantee that our intentions are above reproach."

There was a pause. What did he expect Mary Rose to say? That he was a liar, a cheat, a thief and a kidnapper? The accusations wouldn't hold water. He was nothing but a professor trying to get funding for his pet project.

When she didn't answer right away, he dove right back in. "Give the original back to that little boy. You have nothing to gain from all this. Stop it now."

She still had no answer.

"You can also email me a copy," he persisted. "Dr. Fortuna is eager to translate it. If you like, I'll send you your own personal copy of the translation—plus we'll acknowledge you in our book."

She heard him draw a breath, as though he might be moving to the next level of a difficult negotiation.

"You know," he said, "when your case comes to court, any service you've rendered to the community will look good on you …"

"Oh, so now you're adding blackmail to your own list of crimes?"

"Mary Rose," he said softly, "I'm your friend. Do as I say and save yourself."

CHAPTER 35

▼

When she got to the bank, she felt nervous, as if she were doing something illegal, which was clearly not the case.

Yet, when she presented her identification to the teller and asked to be allowed access to her safety deposit box, she was asked to step aside.

Behind her snaked a long line of customers waiting for service, and it felt to Mary Rose that everyone stared at her as she moved away from them.

"Come with me, please."

She followed a dark-suited woman into a glass cubicle along the wall. It had an uncanny similarity to the prisoner's dock in the courthouse. Mary Rose fought the urge to bolt. "Is there some problem?" she asked with false calm.

The other woman sat behind her desk and motioned for Mary Rose to take the seat opposite. There was so little room that her knees banged against the desk.

The bank official studied a paper with exaggerated concentration. "Ms. Cabrini, I cannot allow you access to this safety deposit box.

"What?"

The woman kept her eyes on the paper in her hand. "The box has been sealed by a court order. No one can gain access without the permission of a judge."

Stupified, Mary Rose protested, "This can't be. How can my personal possessions be seized without my knowledge?"

"Please don't raise your voice, Madam."

"But how can I know the contents are secure? Can I at least have a list of what was seized?" Though she had finally persuaded herself to let go of the document, the thought that it was now completely out of her control filled Mary Rose with panic.

The bank officer shook her head. "Sorry," she said. "I'm sure you're aware that the bank doesn't keep records of the contents of safety deposit boxes. I think you'd have to apply to the court if you want more information."

"This is an outrage!" Mary Rose shouted, jumping up.

But her protest was cut short by a searing pain as her knees hit the edge of the desk, sending her sprawling back into the chair. She sat there shaking for a few seconds before two burly young security guards escorted her out of the bank, frog-marching her past the gaping customers and depositing her on the slushy sidewalk outside.

Her first thought, though she wasn't sure why, was to call Rudi in New York.

Then she remembered the painting on the list of missing art treasures and the comments of the two professors.

Who *was* Rudi Marsh? If he was really a rapacious dealer out to get anything he could by any means, was it possible that he had somehow stolen the document?

But how?

Without warning, an unbidden stream of images began to flow across the screen of her inner vision: skaters whirling beneath the sparkling trees, a glass of champagne lifted toward her lips by a hand not her own, a kiss stolen in a New York limo.

She called him despite her doubts.

But she couldn't get through.

So she called Marlee.

She couldn't get her secretary, either, but she left a detailed message, and within an hour, Mary Rose's cell rang. She dug in her purse, pulled it out and left the Starbucks where she'd been sitting in order to get some privacy.

The sounds of the street made it hard to hear Marlee, but Mary Rose soon got the gist of surprising news.

"The judge who ordered the box sealed is Benedict Semore. That's the interesting part."

"What do you mean?"

"I had to pull a few strings to get all this," Marlee said. She was stalling, waiting for Mary Rose to acknowledge her exceptional skill as an assistant. For the first time, it occurred to Mary Rose that in throwing her own career away, she'd also damaged Marlee's. The thought filled her with new determination.

"I'm sure you did pull strings, Marlee. And when this is over, I promise you that I won't forget ..."

"Thanks. I—"

"Now give it to me."

"Judge Semore signed the order sealing the box and impounding the contents pending a further order from the court. But what's odd here is that he was asked to do so by a lawyer representing the mayor."

"The mayor!"

"Yes. A joint motion was brought before the court by a Di Marino Bianco. You know who he is?"

Mary Rose's mind sped back to the day she'd held the trowel in her hand, the day the ground had been broken for the new courthouse. Once again, she recalled the steady, assessing, frightening gaze of the powerful developer.

"He's a friend of the mayor," she told Marlee.

"He's a lot of things," Marlee answered. "His company has amassed land parcels for municipal development for decades. He was a consultant on the new courthouse. He was personally in charge of the demolition of the buildings that stood on the site of the old Land Titles Office."

"Wow!"

"Even that's not the most interesting part of all this," Marlee went on.

"What else?"

"He's a member of the Community Advisory Committee that had final say as to whether your name could be submitted to the Attorney General for the judicial appointment."

Mary Rose struggled to put all this together. "That can only mean he acted in my favor," she finally said. "The community committee voted unanimously to allow my application."

"So you think he's on your side?"

"He has to be."

"Think again," Marlee said in her sarcastic tone, a tone that Mary Rose realized she had missed over the past few days.

"There's one other thing I found out about him." The secretary paused as if to prepare her boss for the worst. "Di Marino Bianco is a personal friend of the Justice of the Peace who signed the papers charging you with the molestation of Joseph Di Buonna."

A person is only as powerful as his most powerful enemy.

That was something Mary Rose had learned when she'd first entered law school and had had the privilege of hearing one of the last lectures given by Judge Sheldrake Tuppin, a man who, in his own time, had been widely believed to know more about the law than anyone else in the city.

So who was her enemy?

"Marlee, what happened to the records that were stored in the old Land Titles Office? Do you think you could check that out and get back to me?"

"I don't need to check it out. I know for a fact that they were sent to the city archives—that dusty old hole in the basement of City Hall."

"I used to love that place," Mary Rose answered. "All those ratty boxes ..."

"Well, it's long gone now. All the records have been transferred to the new facility." The secretary paused, as if she were unsure what her relation to Mary Rose was at the moment.

"Look, Marlee," Mary Rose said, "I know things are pretty bad right now, but I'm going to straighten this mess out. I just need you to be patient for a little while longer."

Marlee laughed. "What makes you think I've been patient this long?"

The sound of her laughter brought tears to Mary Rose's eyes. But it brought relief, too. As if there were light at the end of the tunnel.

"You want me to go down to the new archives and check for those Land Title records?"

"No, I need you to do something else for me. I need you to find out how Joseph's file came to me."

"I don't get it. Didn't Hunt-Duval assign it to you?"

"Yes. Yes. But what I need to know is why I was chosen in the first place. All the time I was with the orphan office, I was assigned cases in case conference meetings. I never thought about it at the time—I guess because I was so excited about the judgeship—but no file had ever come to me before in such a direct way. You know what I mean?"

Marlee didn't say anything.

"Marlee? Are you with me?"

"Wait a minute," the secretary said. Then the line fell silent.

Mary Rose felt a jolt of fear. In the background, she heard a door slam, as if it had been jerked open and had hit the wall. Then there were footsteps and the sound of labored breathing.

"Marlee—what the ...?

"Sorry," the secretary answered. "I remembered something and I ran out to my desk to get it.

Papers rustled.

"When those OPP guys pick up files, they leave a receipt on my desk. It's a routine thing—a routing chart that shows every place the file has been before it got to us. Our name is on the bottom and ..."

"And what?"

"Let me see. Hunt-Duval's name is above ours and above hers is—hmm ..."

"What? What?"

"Hunt-Duval got the file from Judge Semore."

"Again! Who is this guy?"

"Beats me."

"Get on it, Marlee. Find out who Semore is and why he chose me. Plug into the secretarial network. I have to know everything about how that file came to me." She hesitated before she added, "I'm beginning to think my life depends on it."

"Don't be so dramatic," Marlee answered, but she sounded a little shaky. "I'll see what I can do. You sure you don't want me to check out the archives, too?"

"No," she answered. "I'm fine on that."

Only she wasn't. Because when she tried to access holdings from the Land Titles Office, she found that all the records from 1913 to 1921 were missing.

"Those items were missing for several decades," a lean, eager, young archivist informed her, with such animation that Mary Rose knew he wanted her to press for details.

"Missing?"

"Yes," he said enthusiastically, "but the good news is they've been found!"

"Look," she said, trying to be patient, "I'm sure we all love a good mystery, but could you please just tell me ..."

"Sure," he said. "Here's what happened. The Land Titles Office originally stood on ground near the site of the present courthouse on University Avenue. When the courthouse was built, the older building was demolished. All the records were moved to the archives—or so it was thought. But it soon became apparent that records for some years were missing. Well, they remained missing until the land was excavated for the new courthouse. At that time, a whole cabinet of records was found. Seems they were buried the first time. We're thrilled to have recovered them!"

"I bet you are," Mary Rose said. "What are my chances of having a look at those papers?"

"Sorry. Not available. When they were discovered about eighteen months ago, the city decided to examine and preserve them before committing them to the archives."

"Why?" Mary Rose asked. She was beginning to get a sinking feeling in the pit of her stomach.

"For posterity, of course," the young man said cheerily. Clearly he wasn't the type to question the decisions made by those in authority. He reached over the counter between them and pulled a slick brochure from a standing display. "This will tell you when the city plans on releasing newly restored versions of the missing documents," he offered with strained helpfulness.

Mary Rose glanced at the brochure. Just long enough to see that the restoration project was spearheaded by the mayor. With the helpful assistance of his ally, Antonio Di Marino Bianco.

CHAPTER 36

▼

"Luigi, I found an old receipt among my grandmother's papers. I think it says the Di Buonna hotel closed in 1915."

"Yes." The professor waxed nostalgic. "It was something in its prime. People came from all over the city to hear the boys play and sing. My own great-grandfather visited there as a little boy. He wrote a letter about it that my family kept for years. He said it was the sound of angels."

"Yeah. Yeah, I'm sure it was great. But what I want to know is what happened to it?"

"What happened to what?"

She had invited him out for a drink, deciding to believe his story about the New York limo, figuring that too much water had gone under the bridge for them to be enemies. "To the land? The business? The building?"

He shot her one of those sly, mysterious glances she hated so much. "Don't you know?"

"No," she responded, irritated. "My family hasn't lived here forever. They went back and forth to the old country. I'm sure lots of things happened in the Italian community in Toronto that passed us by."

The professor lifted a small glass of golden muscatel to his lips and took a tiny sip. They were sitting in a café on College Street, one of the few remnants of the thriving Italian neighborhood that had once prospered in that location. The Toronto Italians, like the New York Italians, had grown rich and moved on. "The Di Buonna hotel was one of the most successful businesses in the Ward from 1874 when the old Maestro came here to 1915 when he died. But the land never passed to his children."

"Why?"

"Because, Mary Rose, it was expropriated by the government."

"What?"

"Yes. When the Di Buonna's came, land in the Ward was considered slum. For the most part, it was owned by people who treated it as run-down rental property. But by 1915 or so, it was becoming evident that the area was prospering, that it was about to become the center of a major metropolis. Immigrants like the Di Buonna's lost out. They were smart enough to amass land, but not smart enough to keep it out of the hands of the ruling elite."

"I thought you said the government."

Luigi studied the golden wine in his glass. "Government, ruling elite, same thing."

"It was just snatched away? Can that be legal?"

"Mary Rose," he said, reaching out to touch her hand. She withdrew it before his fingers met her skin. "Mary Rose, you are the lawyer. Surely you must know about the expropriation of land for government use."

"What government exactly? What did they build on the land?"

He looked at her as if to say she could figure it out for herself. After a moment's thought, she did. "The courthouse is built on that land, isn't it?"

He nodded. "Both courthouses—the one that was once Old City Hall and the newer courthouse where you've appeared as a lawyer. Not to mention the planned courthouse that you helped break ground for." He hesitated. "Oh, yeah," he said, "there's also New City Hall."

"All of those buildings are on land that belonged to the Di Buonna's?"

"Maybe. But the expropriation happened a long time ago."

"It doesn't matter."

"What?"

"It doesn't matter how long ago the land was expropriated if it wasn't done properly."

"What are you talking about?"

Mary Rose glanced at Luigi. All her life she had dismissed him as some sort of fool—an irritant, a man to be disregarded and pushed away. The incident in the cab on 51st Street had changed her mind, but his protestation of innocence had changed it back. Maybe he was her friend after all. Maybe he had just given her a clue to the mystery that was consuming her life.

But she still didn't trust him enough to tell him what was on her mind.

"I need to check into a few things," was all she said before she changed the subject. Reaching into her purse, she pulled out a sealed envelope.

"What's this?" Luigi asked, his eyes lighting up.

"A copy of the document."

"But I thought you said it was locked away and that the bank wouldn't let you have it."

Mary Rose shook her head. "True. But I remembered that Joseph opened it on my computer. I found a way to locate it on the hard drive. I made a copy, like you asked."

He grabbed eagerly for the envelope, but Mary Rose held it just out of his reach. "You've got to promise that it's for your eyes only."

Doubt flashed across his face and she realized why. "Yours and Professor Fortuna's," she added.

Later that same day, Luigi called her with his report on the contents of the document.

"There are two parts to this," he began.

"Yes." Mary Rose held her breath.

"The first section is what we suspected it might be," he explained.

"Which is?"

"A labor contract. It states that Giuseppe Di Buonna has assumed legal responsibility for the nurturance, housing and education of the children under his care at the premises he maintains on Crosby Street or at any subsequent location of his choice. It states further that he has a right to any and all of the proceeds from the work that he arranges for them, exclusive of the cost of their upkeep and a modest allowance to be given to each. He swears that all of these rights are his by virtue of the agreements he has made with the parents of said children and in accordance with the sums he has already paid the parents."

Mary Rose tried to get her mind around the implications of such a contract for the children involved. If the Maestro were decent and honest, the children might prosper. If he were dishonest, they would become slaves.

"This part of the document," the professor went on, "appears to have been signed by Giuseppe Di Buonna and by another person, who I take to be a labor agent of some sort—either in Italy or New York. That agent likely provided the children in the first place."

"So that's all this is?" Mary Rose asked, "just an artifact? A historical object? I guess it has no value other than the scholarly value you and your colleague said it has."

She had risked everything for this? A quaint relic from the distant past? So much for fortunes lost and found. She should have known better.

"Not exactly."

"What?"

"That's not all," Professor Giordano said. He paused, cleared his throat. "Remember, it's a two-part document."

Mary Rose fought to control the sudden beating of her heart. "What's the other part say?"

"It's a will."

"You mean like a last will and testament?"

"Yes. It stipulates this, 'I, Giuseppe Di Buonna, having acquired property in my own name, hereby bequeath it to my only living son, Ambrogio, and after his death, to the oldest living person who is his direct descendant."

"What kind of a will is that?" Mary Rose asked.

"Typical Neopolitan. Typical nineteenth-century" he answered. "It shows a desire to control a fortune from beyond the grave and to try to ensure that the fortune stays with the blood."

"So that not Ambrogio but the old man decided who got the property even after Ambrogio died?"

"Yes."

"But what property? Not New York?"

"I don't think so. Could be Italy. Could be anywhere."

"Toronto?"

"Sure. Maybe the old man bought the Di Buonna hotel before he even left New York. Maybe he had planned to come for a long time."

"Where would the record of that land purchase be?"

"I don't know. You're the lawyer. You figure it out."

"The Land Titles Office."

"What?"

"Nothing." She signalled for the bill. "Thanks, Luigi. I've got to run."

"Meet me for dinner?"

"Bye."

Within the hour she was back at the archives. "Even if the records aren't available to the public," she told the archivist, "somebody's got access to them."

"They'll be on public display in a few months," he answered. "I think you'll need to wait until then."

"Look," Mary Rose said, "I'm like you. I love all this old stuff. You can understand how eager I am to see it before the public crowds in here. Are you sure you can't help me?"

He gave the matter a few moments' thought as he straightened his brochure display and lined up all the pencils in the box beside the pile of white researchers gloves. "Well, donors to the archives usually get advance notice of significant events—preview receptions, things like that."

"You mean if I donated money I could have a look at those files?"

"Money? Oh, good heavens, no! I didn't mean to imply that we require money to access our collections! Not at all. That would be bribery. What I mean is …"

"I'll be back."

She went home, went to her closet, pulled the dusty box from its depths and opened the envelope of old photos. She selected a few of her grandmother and her grandmother's friends. Despite the fact that her great-grandfather had been born in Toronto, his daughter, Mary Rose's grandmother had been born in Naples. But she and her husband had been back and forth to Canada many times. In the photos, taken perhaps in the 1970's, Mary Rose's grandmother looked like a stylish North American.

But beside her in one picture was a very old woman who looked like the archetypical old-time native Italian. Mary Rose wondered who this might be. Some old aunt most likely.

She turned the photo over. On the back in faded pencil were several names. One she recognized at once: Mrs. Antonio Cabrini. That was her grandmother.

Beneath her grandmother's name was written *con la sua suocera Mamma (Di Buonna) Cabrini.*

Mary Rose was fairly sure she knew what the word *suocera* meant, but she checked her Italian-English dictionary anyway.

Mother-in-law!

She stared at the photo again. There was no family resemblance that she could make out. But then, a woman is not related by blood to her mother-in-law! The words on the photo clearly implied that Mary Rose's grandmother's mother-in-law had been born Di Buonna.

Didn't that mean that Mary Rose's great-great-grandfather was also a Di Buonna?

And didn't that mean …?

Her head was spinning and she was starting to lose track of the reason she had taken out the photos. She needed something to bribe—uh—donate to the archives. She selected a few more pictures.

Then she shoved them back into the envelope and took out the thing the archivist would be most interested in, the single item that was actually connected to the holdings Mary Rose wanted to get her hands, or at least her *eyes* on. Carefully she placed the old receipt from the Di Buonna hotel between two fresh white pieces of paper and enclosed the whole thing in a clear plastic folder. Then she typed up a letter about the hotel, about the fact that it had once stood very near the Land Titles Office itself, about the fact that it had eventually been torn down so that the great city of Toronto could grow up in the footprint of the old Ward. Blah. Blah. Blah.

It worked.

Within a day, she had an honorary membership in the archives, an invitation to the opening of an exhibit showing photos of the excavation of the land adjacent to what had once been the old Land Titles Office, and a card entitling her to a one-time private visit to the preservation laboratory where the newly-rescued documents were being restored.

She considered going to a camera store and getting a little secret device, but decided that that was ridiculous. Instead, she depended on her powers of observation and her memory to soak in as much as she could as she was shown a few precious documents by the preservationist.

"These are the records of land transfers from this very area from about one hundred years ago," the preservationist said cheerily. Clearly the woman was used to catering to visitors. "This deed is for a small parcel on the corner of Hagerman and Bay …"

Mary Rose could tell nothing from the pristine piece of paper neatly scored by words and numbers written in an old-fashioned hand. A hundred years in the ground had almost seemed to do the paper some good. It was in better shape than the paper the bank was now hoarding.

"Was any of this land expropriated?" she asked, feigning casual interest.

Surprisingly, the preservationist answered quite candidly. "There are a number of letters of protest in these rescued files," she said. "Would you like to see one of those?"

"Sure."

Mary Rose expected to be shown another paper, but that's not what happened.

Instead, the preservationist moved to her computer and clicked. Document after document scrolled up the screen, far too quickly to be read.

"Over the years, scores of people have complained that the government robbed them of their land," the woman said with a smile. "It's an old complaint and one with which the Land Titles Office was very familiar. Naturally when land is expropriated, those from whom it is taken feel cheated, even when they've received full market value for the property in question."

"Is that what happened here?" Mary Rose gestured toward the computer screen. The scrolling had stopped and a single letter was clearly displayed. Unfortunately it was in a language she could not only not read but not recognize.

"I'm afraid I have no idea," the preservationist replied. "For the most part, my responsibilities don't extend beyond the physical properties of these items. Naturally human curiosity compels me to wonder what happened to some of these property owners—where they went, what property they were subsequently able to acquire. If any ..."

"Are these the only copies of the letters that would exist?"

"What do you mean?"

"Well," Mary Rose said, "if a land-owner were protesting the expropriation of his land, who exactly would he be protesting to—City Hall only, or someone else besides?"

"I'm not sure," the preservationist answered, "it's an interesting question." She smiled again. "Ironically, the chambers of City Council sit on some of the very land that was expropriated. I mean the present chambers in New City Hall. A hundred years ago, the municipal seat was located in what we now call Old City Hall. Though this was well before the age of computer print-outs or photocopiers, there were ways to make copies. I suspect that in addition to being sent to the mayor or the city in general, some of these letters were sent in duplicate, most likely to individual members of the city government in power back then."

"If that had happened," Mary Rose asked, "where would those letters be now—I mean if they hadn't been lost or destroyed?"

The preservationist thought about the question for a moment. "I think they would have ended up in the city archives at Old City Hall. Which would have ended up in the archives in the basement in New City Hall. Which would have ended up here."

Back to square one!

He didn't say, "What now?" but Mary Rose could see that the formerly eager young archivist was starting to lose patience.

"I need to see letters that citizens sent to individual city officials in 1915."

"Are you kidding? There are thousands." He shook his head. "You'll have to search the data base for yourself. And if I were you, I'd spend a little time figuring out how to narrow the search. You can't just dive in. You need a few keywords."

She tried Di Buonna Hotel. Giuseppe Di Buonna. Di Buonna orchestra.

But she found nothing.

Until, with some embarrassment, she had to ask the archivist to try to check the address on the old receipt she'd donated. Once she keyed in the street number of the hotel, a list of citations jumped onto the screen.

Except for the first citation, which was in Italian, all the others were in English. From the second item on, the citations seemed to represent correspondence between an A. Di Buonna and Mr. W.L. Adams.

Mary Rose was uncertain as to the composition of the city government back then. Could it be that a single city councillor had been involved in the expropriation of the property on which the hotel had sat? That seemed highly irregular.

She clicked on the first entry on the list. She expected a typed transcription of some old letter, but what she saw was the familiar handwriting of Giuseppe Di Buonna. It was unmistakable, though even shakier than the second paragraph of the only other sample she'd seen of his writing. As had happened before in her research, she struggled with the Italian, but even her limited knowledge of the language was sufficient for her to figure out that the Giuseppe Di Buonna who wrote in 1915 was a more modern man than the one who had escaped from New York so many decades before.

And he was a very old man. The gist of his letter was that no city worker was going to steal his property, even if he was near the end of his days. He swore that his son, Ambrogio, would make sure of that.

The old man's determination seemed to reach out to her across the years and infuse her with renewed determination of her own.

Reading the letters, she could understand why the family had failed to get the expropriation of their land reversed. They had argued on the basis of a sentimental attachment to the property rather than seeking counsel to vigorously defend their position on legal grounds. Mary Rose made a note to consult a modern expropriation lawyer. Land was forever. It was never too late to correct some mistakes.

When the archives closed, Mary Rose made her way toward the parking lot where she had left her car. Her head spinning with all she'd been reading, she decided to take a drive down to the bottom of the city where the eastern beach rimmed Lake Ontario. It was the dead of winter and the beach would be cold, but the calming waters seldom froze.

Was it possible that the old man had lost everything in some sort of illegal transaction? Mary Rose was no real estate lawyer, but it seemed to her that if the expropriation had been illegal and the will legal, then the legitimate heir, that "eldest living descendant", that "blood of my blood" would now own not only the land the hotel once stood on, but also the land occupied by new City Hall, the present courthouse and even the new courthouse. It could be worth a couple of billion!

Suddenly she realized what all this had to mean. The ancient man that Joseph had met in New York thought that Joseph must be that heir!

On the walk to the car, a few blocks, she tried mentally to run through all she had learned about the geneology of the Di Buonna's. Dr. Fortuna claimed the old mestro, Giuseppe, had daughters, but did they count? Italians had rules for the naming of sons. Guiseppe must have had a son before Ambrogio, a son named Giuseppe, the first-born who would have carried his father's name. For Ambrogio to have been made the heir must mean that the oldest son had already died at the time the will had been made.

Ambrogio Di Buonna. Gio Di Buonna.

That name rang a bell. But why?

The names spun in her head, running into each other, generations jumbling. Different people with exactly the same name. Different names for the same people?

I need a break!

Before she made it to the car, however, her cell phone rang.

She almost didn't recognize his voice, but when she did, she was astonished at the powerful feeling that overtook her.

"Canada. I miss you. Fly to New York tonight. Just get to the airport. Everything will be arranged."

"Rudi, I—"

What was she about to say?

She didn't know herself.

Probably yes. Probably it doesn't matter what doubts I have ... "

Suddenly, the phone clicked and the connection disappeared. It had been only days since she'd been in New York, but it all seemed a long time ago.

As she caught her breath, it began to snow. Not the sparkling whiteness of Central Park in the sun, but a damp, gray, blowing half-drizzle that stung her face.

When the phone rang again, she grabbed it, held it to her wet cheek. When she opened her mouth to speak, snow touched her tongue.

"Rudi, I'll—"

A deep, familiar voice demanded, "Give up this digging around. Stop what you're doing. You're never going to sit on the bench. You're going to end up in jail. Or worse. Much worse. Stop now." There was a pause. "Consider this a warning. Consider yourself lucky that I called."

Her own lawyer! She was being threatened by the very man she had hired to save her.

"Whose side are you on?" she demanded. "And how do you know what I'm doing?"

There was no response.

"I'm way past worrying about being a judge," she told him. "And I'm rapidly getting past worrying about going to jail, too. Something's going on here and I'm going to figure out what it is."

Still no response.

"As for you," she nearly shouted, "you should think about the possibility of going to jail, too, you … you shyster! And in the meantime," she added with vehemence, "you can go to hell!"

She slapped down the lid of her cell phone, gasping, drawing the moist winter air into her lungs. Her heart was pounding. Land worth a billion dollars. That's what was at stake now. And real estate manoeuvring that reached back more than a century. For the first time in all this, she felt out of her league.

She reached her car and slid behind the wheel, her phone still in her hand.

She dialled Rudi.

But there was no answer.

So she called someone else.

CHAPTER 37

▼

"Mrs. Stein, can I see you today? I need to speak to you. It's urgent."

At the older woman's invitation to come over at once, Mary Rose pulled away from downtown and headed north. She had a feeling she'd never had before, the feeling that she was being followed. She remembered how Rudi Marsh's man had known about the autograph dealers she'd visited in New York before she'd even met Rudi.

Had she been followed the whole time—ever since the day the Di Buonna file had landed on her desk?

It occurred to her that Marlee hadn't yet called with any additional information about the elusive Judge Semore.

She glanced in her rear-view mirror. There were so many cars behind her in the crowded mid-day streets that there could be ten people following her!

But by the time she pulled in front of the stately home of the Steins, hers was the only car on the street.

As she stepped to the door, she looked up. Joseph was staring at her from a second-story window. She waved, but he disappeared.

She rang the bell, expecting the maid or the nanny to answer.

But Mrs. Stein came to the door herself. As always, she was beautifully dressed, this time in pale blue wool slacks, a pale blue sweater and an Hermes scarf.

She ushered Mary Rose in, invited her to sit, and served tea herself. There didn't seem to be anyone in the house but the two women and the boy.

"Thanks for seeing me right away," Mary Rose began.

"Is something wrong?"

"Yes," she answered. For a second, she hesitated, trying to decide how much to tell the older woman.

"Mrs. Stein, Joseph's in danger. There's far more at stake here than I first realized."

"Danger? From whom?"

"From people who have reason to believe that he's the heir to a great deal of money."

The other woman laughed. "This is all starting to sound like the movies. What money?"

"Has anyone come around here?" Mary Rose interrupted, "I mean strangers in front of the house?"

"Of course not!"

A grim realization hit Mary Rose. *She* was the only connection between Joseph and the people who were pursuing *her.* By coming here, she had put the boy directly in their path.

"Listen, Mrs. Stein, I can't stay and I can't come back. I need two things from you."

The woman had every reason to distrust her, but she reached out and took Mary Rose's hand. "What do you want? If I can give it to you, I will."

"The first thing is that you need to keep Joseph here at home until I figure out a way to get some protection for him."

"Protection?" Mrs. Stein repeated with alarm.

"I can't say why just yet. You have to trust me. Just keep him inside."

The other woman nodded. "What else?" she asked.

"I need you to tell me everything you know about the Italian side of Joseph's family. I need the full names of his father, his grandfather, great-grandfather—as far back as you can go. I need to know where these people were born and where they ended up."

"I'll try," the other woman answered, clearly distressed, "but if Joseph's safety depends on my memory, I'm really concerned. It would be better for you just to look it up. Didn't they give you all this information in Joseph's file?"

"I can't get that file, Mrs. Stein. It's secure and it was handed back to the Orphan Advocate Office weeks ago. Joseph himself gave me another item, but it's locked up at the bank. For me to see papers regarding Joseph would require a court order."

She didn't add *And with child molestation charges against me, no court would give that order.*

"I can remember part of the family list in the file," Mary Rose went on. "In fact, I have a vague recollection of a familiar name or two. I didn't make much of it at the time, but now I wonder whether one or more of the family names might have led someone to erroneously believe that I was in some way related to Joseph."

Mrs. Stein smiled. "My dear son-in-law used to joke that all Italians are related," the woman said softly. "I'll try to tell you what I know. You better fill your teacup, this might take time."

"The Di Buonna family," she began, "came from a town in southern Italy called Laurenzana. Like a number of such places, it sent its native sons halfway around the world looking for work."

"How do you know these things?"

"When Joseph was born, Joey Di Buonna, Jr., Joseph's father, told me that he wanted to name the boy with his own name because every first son of a first son had been so named since the Middle Ages. He also said that every Joe Di Buonna ever born had been a musician, as he, of course, was himself when his duties as a doctor permitted him any spare time. I asked him how his family had come to Canada."

She lifted her cup and took a sip of tea. Mary Rose waited.

"The story he told me was rather fanciful, I thought." Mrs. Stein smiled again. "As I said, the first Giuseppe Di Buonna to come to the new world was a musician. Laurenzana was famous for exporting harpists and accordion players—child street performers who travelled around the world, playing and begging, and, on rare occasions, breaking into the professional world of music."

"And this Giuseppe became a professional?"

"In a manner of speaking. What he became was an impresario—or at least that's how Joey phrased it. Joey said that Giuseppe was always referred to as The Old Maestro. He'd started recruiting and training child musicians in New York before the turn of the century. Joey didn't say exactly why, but the maestro had to leave New York in a hurry. Somehow he ended up here, in Toronto, with quite a number of the little boys in tow. He was also accompanied by his adult son."

"Also named Giuseppe, of course?"

"No," Mrs. Stein answered. "Joey told me that the maestro's first son—yes, Giuseppe—had died in New York, leaving a son of his own, a little boy who someone got lost in the shuffle and was left behind. That child, that little Giuseppe, struck off alone and more or less single-handedly founded the American Di Buonna family. Apparently, though, that child eventually had a son—

whose name was Americanized to "Joe". Joe came up to Canada briefly. The old maestro, had he 'remained' Italian would have considered Joe, his great-grandson by his first son, his heir. In the absence of a will, it would have been assumed that Joe and his heirs would inherit whatever the old maestro had acquired in Canada. But that's not what happened."

"Instead, he had another son …"

"Yes. Gio. Ambrogio Di Buonna, the second son. The story goes that before he left New York, the maestro gave up the old idea of leaving everything to the first sons of first sons. Gio had been faithful to him. Giuseppe had died long before and Giuseppe's children and grandchildren were American. The old man made Gio's children his heirs."

"But what did he leave them?"

Mrs. Stein sighed. "Italian family legends are imaginative and romantic. According to my late son-in-law, Giuseppe left all future Giuseppes the greatest gift he had. Not the money, which somehow disappeared when the old man died, but the music."

"The music?"

"Yes. Joey, my son-in-law, was a doctor, as you know. But you should have heard him play the cello." The corners of Mrs. Stein's mouth fell, but she shuddered, squared her shoulders, controlled herself. "Joseph is gifted also. And as soon as he gets over the tragedy of his parents' death, he'll resume his musical studies. We intend to keep his Italian heritage alive for him through his musical talent."

"Mrs. Stein," Mary Rose said, "the day is going to come when this mess over the document and the charges is straightened out. When it's all over, I'm going to help Joseph, too. I promise."

"What document? What charges?"

Mary Rose remembered that Mrs. Stein had not been the one who'd alerted the police regarding her meetings with Joseph, but she'd forgotten that, except for one fleeting mention, the woman knew nothing about those charges. And of course Mrs. Stein had no way of knowing anything about the document that had started all this. The woman was still working on the assumption that Mary Rose's interest in Joseph stemmed only from her responsibilities with the orphan office. Mary Rose gained new respect for Joseph and his dedication to his ancestor's requirement to keep the family's secrets.

But she also felt renewed fear. She, herself, had not kept the secret.

If deadly consequences resulted, she had no one to blame but herself.

"Mrs. Stein, are you telling me that the American branch of the Di Buonna family didn't care about the inheritance?"

"There isn't an inheritance. That's I'm telling you. And anyway, Americans don't think about anything that happens in Canada, do they? Besides, there are hundreds of descendants on the American side. There were only the two sons, Giuseppe and Ambrogio, but there were a lot of daughters—four or even six. They all have descendants."

"What about the descendants of Ambrogio—or Gio?"

"I don't know about them," Mrs. Stein replied. "I never knew Joey to say a thing about those long-ago relatives. He did say that he had distant cousins in Toronto, but I never met them and Joey and my daughter certainly never made any effort to introduce Joseph to them."

"Distant relatives?"

"Long-lost cousins," Mrs. Stein said with a little laugh. "I never met a Jew or an Italian who didn't have plenty of those ..."

CHAPTER 38

▼

"Little brother, I need your help."

"Mary Rose! Did you get that package I sent you?"

"Yeah. Thanks. Listen ..."

"What's inside? Junk, I bet. Gramma was always saving weird stuff from the old days."

"Gene, I'll tell you all about the box. There's something in there I think you should know about—"

"Something worth money? An antique?"

"Yeah. But I'll tell you about that later. I need you to remember something."

"What?"

"Anything Gramma ever told you about our ancestors."

There was silence on the other end, as if her brother had been running the family tree through his mind.

"I don't know if I can do this," he finally said. "Can't you look it up on the internet or something?"

"Not until I know where to start. Who was our grandfather on Dad's side?"

"You know that one. Dad's father was Antonio. He was born in Naples."

"Right. I did know that. Who was his father?"

"He was a guy that came to visit when he was really old and Dad was a little kid. He brought Grampa some skinny, smelly cigars. Dad never forgot the stink of them."

"What was his name—that really old guy?"

"He would have been our great-grandfather?"

"I guess so." Mary Rose counted on her fingers. "Yeah. Daddy was born in what—1930?"

"Yes."

"And his father would have been born about the turn of the century, thirty years before—say 1900. That's Antonio Cabrini, our grandfather."

"Right. And his father might have been born another thirty years before—around 1870."

"It's not his father. If his father had been a Di Buonna, we would be Di Buonna's."

"What?"

"His mother," Mary Rose said, "I need to know the name of his mother."

"Why don't you look in that box again," Joe said. "I remember that Gramma used to have old pictures with people's names on the back."

"Di Buonna. I saw a picture of an old Italian woman who was probably our great-grandmother. The picture said that her maiden name was Di Buonna."

"So her father was a Di Buonna. And he would have been born maybe in the 1850's."

"I wonder what his first name was?" Mary Rose said. "That's what I really need to know."

"Gio."

"What?"

"His name was Gio."

"How do you know that?"

"I don't know how I know, but I remember that Gramma always used to say that it was a shame I didn't have a little brother because then his name could have been Gio. I remember her saying, 'Nobody knows how to name their kids anymore.' Crazy, eh?" Anyway," he added, "those people came back and forth to North America a dozen times over the years. They always ended up in Canada, but maybe they came through New York. Why don't you check the Ellis Island website?"

She did.

Which is how she figured it out. Her father was Eugene Cabrini, born in 1930. His father was Antonio Cabrini, born in 1900. *His* mother was Maria Di Buonna Cabrini, born in 1875. *Her* father was Ambrogio Di Buonna, nicknamed Gio, second and last surviving son of Giuseppe Di Buonna, the Maestro of Orphans. She had no cousins older than herself. That made Mary Rose Cabrini the legitimate heir of old man Di Buonna.

She shut down the computer, grabbed the phone and called Marlee.

"I'm sorry, I just wasn't able to find out why ..."

"Forget it, Marlee. I know why that file came to me. I need you to help me one more time, then I'll be off your back."

"You're not on my back. In fact, I miss you. Is there any chance of your coming around—at least to get your books and papers?"

Mary Rose laughed in spite of herself. "I'm not done, yet, Marlee. Not by a long shot."

"What can I do for you then?"

"I need you to get Judge Semore on the phone. I have to talk to him right now."

"But I don't think he'd ..."

"He'll talk to me when he realizes that I know what he and his buddies John Franklin and Antonio Di Marino Bianco are up to."

"That's a stupid thing to say over the phone," Marlee answered. There was a sudden coldness to her tone, a coldness that Mary Rose had noticed a few times before but had never been directed at her. "If I were you," the secretary continued, "I'd forget about talking to Semore. On second thought, I wouldn't come around here after all. Maybe you better send somebody to pick up the things you've left lying around the office. I packed them all up for you. You won't be needing them anymore."

These chilling words struck Mary Rose dumb.

But only for a second.

"You're in it with them, aren't you, Marlee?" she accused. "All these years you've acted like the good and faithful servant when really you've been seething with resentment. You're a pretty good actress. It was you, wasn't it? It was you who manoeuvred things so that Joseph's file would end up on my desk. You who reported me for meeting with Joseph. You who made the appointment with the lawyer who intended to do nothing to help me. What are you going to get out of this? A new job? A piece of the action? How much was it worth to betray me?"

"Don't be ridiculous," the secretary answered, "I'm doing you one last favor. Get out of this now. If you back off, I'm sure it's not too late. You might not be a judge here in the city, but this is a big province."

"And all I have to do is forget that I probably own a big chunk of downtown Toronto?" Mary Rose laughed. "Why should I do that?"

"Because you like life?"

"Don't threaten me, Marlee. You can't hold me hostage."

"I don't need to. You're your own hostage. You don't know the difference between your enemies and your friends."

The line went dead.

Mary Rose put down the phone and glanced around her apartment as if the neat little place could provide some clue as to what she should do next.

Without knowing why, she went back to her closet and took out the dusty old box one more time.

She removed the envelope of photos without opening it. She set aside the other envelope, the one with the old letters.

Carefully, she lifted the paper-wrapped package from the bottom of the box.

The battered little white harp lay in her lap, its delicate curves still as lovely as the day some unknown hand had carved the wood, a hand warmed by the sun of an Italy gone forever except where it had been captured and held in art—and in artifacts like this one.

She touched the rough strings. They curled around her hand like the responsive fingers of a baby.

She thought about what Mrs. Stein had told her. Someone had been left behind. Some boy, some little musician of the street had come home one night to find that everyone had gone without him. All her life she'd heard jokes about a situation like that. But now she could see the reality of it, feel the shock of the child, the overwhelming sense of loss.

He turns the corner of Crosby Street. Already he knows something is wrong. When he gets to the front door, he sees it's open. When he climbs the stairs, he hears the echo of his own footsteps in the terrible silence. There are no voices, no songs, no squeal of animals trained to dance. When he gets to the top of the stairs, he enters a deserted room. He goes to the window. The yard is empty. A few white rags hang on a line, but there is no wind and they do not move. He looks across the yard. All of New York City is out there. Now it belongs to him. And he belongs to it.

If she had learned anything in her years of child advocacy, it was that children are remarkably strong, resilient, resourceful. Joseph Di Buonna was trying to save himself. And maybe Mary Rose Cabrini was trying to save herself, too. Not from poverty. That wasn't what the document and its strange history were about.

They were both trying to save themselves from losing their past, from being cut off from all the years that had gone before, from their own history that stretched back further than any living person could know.

What they did know was that both of them, Joseph and Mary Rose, came from strong and determined people, people who had done what they had to do despite fear, the fear of banishment, even the fear of death.

She touched the little harp one more time—for strength. Then she put it away and prepared to do what she had to do.

She picked up the phone and called Mrs. Stein. When the woman answered, Mary Rose gave her the address of her bank. "Meet me there in twenty minutes …"

CHAPTER 39

▼

She didn't know whether she'd be re-arrested, so she left her car at home. She cleaned out her purse so that her credit cards and I.D. would be safe if they confiscated what she was carrying. She soaked her houseplants, though they'd die for sure if she were taken away. She called her brother and left him a message. Then she called New York and left Rudi Marsh a message too. He deserved a decent goodbye.

If this were a movie, she thought, *I'd have a gun and I'd bring it.*

But it wasn't and she didn't.

She took the subway to the bank. It gave her a few extra minutes to think about how she was going to manage to storm the vault to claim what was rightfully hers.

Only then could she do justice to any claim that Joseph might have.

As she exited onto the wide avenue on which the bank sat, she was surprised to feel the warmth of the sun on her face—as if now, in the dead of winter, there were some promise of the spring to come.

Well, most likely she'd be spending spring in jail.

She couldn't think about that now. All she could do was hold her head high, like any other customer rich or important enough to have items to store in a safety-deposit box.

As she entered the cool banking hall with its high, ornate ceilings, she felt a shudder of fear. For the first time, it struck her as a little ridiculous that the place still looked like a palace. How appropriate, though, for a person about to be sent to the guillotine!

Again she saw the long line in front of the teller's window. Beyond the line, a well-dressed woman stood behind a high marble counter. Mary Rose had never seen this bank employee before, which probably meant that the woman had never seen *her*, either. Marshalling her best lawyer skills, she strode past the waiting customers and headed straight for the counter.

"I wonder if you'd be so good as to assist me," she began. The woman looked up. She glanced at the line, as if considering whether to tell Mary Rose to get into it like everybody else.

In that moment of hesitation, Mary Rose took a quick look around. The area was so secure that she would have needed a tank to breach the marble counters, the wooden desks, the screens, pillars, displays and potted plants that stood between her and the metal grill in front of the safety-deposit box vault.

"What is the …"

Whatever the woman behind the counter was about to say to Mary Rose was cut off suddenly by the sound of a child screaming.

But this was not the sound of an infant or an obstreperous toddler.

"It's mine. I know it's here. It's stolen property and you are holding it against my will. I demand that you give it to me right now."

Everybody in the bank turned toward the source of the commotion, including Mary Rose. Immediately, she decided what to do. "What I came to tell you," she said, "is that that young man is a client of mine. I'm a lawyer with the Orphan Advocate Office. I'm here to help him. He gets out of control every so often. If I can show him that what he wants to take with him is more secure here in your safety deposit vault, he'll stop screaming, but I need to speak with you first—confidentially." She nodded toward the area behind the counter.

The bank employee looked back at Mary Rose. "Thank goodness you got here," she said, as she turned an invisible key and opened a section of the marble counter, allowing Mary Rose free entry.

But before anyone could stop him, Joseph saw his chance. He darted after the two women.

And behind him came not Mrs. Stein, as Mary Rose hoped, but a man who chased the running child, grasped him and tried desperately to calm him.

He was a handsome man, well but not expensively dressed, middle-aged. The more he spoke, the more it became apparent that he had an American accent.

"Joseph," he said, "we're going home. This isn't the way to get anything, whether it's really yours or not. Your grandmother's worried about you. Both grandmothers. And me, too. Come on, son. Let the adults straighten this out. That piece of paper isn't going anywhere."

An armed guard stood beside the door to the vault, but he seemed unaffected by the scene before him, as if he considered a hysterical twelve-year old to be no threat to the security of the bank.

Mary Rose stepped past the guard and walked toward Joseph.

She had seen a lot of hateful little faces in her years as a lawyer, but she'd never seen the pure rage that filled Joseph's face the minute he set eyes on her.

"You betrayed me!" he hissed. "You stole my document. You told my secret to everybody! And now you're keeping me from everything that's mine!"

He lunged at her.

Mary Rose stepped back.

"I'm sorry, Miss," the American said, "but I think it would be best if you got out of here."

"Who are you?"

"Joey Di Buonna—from New York. I—"

"Don't talk to her. Don't tell her one more thing about our family. Get away, Grandpa. Get away!"

With those words, Joseph Di Buonna lunged again.

This time, he jumped toward the guard. The boy was so small, so quick and so determined that he managed to disarm the guard before the man even knew Joseph was coming at him.

Time stopped.

Mary Rose saw Joseph. She saw the gun. She saw the guard make a motion as though to retrieve his weapon. Then make a motion away. She saw the bank employee glance desperately beyond the counter that separated the boy with the gun from more than a dozen customers near enough to be shot dead by a stray bullet.

She saw her past stretching toward this moment, and it seemed almost funny that all the struggles of the Di Buonna's—their fight to make a life in the new world, their musical success, their ability to amass property, their inability to hang onto it—that all that should culminate in this absurd confrontation between a distraught little boy and a washed-up lawyer.

"Give me the gun," Joseph, she said as calmly and as simply as she could, "and I'll give your grandfather the paper."

Above all, remain calm.

How many times over the years had she had standoffs with children out of control? Children lying stiff, prone and resistant in the foyers of expensive homes. Children screaming in the middle of church services, in libraries, in courts. Even children who had roped, chained and otherwise fastened themselves to immoveable objects. The trick was to remain an immovable object oneself.

"Joseph, I am not going to change my mind about anything just because you have a weapon. Put it down and we'll talk."

Her voice didn't shake, but his hand did. Her heart skipped a beat then, but she kept her eyes focussed on his. "You are right," she said, "I *did* reveal your secret to other people. That was wrong, and I apologize for not seeking your permission. But now it's my secret, too."

The boy's eyes widened in surprise, but he said nothing. At least she knew he was listening.

"You didn't betray anybody, Joseph. That document affects us both. I'm willing to share it—willing to share everything it represents about our family. I asked your grandmother to come here today to prove that I will never keep something for myself that belongs to us both." She didn't take her eyes from the boy's face as she added, "I see that your grandfather came with you. That's fine. If the bank allows, he can take the paper and he can keep it until you and I decide what we'll do. Will you accept that, Joseph? Will you put the gun down if the bank turns over the paper to your grandfather?"

He didn't agree at first, but after a few more attempts, he let the weapon slowly slide to the floor, and then he slid to the floor himself, collapsing in a heap, sobbing.

Without a word to anyone, Mary Rose turned and walked out of the bank.

And into the arms of the police, who arrested her for contacting Joseph contrary to the conditions of her release.

As they politely, but firmly pushed her into the back seat of the cruiser parked at the front of the bank, she realized she had no one to call. Certainly not her lawyer. Not her brother, who was far away, or Rudi, who was just a foolish dream.

She'd burned her bridges with Marlee—fairly or unfairly.

Luigi Giordano?

What could the Italian professor do to save her from the ignominy of being in jail? She had no excuse. There were charges against her and she had gotten in trouble again and now there would be no bail, no matter how many professors stood up for her in court.

Thinking these grim thoughts, she was startled when the police cruiser went only two blocks before it screeched to a halt, the door flew open and she was unceremoniously pulled from the car and shoved with painful violence into another car.

That car, too, only went a few blocks. Out of the bright winter sun and into some dark dungeon that Mary Rose didn't recognize at first.

Then she saw the characteristic markings on walls and pillars and realized she was in the parking garage underneath Nathan Phillips Square in front of New City Hall.

The car jerked to a halt, and once more she found herself hauled out. She struggled, but her flailing arms were soon caught behind her back and cuffed there. As she kicked and tripped, her abductors, who stayed behind her, keeping her from seeing their faces, dragged her to a dark corner of the garage, a space reserved for dignitaries visiting city hall. There wasn't a car anywhere nearby.

"Give it over," a rough voice demanded. Mary Rose had never heard that voice before. There were no longer many uncultured thugs around in the sophisticated city. This voice sounded like something out of mafia movie, and Mary Rose almost laughed in spite of her desperation.

"Allow me," said a very familiar voice. Shocked, Mary Rose pulled sharply away and turned.

She found herself facing the mayor.

"Give us the paper and we'll set you free," he said simply.

She almost believed him. But she didn't have the paper. Her stomach began to knot in fear and the saliva dried in her mouth. But before she could try to wet her lips and make an excuse for herself, she heard footsteps approach.

The garage lighting was dim and the space was vast, so at first, all Mary Rose could see was a tall, slim male figure slowing making his way toward her. He was in no hurry. Why should he be? He was in charge.

The thug waited. The mayor waited. Mary Rose's heart beat so loudly that it nearly drowned out the sound of his footsteps in her ears.

The intermittent light fell on his good haircut, but darkness still embraced his features.

Until he was only ten feet away.

He raised his face into the light.

"We meet again," the man said, as if this were some sort of classy reception.

"Apparently," Mary Rose retorted. The sight of him made her sick.

"The first time I saw you at the ground-breaking, I knew I had a powerful foe," he said with a slick smile. "But perhaps I overestimated you. I didn't think you'd be this easy to trap." The developer, Antonio Di Marino Bianco, gestured to the expanse of the parking lot as if he owned it.

It occurred to Mary Rose that that ceremony, in which she had noticed for the first time, the calculating coldness of his demeanor, had taken place almost directly above them. But that had been in the open air.

"What do you want?" she asked Bianco.

"That's obvious, isn't it?"

Yes. It's obvious. You want me dead.

"I don't have the document. It's in safekeeping at the bank. But then you know that, don't you? You and your friend the mayor here are the ones who managed to have my safety deposit box seized." She glanced from one man to the other. Even if they killed her now, she wanted them to know that she was aware of what they'd done to her.

"You knew there was a likelihood that the expropriation of this area of the city was illegal the minute those old Land Titles Office files were discovered at the excavation site. You did some research—the same research that I eventually did myself. You knew I probably own this land. But you also knew that once it could be proved that the land was privately owned, you could find a way to get it yourself, to sell it back to the city and the province for the billions it's worth. You figured that if you could get your other pal, Judge Semore, to set the wheels in motion to bribe me with a judgeship, I'd stay away from the land ownership claim. Well, you figured wrong."

"That's a nice theory and a nice speech," the mayor interjected. "Too bad there's no audience for it."

The developer laughed. "Yes," he said. "Let's go. The time has come to let our little would-be judge fend for herself."

The two men began to walk away, and the third, the awkward outlaw, followed behind.

At first, Mary Rose felt relieved.

But then she remembered that after 9-11 security measures had been greatly increased in this underground garage. It was one of the reasons she never parked there herself anymore. The whole place was compartmentalized. At any sign of trouble, steel doors sealed off every section.

One by one, she began to hear those doors slam shut.

First, far in the distance.

Then, closer.

Then, almost in front of her face.

CHAPTER 40

▼

In the complete darkness, it was almost as if Mary Rose could read the newspaper headline that sprang into her mind, "Prominent Lawyer Found Dead After Garage Robbery." It would make perfect sense. She had nothing with her. She worked near city hall ...

Why else would she be locked alone down there unless her killer were on his way?

She decided the only thing left to do was to make peace with God.

After what seemed like eternity, she heard doors begin to open in the distance. And the unmistakable roar of the engine of a powerful car.

Absurdly, she cowered and tried to make herself smaller, crouching down into the dank corner of the small space in which she was trapped.

The sound of the car came closer.

Stopped.

Simultaneously, the metal door in front of her swung upward and away, and she found herself trapped now not by metal, but by light—the glaring headlights of the car.

Silhouetted against that light, she saw two figures. A tall lean man. A shorter, squarer, stouter accomplice.

Weakened by fear, she made a vague, vain effort to spurt past them into the emptiness of the garage, but the lean man grabbed her and held her tightly against his chest.

She felt a rough, burning sensation at her wrists. She yanked away from whomever it was who pulled strongly at the cuffs.

And to her astonishment, she realized her hands had been freed. She pulled them in front of her and pushed weakly at her captor.

"Mary Rose," a low voice whispered. "I'm here. You're safe. Don't fight now. You're safe."

The darkness became a deeper black. Her eyes closed involuntarily, and she swayed, about to faint.

But the strong arms held her up. And the scent of citrus and vetivert filled her nostrils.

It was only then that she recognized who it was who held her.

"Rudi," she said, "you're here. Why are you here?"

Before he could answer, she fainted dead away.

When she woke up a few minutes later, she was already in the back of his limo, her head in his lap, his hand caressing her hair, her cheek.

Another, rougher, hand reached over the back of the front seat and dropped a small, old, but still intact piece of paper into her upturned palm. "I told you once before to be more careful about hanging on to your stuff."

"Quiet," Rudi warned his assistant. "I think my Canada needs her rest."

EPILOGUE

Eighteen months later, the mayor and his friend the developer had their trial in the new courthouse. A good part of the case against them came from evidence Marlee was able to supply about their efforts to sabotage her past—and current—boss, Judge Cabrini-Marsh.

Mary Rose herself took a day off from the bench to testify.

As she stepped down from the stand and exited the courtroom without so much as a glance at the people who had tried to rob her not only of her profession, but of her birthright, she and her husband joked a little about the fact that she owned the land they were walking on.

Not for the first time, she thanked him for saving her life, and thanked him too for the five hundred thousand dollars he'd spent acquiring the little document from the Cabrini-Stein Trust and donating the paper to the professors' universities so that they could preserve it and complete their studies about it. She no longer needed the paper itself to prove that she was the legitimate heir.

The Trust also set up a scholarship for Joseph to resume his musical studies as soon as he was well enough, which everyone agreed would be soon.

As for the battered white harp, Mary Rose and her brother had decided that it would remain in their family—forever. Rudi Marsh's family understood the value of hanging onto family treasures. That was why his father had managed to save his most precious painting from Nazi marauders during the war. It had indeed belonged to a prominent Jewish family, just as Mary Rose had suspected. *His* prominent Jewish family.

As husband and wife left the courthouse square together, one of the court officers came running after them waving an important-looking piece of paper he said he'd found on the floor of the courtroom near where Rudi had sat.

It looked nothing like the piece of paper that had started this whole adventure, but it was old.

And in Yiddish.

Mary Rose glanced at it. She felt a little jolt of fear.

Rudi Marsh glanced at it, too.

He seemed puzzled.

Then he smiled, wrinkled it into a ball and tossed it away.

THE END

978-0-595-45412-9
0-595-45412-7

Printed in the United States
82175LV00003B/223-246